Once Upon a Pirate

◆ NANCY BLOCK ◆

HarperPaperbacks
A Division of HarperCollins*Publishers*

HarperPaperbacks   *A Division of* HarperCollins*Publishers*
10 East 53rd Street, New York, N.Y. 10022

Cover illustration by Jean Monti

First printing: April 1995

Printed in the United States of America

HarperPaperbacks, HarperMonogram, and colophon are trademarks of HarperCollins*Publishers*

❖ 10 9 8 7 6 5 4 3 2 1

DEDICATED TO JEAN PAWLOWSKI

HAPPY BIRTHDAY, MOM

I LOVE YOU

Acknowledgments

To my dad, Gene Pawl—after all you've done for me, this is the thanks you get. The western is for you. A zillion kisses to my husband Bruce, and to Holly and Greg, my wonderful, obedient kids. Okay—so I lied about obedient. Thanks guys, for putting up with a nutcase at times. And to my little brother, Dave Pawlowski—I love the laser printer. All other family members on hold till next time.

Special acknowledgment to critique members, past and present. And a salute to the Connecticut chapter of Romance Writers of America, one of the greatest support groups there is.

Hugs to Julie Caille, Zita Christian, Leslie O'Grady, and Leigh Riker for the best quotes money can buy. The checks are in the mail.

And finally, to Julie Caille (again) and Sharon Schulze—friends, critique partners, and sisters of my heart—thanks for believing in me. But more importantly, thanks for kicking butt!

1

Zoe swept an errant curl from her eyes and looked upon Ravenscourt for a final time. Weeds poked out from the dips and hollows of the circular stone drive. The overgrown landscape practically obscured the view of the inlet, and the constant winds of the Atlantic had weathered the stately facade of the Tudor manor house until it appeared abandoned.

The estate had never been in perfect repair, but in the last few years it had fallen onto hard times, looking just as disreputable as her former husband. He had asked her—no, begged her—to stop by one last time before returning to the States. Most likely to persuade her of her folly in leaving.

Hands trembling on the wheel, she almost turned around, tempted at that moment to head straight to the airport and avoid the inevitable confrontation with Jon. She hated their fights. Not that he was an ogre or vicious in any way; he was exactly the opposite—reasonable, calm tempered, and logical to boot. But each and every time he asked her to stay, he called to mind their sweeter memories, which had Zoe swaying, her resolve weakening.

She'd never understand the man—not even if she lived beyond eternity. Jonathan was the most complex person she'd ever known. The charming exterior that had attracted her when they'd met was as appealing now as then. He'd never been anything less than a gentleman, constantly attentive, witty, urbane. And he'd always shown a fondness for their kids.

It seemed a match made in heaven; it had been a marriage forged in hell. Not that anyone in their circle of friends would have guessed . . . not even Jonathan had. But beyond that polite and oh-so-correct veneer lay an emptiness that had sucked at Zoe's soul till there was nothing left to give.

Love—that was all she wanted from him. All she had ever wanted. And Jonathan was not capable of it.

It had taken her a while to examine the frayed edges of their relationship. At first she hadn't wanted to believe his lack of emotion—he seemed the perfect husband, the perfect man. She'd felt lucky to have been chosen by him—the same sentiment held by those who knew them.

But over time she'd seen past the slick exterior of the man to the center of his hollow core. Through sixteen years of marriage she'd given him her all, and it had been lost forever in that empty whirlpool of a heart.

For the children's sake she'd tried to make do, but when Jon had enrolled them both in boarding school, she'd known that was it. They were all she cared for, all she loved. A woman like her could not exist without love—it was a necessity, nourishment for her soul.

And she was slowly starving to death.

Jonathan never seemed to notice, and if he did, he didn't care. When the recession hit, she'd stuck by him—loyalty, after all, was a hard thing to kill. But as the family business continued to spiral downhill, Jonathan's depression, and subsequent obsession, finally drove her over the edge. She couldn't stand by and watch him descend into insanity.

Oh, she'd tried to get him help, had urged him to seek it himself. But nothing could persuade him to give up his obsession—his quest for buried treasure.

Black Jack Alexander, ninth earl of Ravenscourt, Regency rake. . . and his damned buried pirate's loot. If she had the bastard at hand, she'd wring his neck.

Her marriage to Jon might have been a dismal failure, but she didn't want to see the father of her children dragged off to a modern-day Bedlam. If he kept up this incessant search for old Black Jack's treasure—the salvation he saw to both business and marriage—he would be in a straitjacket within the month.

Zoe stepped out of the rental car and automatically grabbed her bag, a combination purse and carry-on. After slinging it over her shoulder, she straightened her Yankees jacket, smoothed her jeans, and tugged down her baseball cap, then headed for the door. She knew her casual attire would irk Jon, but she'd be damned if she'd sit on a plane for over eight hours wearing a dress and hose. Besides, sporting her favorite teams' logos was her way of saying good-bye to England and declaring the resurrection of her independent American nature.

Zoe walked up the steps, pausing to take a deep

breath. Although the bell was broken, she didn't bother to knock—the servants had been dismissed years ago, and Jon would never hear her in the cavernous monstrosity of a house. Instead she marched in, calling for her ex-husband, her voice echoing from the high ceilings as she looked for him in each room.

Most of the furniture was gone, long since sold. What was left loomed like dormant ghosts under the dust-laden sheets. Jon was nowhere to be found.

Knowing his habits as well as her own, she took the stairs to the second floor and headed for the master suite. She wouldn't put it past him to try to seduce her into staying; after all, he'd tried it the last time and it had worked. In fact, it had been the only area of their marriage that had worked.

She'd never confuse passion with love again.

"Jon, where are you?" Zoe pushed open the door to the bedroom, pushing back her bittersweet memories as well. It appeared he'd been there recently—she could still smell the spice of his expensive after-shave lingering in the musty air.

Across the room she spied an opened secret panel that led to the hidey-holes inherent in a house of such age and history. She'd explored them as a newlywed and years later with the children. Jon hadn't been much interested in such pursuits until his obsession with finding Black Jack's treasure had hit its zenith.

It looked as though she'd have to drag him out again.

Zoe walked through the opening, ducking her head till the tunnel grew more spacious. She could hear Jonathan's elegantly accented curses grow louder the deeper she entered the bowels of the passage.

"Jon! It's Zoe," she called ahead, not wanting to startle him and get clubbed by a shovel. He'd been digging holes all over the place for the past year. Luckily he'd installed some haphazard lighting, or else she'd have broken her ankle by the fourth pothole. Floorboards had been loosened everywhere, and whole portions of wall paneling were propped precariously along the way. As she approached ground level she could hear Jonathan's banging and called out to him once more.

"Zoe, luv!" he answered. "That you?"

His melodic voice echoed through the passage, grating on her nerves. *Luv?* She thought it ironic that a man incapable of love would use such an endearment.

"Yes," she said. "Where are you? I don't have much time if I'm to make my flight." She could hear a softly muttered oath.

"At dungeon level, I suppose. Take a right at the fork, past the broken lamp. I've opened an old passage on the left."

After stepping around the debris, Zoe veered right as told, the light fading with each step she took. She wedged herself through the opened panel and caught sight of Jon's disheveled dark hair. As he turned toward her, a bright grin upon his face, she couldn't help but smile. His mismatched eyes would have scared the heartiest stranger in that dull light—one shining an unearthly blue, the other the dark glow of the devil.

"Look, Luv," he said. "I think I've found a hidden latch. I can almost smell it—Black Jack's treasure. The business will be right as rain in no time at all, and there'll be no need for any of this divorce nonsense." He turned away, edging his fingertips around the paneling.

Zoe shook her head. The man was a hopeless case. No matter how many times she told him that money, or the lack of it, had nothing to do with the demise of their marriage, not a whit of it sank into Jonathan's thick skull. Just as she began to refute his assumption for the final time, the panel collapsed inward with a frightening groan.

Very dramatic, she thought.

Jon plunged through the portal, his whoop echoing more eerily than the door. A sudden rush of fear clawed its way up Zoe's back, and an awful, sickening feeling tightened like a fist around her chest.

"Jon, wait! It could be dangerous." Her shouts fell on deaf ears. She could hear him forging ahead, then suddenly come to a halt. Total silence reigned just before a loud crash and Jonathan's scream simultaneously filled the stagnant air.

Zoe ran to the opening without a moment's hesitation—she'd never heard Jon scream in her life, not even when his appendix had burst while on the way to the hospital.

But before she could reach him, her sneaker caught on a loose board. Zoe's hollow scream blended with the fading echo of Jon's, damning Black Jack Alexander and his pirate treasure as she plummeted headfirst into an endless abyss darker than the halls of hell.

Thunder boomed like cannon fire in an ink black sky as the first cold droplets of rain tapped across Zoe's body. The wind whipped over her where she lay, smacking her face with a salty spray, helping revive her senses. With elbows and forearms, Zoe pushed her upper body from the slick planks and surveyed her surroundings.

Overhead, sails flapped angrily on the masts, shaking in the same rhythm as her arms. When the horizon dipped into the sea, dizziness assailed her as relentlessly as the ocean waves battering the creaking timbers beneath her. Her stomach rolled with each crest of the tide.

How the hell had she gotten onto a ship?

The last thing she remembered was being at the estate to say good-bye to Jon. But that seemed to have happened an aeon ago. She must be caught in a bizarre dream. . . . Or had just entered the twilight zone.

Zoe moaned.

The waves continued to crash against the ship, tossing it from side to side, pulling the deck out from under her. She lowered her head to her arms, took deep cleansing breaths, willing the nausea back down her throat. Icy goose bumps crawled down her spine.

This isn't a dream, she thought, it's a nightmare.

A flush of heat stole over her body, covering her skin with clammy sweat. Saliva pooled in her mouth. Amid the surreal screams of men and sails, a firm step drew steadily closer. Zoe swept the sodden bangs from her eyes, startled to see the tips of two scuffed black boots inches from her nose. She followed them with her blurry gaze from toe to ankle and up their long length.

They seemed to go on forever.

When boots gave way to tightly clad fabric, she hesitated, admiring the view. The legs beneath those snug pants were enough to make a nun take notice.

Hard, heavy muscles tightened and relaxed with each deep sway of the ship as their owner balanced smoothly on the tilting deck. Stifling her stomach's protest, Zoe continued to gaze up . . . over the loose white silk that covered a lean, hard-muscled torso. In the deep vee of a poet's shirt lay a luscious expanse of sun-bronzed skin, the magnificently powerful chest adorned with a thatch of black hair sprinkled liberally with silver.

Silver?

Intrigued by this unusual twist to every pirate fantasy she'd read, Zoe looked up at a chiseled face that stole the breath from her lungs. Sharp angles defined a set of features that played pure havoc with her senses. Her gut knotted up again—this time in anticipation.

The man wore a speculative look as he stared down at her, one dark eyebrow raised in question. Devil and angel met in the enticing vision that skimmed over her body from head to toe with a cool, critical gaze. An eye patch secured round his windswept face only added to his mystique, evoking further images of all the pirate heroes she'd seen slashing their way across the silver screen.

Around them the elements wreaked vengeance upon the ship, ripping at the sails, tearing at the rigging. Yet those sights and sounds receded completely as the pirate's gaze met Zoe's. It seemed as though she had known him forever. A name, a familiarity, lingered at the edges of her mind, but she was unable to call it forth from her aching head. Lord knew she'd never seen such dark beauty on anyone, anywhere.

It was sinful.

And she wanted to dip into that sinfulness, brushing her fingers through those thick ebony and silver waves of hair. Gliding across those sexy laugh lines with a trail of soft kisses. Stopping atop those full, firm lips with her hungry mouth and tongue.

His eye, so dark brown it appeared to be black, deepened to the shade of night as his lid lowered seductively. Zoe licked her dry lips with the tip of her tongue, her gaze shifting to skim down his body.

Though her head began to droop once more, she didn't fail to notice the impressive bulge that had arisen beneath those wicked, form-fitting pants.

Her stomach twisted with desire. An ache spread through her body, and a gnawing need arose . . . for a bucket, as she spewed the contents of her fast-food meal over the scarred boots of the fallen angel. Zoe's aching head dropped back to her arms.

"Shit."

It was the last thing she uttered before her fantasy ended and total blackness consumed her.

Winn glanced down at his soiled boots before attending to the unconscious form that sprawled upon the deck. Around him the wind whistled, timbers shuddered, and the sea tossed its angry foam against the ship while his men scrambled about their duties.

But in the few feet of space surrounding Winn, it seemed as if time itself stood still.

He took a quick look about, noting the men at their duties. Nary a glance turned his way. Had they not seen the apparition crash to the floorboards? Or was it only he who had witnessed that devilish sight?

He swept a shaky hand through his hair. It had been a long night—too long—a night fraught with intrigue and darkened by blackmail. After all that had occurred, he was so tired. Perhaps he was hallucinating and she was only a vision. . . .

Winn crouched down, gingerly extending a hand toward the sun-streaked curls that framed the woman's face like a halo.

Ah, hell. She was real.

He would have preferred hallucinations.

Winn rubbed his pounding temples. God, he was

getting too old for surprises. As the deck tilted violently, his stomach lurched.

He was getting too old for sailing, as well.

A mirthless laugh escaped him as he kept the woman from sliding overboard. Who would believe it? A pirate suffering from seasickness!

This latest encumbrance to his health was pure agony—something he'd wish on only the staunchest of enemies. He looked at his boots—the mess had washed away with the rain—and took pity on the small form beside him. If anyone could relate to such misery, it was he. But it seemed the chit was in more dire straits, having bounced against the deck with her sudden appearance.

Winn pushed the wet hair from the woman's face. A dark bruise already formed upon her cheek. Damn. There was nothing for it but to take charge of the situation . . . and hope she wasn't a disciple of hell.

With one motion Winn scooped her into his arms and stood. Though air and sea raged around him, he balanced easily against the roll of the deck, automatically shouting commands to his crew.

"Mr. Turcotte, use your agility to untangle that sail. Mr. Leetch . . ."

"Aye, Captain." A sandy-haired man smoothly appeared at Winn's side.

"Your deft hands and intelligence are needed." The young man nodded solemnly. "Can you get this leaky barrel secured and head her out to sea?"

"Yes, sir." Leetch presented him with a neat salute.

Winn glanced down at the woman in his arms before focusing his attention on the young lieutenant. "The command is yours. I have pressing matters to attend below deck." He watched, amused, as his words registered. A wide smile curved upon the stripling's face.

"Aye, sir. Thank you, sir."

Leetch took the helm before Winn reached the hatch, and he'd eased the ship's rolling before his captain hit the lower deck.

Thank God for the youth's skill, Winn thought. It was a damn sight difficult climbing down a ladder with the ship rolling and an unconscious woman draped in his arms. She was slim but muscular and weighed more than he'd thought—though she'd have been heavier if she'd been wearing rain-soaked skirts. What in hell was she wearing, anyway?

Winn strode down the corridor and kicked open the last door. "Mr. Graves!" he bellowed as he entered the room. Using his boot to hook the rung of a chair, he turned the seat toward him. With a painful grunt he dropped down, still holding the woman in his arms.

"Mr. Gra—"

His shout was interrupted by the headlong charge of his towheaded cabin boy.

"Yes, sir," the boy said, eyes widening as he spied the woman. "What ya got there, Captain?"

"You realize, Mr. Graves, that it is impertinent for a mere cabin boy to question an officer." Winn put on his sternest facade. "This could be the devil's daughter, for all you know—you shouldn't even ask her name."

"Yes, sir," the boy said, a look of contrition upon his face. It was followed by wide-eyed awe. "Is she, sir?"

"Is she what?"

"Is she the devil's daughter?" The little boy asked the question with such ghoulish expectation that Winn had to suppress a chuckle.

"Yes," he growled. "And if you don't find her a towel and some dry clothes, she'll likely snap off your head when she wakes and chew it into little bits."

The boy scrambled out the door without a word. Winn leaned back on the seat, chuckling at the youth's innocence. The body in his arms was far too warm and solid to be that of the devil's daughter, providing the devil had a daughter. Still, who was she, and if she hadn't come from hell, then where?

Winn abandoned his introspection as his cabin boy entered the room on the run and skidded to a stop before him. The boy held out a clean towel in one hand and a pile of clothes in the other. He didn't say a word as Winn took the towel and nodded toward his bunk.

"Put the clothes on the bed, boy. This also." He eased the woman's satchel from her arm, and the boy did as told. "After you turn down the sheets, have one of the middies check on Mr. Leetch's progress, then hightail it to Cookie for a pot of broth and three bowls. It should still be warm—you know how he dawdles at putting the fire out."

Graves nodded when there was no further instruction and headed out on his errands. But as he reached the door, he hesitated and turned to Winn, consternation clear on his cherubic face.

"Three bowls, sir?"

"Aye." Winn nodded. "One for me, one for the devil's daughter here . . . "

"And?" the boy prodded.

Winn's voice lowered ominously while he scanned the dark corners of the cabin. "And one for the devil himself," he whispered.

The boy lit out of the cabin as if his drawers were on fire. Winn's laughter rang through the room, but a drowsy mumbling interrupted his amusement and he looked down at the woman on his lap. She appeared to be coming to. Not wanting to be caught in an indelicate position, he quickly patted the water first from her shapely but scandalously clad legs, then over the rest of her odd garments and up her body. As he ran the towel over her tangled length of hair, big green eyes the shade of the stormswept sea looked out from under her rain-spiked lashes. Incredibly, those eyes widened further before they narrowed into angry slits.

"You've gone too far this time, *luv*." The endearment sounded like a curse on her tongue. "A phony eye patch won't help your masquerade."

At the comment about his patch, Winn inadvertently tightened his hold on her. He could feel the color drain from his face. But the spitfire didn't seem to notice as she continued.

"Even if you're the bloody reincarnation of the once illustrious Black Jack Alexander, you can't seduce me into having anything to do with you again. I'll go to hell first."

Reincarnation? Whatever did she mean?

A crash at the doorway interrupted Winn's thoughts. His gaze left the little virago's angry face to survey the damage. Graves had already scooped up the broken bowl and was mopping some spilled soup from the tray.

"Sorry, sir." His face ashen, he gripped the pieces of the crock. "But if she's going back to hell, then maybe her dad could use her bowl."

Winn flashed him a grin. "That won't be necessary, my boy. Her, uh, dad isn't coming." The woman gasped in protest, and the boy's face paled even further. "Perhaps you'd like to get another bowl and join us?"

he asked Graves. After all, it had been his original intention. He didn't want the boy sick from the dampness. Graves shook his head emphatically.

"No thanks. Sir?"

"Yes?"

"Mr. Leetch is doing just fine. He said to take your time, he could go on for hours."

"He did, did he? Replacing me already, the scamp." Winn smiled to himself. Leetch had waited patiently to take command. But knowing it was his last mission, Winn had been loath to turn it over.

He looked down again at the woman in his charge. Her lids had drooped nearly shut. Winn shifted her to a more comfortable position and winced—his shoulders were beginning to ache from the rain. Perhaps it *was* time to give over charge of the ship. He heard Graves clear his throat, and he turned.

"You wished to say something, Mr. Graves?"

"It's just that, well, nobody could replace you, Captain."

"Is that so?" Winn asked softly. Graves nodded. "Thank you, Adam." Noting the color that crept up the boy's face, Winn said, "You are dismissed until Mr. Leetch's next report. And Adam," he added, stopping the boy's exit. "You might want to join Cookie for that bowl of soup. . . and have one of my jellies for dessert."

"Aye, sir. Thank you, sir." The boy grinned, giving him a flourishing salute before dashing out of the cabin.

Winn's thoughts returned to the woman and how quiet she'd become. He held her wary gaze as he spoke. "Now, tell me, *luv*. Just how did you discover that I'm Black Jack Alexander?"

*   *   *

Zoe closed her eyes for a moment and took a deep breath, willing the nightmare away as unsuccessfully as she had her earlier nausea. Muddled as she felt, she had to sort things through. What had happened to her?

Her body ached all over. The last lucid memory she had was of tripping and falling through a deep hole in the tunnel. Right after Jonathan fell through the same hole . . . or right after he hit her on the head and carried her off.

But where was she?

Zoe stretched her arms and moaned. She felt as though she'd been run over by a truck. No—more likely a steamroller.

Though her lids felt as if they'd been hammered shut, she could still smell the musty dampness of the sea infiltrating fabric and wood. Could taste its salt upon her lips and feel its cool wet touch upon her skin. Could still hear the groan of timber and sails creaking under the ocean's roar. She was definitely on a ship, and the deep roll of the waves told her they were already at sea.

Her eyes snapped open at that thought, and she surveyed her surroundings. Rich paneling lined the walls. Through an open doorway she could see a study with a row of windows looking out into the blackness of the storm. The furnishings, though spare, were elegant, refined, and decidedly masculine. There was a wide, carved mahogany desk beside the open door, and on it lay a pile of charts, a compass, and a sextant.

What was Jonathan doing in the captain's cabin? And what was he doing in that ridiculously sexy outfit?

She peeked at him out of the corner of her eyes, her head resting against a chest that had always been large but now fairly burst with muscles. The last few years Jonathan's body had gone to rack and ruin, looking unkempt and soft, but it had been six months since she'd seen him. With his obsessive digging around the estate it was feasible he could have developed a better physique. But could a man change that much?

Suddenly aware of his scrutiny, she shifted on his lap—and immediately regretted the action. Her cheek brushed against his hard chest, and the salt-and-pepper curls tickled her nose. Zoe sneezed, practically jerking upright in his lap. Two things crossed her mind with lightning speed.

She liked Jon's hair dusted with silver.

And the hardness her rump pressed against was definitely not his belt buckle.

Zoe tried to squirm out of his arms but could feel that pressure growing beneath her. She sat totally still, unsure what to do next but certain that she had to stay immune to Jon's all-encompassing spell.

She would not give in to the lure his body had on her. Would not be manipulated by that languid stare, those firm, full lips, those tawny cheeks. God save me, she thought. The man was as alluring as ever.

Even more so.

Zoe shuddered as his eye twinkled and a crease that looked suspiciously like a dimple appeared at the corner of his mouth. This was worse than she'd thought. Jonathan had never looked at her that way in her life.

He had just turned from alluring to irresistible. And was becoming more dangerous by the minute.

She pulled herself together under the mantle of righteous indignation. She would not fall into her ex-husband's traps. Or at least not farther into his traps, she thought ruefully.

"Enough is enough. Release me, Jonathan."

Two dark eyebrows raised in confusion. "Who is this Jonathan?"

"*Now*, Jonathan." She pushed against him, and his hold loosened. A scowl crossed his face as she tumbled to the floor.

"Woman, you are a stubborn one. You'll be nothing but a mass of bruises with this penchant of yours to fly through the air."

"What are you talking about?" Zoe scooted backward along the floor until she rested against his bunk. She had no patience for this nonsense.

"The way you drop from thin air onto hard surfaces like my cabin floor . . . as well as the deck." His left eye narrowed. "Just how the bloody hell *did* you do that?"

"What?"

"Fly onto my deck. One moment the deck was clear, the next you were there. Appeared just like that." He snapped his fingers. "Right before my very eyes. Had I not seen it for myself, I'd never believe it."

Zoe leaned her throbbing head against the mattress—it ached in earnest now. "Just give it up, Jon. I'm in a bitch of a mood."

"A bitch, or a witch?" His voice lowered mockingly. "Had you appeared so precipitously not many years ago, you'd have been tossed overboard for witchcraft."

Incredibly, his eye twinkled more merrily than before. He was too damn appealing, and it rankled.

"You know I'm a patient person, Jon. But I've developed a vicious temper in my old age. Especially when engaged in tedious games of this ilk."

He merely raised an imperious brow, the picture of innocence. But he didn't fool her. Not one bit.

"Jonathan, for the last time," she enunciated slowly,

"I will not return home, I will not resume my role of devoted wife, Black Jack's treasure has no lure for me, and I demand to be released immediately."

There. That ought to teach him. God, she hated to be brutal, but the man had to face the facts. Abduction was bad enough, but if he thought he could actually keep her, he was definitely off his rocker. She had a plane to catch—

"Shit."

"A favorite word?"

"Dammit, Jon. You've made me miss my flight." She scowled up at that self-satisfied face.

"Another flight? Where to this time?" he asked curiously, almost as if he'd forgotten.

Conveniently forgotten, most likely. "To the States. You know, as in United States of America. I'm going home, Jon."

His face split in a wide grin, teeth flashing brilliant white against his deep tan. "Don't your arms get tired?"

"Whatever from?"

"Why, from flapping them, of course." His chuckle was beginning to grate on her nerves. "Or do you just glide?"

She gave him what she hoped was a scathing look and gritted her teeth. His sarcasm always drove her bonkers. "I've had enough of this nonsense, enough of you, and enough of England. But *you* know that. You've known it for a long time."

"Have I?" he asked, brushing his fingers through his dark, wavy hair. He leaned back against the chair, crossing his booted legs at the ankles. "Who is Jon? And how do you know about my treasure?" he asked in a deceptively soft voice.

She recognized that tone, and it raised the hackles on her neck. *My* treasure, he'd said.

"So—it was all a lure, a put-on. 'Come see the secret panel.'" She watched as his eye darkened to the dead of night. "Of course you'd already found the treasure. How else could you afford a boat like this? Unless you rented it from someone."

"Rent." He frowned at the word. "I'll have you know I own this ship. And it takes a damn sight more money than most would believe to outfit one. Happens I've secured a number of 'treasures,' as you so quaintly put it. Most would call it privateering."

An ominous chill swept through Zoe's body. My God—he wouldn't actually commit piracy. Would he? Her voice quavered despite her resolve to stay calm.

"What exactly do you mean by privateering?"

He smiled that rakish smile and leaned forward, elbows resting on his muscled thighs. She looked away quickly from that distraction, staring out the windows toward the sullen sea, and he had the nerve to chuckle again.

"Some would call it piracy. The less charitable—looting."

"That's it." She sprang from the floor the minute the words left his mouth. "Enough of this Regency rogue scenario. I've about run out of adventures, Jonathan. I can't take any more."

"Easy, tigress."

She eyed him warily as he stood and moved toward her with a smooth stride. He seemed to be a part of the ship, while the roll of the waves made her dizzy. The moment he pulled her in his arms she knew she should have stayed on the floor. Instead she leaned against his solid chest, fighting an overwhelming attraction as well as vertigo.

"You know," he said, "you have the eyes of a cat . . . or an enchantress. Is that what you are, why you've come to me? To enchant me with your spell? To win my fortune? For I'd give all I own to have a woman like you."

His voice was a rasp, so unlike the trim smoothness of the Jonathan she knew. Perhaps he was getting a cold.

Zoe sighed, soaking in the warmth of that rough voice and the enticing heat of Jon's hard male body. She knew she shouldn't stay there in the dangerously secure circle of his arms, but she was feeling sicker by the moment and needed to rest in his comforting embrace.

"You always were a rogue, Jon." She sighed and snuggled closer.

"Aye, a rogue," he rumbled. "But not Jon. Nor Jonathan." He nudged her chin up with his hand and held her gaze. "May I formally introduce myself? Captain Black Jack Alexander, at your service, madam." He grinned as she stared at him in horror. "Rumors that bad, eh?"

There was not the smallest sign of dissembling about him, only blatant pride. Zoe groaned. Oh, Lord. It was worse than she thought. He had finally flipped and actually believed he *was* Black Jack.

Unless the nut routine was a ruse to gain her sympathy.

"Should I call you Black, or Jack?" she asked nonchalantly.

Jonathan's chest rumbled once more with quick laughter. "Darlin', you can call me whatever you want." He pressed the back of her knees against the bunk, and she tumbled to the mattress, Jonathan following to hover over her. "As long as you call me often, and call me to your bed."

Zoe stared at the latest edition of her ex-husband and almost lost herself in his spell and in the black depths of his exposed eye. She'd always been attracted to his mismatched eyes, the contrast between light and dark. The patch was ridiculous, of course, but it highlighted Jonathan's rich tan and his new, dangerous aura. Seeing just the one eye sparkling at her like polished onyx, she could almost believe he was Black Jack.

Almost.

Zoe scooted back on the bed, groping for her purse. Jonathan didn't waste a second, insinuating himself against her as if they were attached. Ah, but he felt so good. The length of him, the weight of him. And he smelled better than ever, still hinting of spice, but with the honest musky tang of wind and water and hard work.

There. She finally found her purse. But Jonathan had found her lips. His own pressed against hers, firm and full, teasing, coaxing, sweeping her up in desire. His tongue glided over the seam of her mouth, again and again, moistening her lips as the rest of her moistened, shivered for his entry.

He pressed against her with his tongue, sliding slowly between her lips till he gained sweet access to her mouth, meshing with her softly, sinuously.

Driving her wild with need.

His hands opened her jacket, found their way beneath her shirt. They cupped her bare breasts reverently as his fingers stroked the tips into buds. Heat spread throughout her body at the delicious sensation. She pressed up into his hands, wanting more. Craving more.

For one blind instant Zoe gave in to desire, aroused more with that one kiss and gentle touch than she'd been in years. She pulled him closer, clung to him, twined her tongue and legs about him. Feeling the hardness of his own need, she moaned—and came to her senses.

He'd done it again. Made her a slave to her passionate nature.

She wouldn't waste another sixteen years waiting for him to change, looking for a love he couldn't give, was incapable of giving. She'd vowed to herself that she'd start a new life, learn to love herself more, live on her own. She wasn't about to blow all her hard work now.

Zoe found what she was looking for, pulling her hand from her purse even as she pulled away from Jonathan. He tried to follow her, recapture her lips, but she shoved against his chest with her free hand.

It took a moment for the glaze of passion to leave his eye, for his thoughts to turn lucid. He looked down at her, clearly puzzled, his hands still lovingly cupping her breasts.

"Get off me. *Now*, Jonathan, or Black Jack—or whoever the hell you are at the moment."

He didn't move, but his brows beetled in a flush of anger. "No, my cat. You'll not tease me, promise me your lush loving only to withdraw it."

His fingers resumed their sweet motion, caressing her budded nipples till they ached. She squirmed beneath the assault, loving and hating him. Then she raised the small spray canister before her.

"Leave me alone, or I swear I'll shoot." She aimed

squarely at his face, her hands shaking with both outrage and need.

Jonathan's head jerked back, a new awareness in his eye as he took in her pinched features. "What form of firearm is this?"

"It's the latest technology. Packs a punch worse than mace."

He braced himself onto his forearms, her breasts forgotten in light of this new development. "As hard as a mace? Surely you wouldn't use such a weapon on me."

"Surely I would."

He swooped down, intent on finding her lips once more. Zoe shot a spray straight at his eye, immediately regretting the action when he flew off the bed, howling.

"Damn you, woman. You've blinded me!" He stumbled over to a basin fastened to a set of drawers and splashed water on his face, over and over, cursing her a blue streak all along.

Lord. She knew breath spray wasn't toxic, but could it blind? Zoe didn't move, paralyzed with shame. She didn't mean to hurt him, but dammit, he'd had it coming to him when he didn't stop as she'd asked.

Still gripping the breath spray, Zoe practically jumped out of her skin as the object of her thoughts materialized beside her. The man was a natural predator—she hadn't heard a thing.

Through his bleary eye he looked down at her, myriad expressions flitting over his face—anger, hurt, surprise—and desire. His rueful grin hinted at the strength of that unbidden passion. When he bent over her she flinched, not knowing if he would continue his sensual game.

But the hands that reached toward her merely

tugged the bottom of her shirt back over her breasts. One eyebrow suddenly winged up, and his expression warmed to a smile.

"For once we agree, madam." His voice grew soft as velvet, deep as midnight. "They most definitely are." And with that cryptic message and a graceful bow, he bade her a pleasant rest before walking out the door and locking it behind him.

Zoe stared after him for some time, pondering his odd change in attitude. It wasn't until she tucked in her shirt that she remembered what she was wearing—and finally realized what he'd meant. Although she was alone in the room, her entire body heated in a blush.

Emblazoned in red, across the damp material clinging to her chest, was the name of her favorite NFL team.

Giants.

2

Winn stepped onto the deck, the cold rain lashing his face a welcome relief to his stuffed-up nose. At least his eye had stopped watering. Though it made bloody little difference in this squall.

He surveyed the ship, automatically saluting the quarterdeck where the Stars and Stripes, symbol of the United States, usually waved its majestic greeting. An American privateer in English waters, he chose to hang his own standard instead. The Ravenscourt coat of arms flapped arrogantly in the wind, its stark black raven on a field of red as formidable as his title of earl.

He didn't like the display of aristocracy—not when he'd committed his very soul to the freedom his adopted country professed. Yet he flew his standard, proud of his heritage, to gain easy access to the country of his birth. And to conceal the mission he'd undertaken for the young nation that held his heart.

Wind and rain lashed at the rigging, making the

night darker than Hades as Jonathan Winnthrop Alexander Dunham, ninth earl of Ravenscourt, carefully picked his way across the rolling deck. The footing was treacherous in conditions like these, and he'd no desire to be washed to the sea that boiled around them like a witch's brew. The ship appeared as well as could be; he knew his crew would have all in hand. They were a good lot—dependable, totally loyal—and certainly seemed capable without him.

Sometimes he wondered if he was needed at all.

As far as he could see, all the necessities had been taken care of. Everything loose had been battened down. The mainsails and topgallants had been furled and secured. Only the topsails flapped in the wind, alternately billowing and eddying with the unpredictable crosscurrents brought on by the storm.

Winn made his way to the quarterdeck, ready to relieve the helmsman on duty. It was well into midwatch. Two bells had sounded as he left his cabin, making it close to a quarter past one. To his surprise, Leetch still stood at the wheel with not a crease of worry upon his face. Instead the young lieutenant wore a look of such sheer delight that Winn regretted not having relinquished command earlier. When Leetch caught sight of him, Winn could sense the young man's disappointment.

"Still at the wheel, I see, Mr. Leetch. Was there some trouble with the helmsman?" It was all Winn could do to keep his smile to himself. As it was, the corners of his lips twitched uncontrollably. He most likely appeared to have an affliction.

But Leetch didn't notice. He was too busy hiding a sheepish expression of his own.

"Sent him on down, sir. No need to double shift

when I have to be on deck in any case. Besides, I don't feel a bit tired."

"Good. Then if I relieve you now, you can take over again for my regular shift and I'll double up on my sleep. Haven't seen my cot in two days, what with playing games with those merchantmen and my rendezvous ashore."

"Aye, Captain. Gladly." Leetch's eyes lit up. He strode from the quarterdeck and saluted again before scurrying down the hatch.

Winn sighed. Oh, to have another chance at such robust energy. It had been so long since he'd felt that way, he could scarcely recall the feeling. Why was it such energy was wasted on the young? All of life seemed one compensation after the other—vigor for those who lacked maturity and experience for those who lacked vigor. It seemed a damned shortsighted arrangement by the powers that be.

Here he had all the experience and control a man could wish for, and he found himself wishing for a new body instead. He shrugged his shoulders as he steadied the wheel, loosening the tightness that constantly assailed him.

Ah, well. It could be worse. At least all his parts worked—that is, all the parts that still remained. He'd had evidence of that before in his cabin. Amazing the chit could arouse him so easily.

Then again, she really wasn't a chit, was she? No. She was a woman—a woman in her prime—and that's what had attracted him most. No simpering stares or vacant eyes, no primping or teasing in her demeanor, she proved as straight a shooter as his western frontiersmen.

Aye. And it seemed her shot had gone unerringly to his groin.

Winn's wry laugh slipped away on the breeze even as he tamped down the makings of a dark mood. No use whipping himself over the irony of his own thoughts. What remained of him was still useful for begetting pleasure, if not children, and since he'd no one to call wife, even that was not a problem.

The problem was, for the first time since his injury he was truly interested in using the tools of manhood that God had given him. The real irony being, for the first time in his life he was ashamed of his body.

Winn shook his head, battening down his morose introspection as tightly as the crew had battened down the ship. He turned his attention to the sea, noting the waves rising higher around him. Then his gaze focused downward to the rain-spattered compass, discerning his direction in the wavering lamplight.

If he continued their course at this speed, the waves would soon overtake the ship. He needed enough lofty sail to keep her safely before the sea. Calling to his most experienced topmen, he ordered them aloft, then watched as they climbed up the ratlines on the windward side of the ship. As soon as they reached the highest yard and took their positions aloft, he commanded them to let fall the sails.

The topgallants quickly filled with air, billowing in their race against the sea. Within minutes the ship scudded ahead and the men scrambled to the deck, congratulating themselves on a dangerous job well done. And so it was, thought Winn.

They were a canny bunch, working together as one, sensitive to his needs and desires. But right now his needs and desires centered around the soft curves of the woman he'd left behind in his cabin—on his cot. His groin tightened at the picture that thought painted.

Could it be his foul mood of late had sent the men on an errand of mercy? Who was to say they hadn't gone ashore after him, sneaking into town while he met the regent's man, bringing the woman aboard to lighten his mood? Leetch had seemed especially happy with the events of the night. Could that sober young man have orchestrated such a feat?

While it wasn't beyond his crew's ability, such a theory was leaky as a battered hull and farfetched in the bargain. The woman seemed no doxy and was quite loath, in fact, to have him touch her.

Was it only his touch that offended her, he wondered, or that of all men? For a moment his self-esteem suffered, thinking her repelled by his injury. But no, only the surgeon knew of his loss, and McCairn was a loyal friend—as tight with his tongue as he was with his money.

A doxy who wouldn't service a man was either independently wealthy or terminally stupid. It made no sense. But if she wasn't a light-skirt, the men wouldn't have taken her. As rough as some of them were, his entire crew knew how to treat a lady; he'd stake his life on it.

Yet there was no explanation as to her arrival, appearing before him as if conjured, which he believed a patently ridiculous idea. He was a man of science, a believer in logic.

Winn pulled up the collar of his tarred coat. Despite his fisherman's hat, he could feel the rain upon his neck. The men had laughed the first time they'd spied his odd attire, bought from an old fisherman up Rockport way, but they'd seen the sense in it the first storm he'd worn it and now sported such strange outfits themselves.

Yes, Winn thought, he was a man of logic.

Which had him wondering about the strong smell of mint.

Zoe rummaged around in her bag, looking for a snack. She hated airline food and always came prepared for the worst. She found an apple, a pear, a granola bar, and a sandwich and tossed them onto the bed where she sat. The broth had tasted delicious, but she was looking for the hard stuff, something to drown her sorrows with. Or at least to soothe her mind.

Ah. Paydirt.

She pulled out her prize, tearing the wrapper off the flattened Yodel and shoving the cake into her mouth. There was nothing like a chocolate fix to make things look better. She scooped the crumbs from the wrapper and licked her fingers clean while contemplating the day's weird events.

However it was she had landed on this damn ship, it had something to do with Jon and his obsession with his revered forebear, Black Jack Alexander. The man she had once married had finally broken his tether, gone off the deep end . . .

Was certifiably nuts.

Perhaps it was schizophrenia—after all, he seemed like a different man. He'd changed much in the last six months, and not only physically. Yes, she thought. It was as if Jon had become a stranger.

He'd taken on the persona of a pirate, his rakish attire and the ship testimony to that. Yet it was more than accoutrements that marked the change. It was his attitude, that naughty twinkle to his eye. The way he looked at her, boldly, in command. It was also the way he had stirred her senses. She'd always found him attractive, true, but now his appeal overwhelmed her.

Nothing had altered remarkably, yet the subtle differences added up. Even his hair seemed thicker, darker where it wasn't glinting with that remarkable silver. Funny. She hadn't noticed that in the tunnel. Must have been the poor lighting.

His shoulders appeared broader, and he seemed to tower over her even more so than before, but that was nonsense—unbridled imagination. And no wonder, when she'd been pressed against that newly developed, hard-muscled chest.

The memory still made her tingle.

All were part and parcel of a well-exercised individual. Perhaps Jon had taken up weight-lifting. Then again, there'd been all that shoveling on the estate. Most of the changes could be explained.

What she couldn't dismiss was the sheer magnetism of the man, the monumental appeal he presented— that swashbuckling aura she could never have imagined Jon possessing or pretending to have. He'd shed the personality she had known and had taken on a new one.

One she found intriguing.

One she'd have to fight tooth and nail.

For she wouldn't succumb to Jon's charm again. Her own character and self-esteem had suffered too much to have it broken once more. She'd rebuilt in the past, but another crack in the foundation would have all her efforts tumbling to dust.

No. She couldn't afford to fall for this scheme.

He was playing out all her romantic ideals. Every quality she'd admired in him seemed to have met with the ones she'd hoped for all those years, and every fiber of her being had responded to him. With a snap of his fingers she'd be in his arms, and she'd vowed never to give him that power again. . . .

007-in-an-eye-patch or not.

Zoe chewed pensively on her bottom lip, startled to find the taste of salt and pirate upon it. The roar of ocean and storm filled her ears, the waves slapping rhythmically against the ship as she surveyed the room. One aspect of Jon's personality remained—the pristine condition of his cabin proved him as meticulous as ever. So much for her fantasies of a completely changed man.

Zoe rubbed her arms against the chill of dampness, then put her snacks back in her bag. It seemed like years since she'd driven to the estate that morning, and she was tired as hell. Besides, she ached from teeth to toes, evidently having fallen to the deck—she'd remember it all in time.

She glanced around the room, looking for a change of clothes, but the trunk was locked. More than anything she needed sleep, and as long as Jon played the pirate there was nothing she could do besides accept his hospitality. She snuffed out the wick of the lanterns, extinguishing the lights. Then she tossed off her sea-laden clothes, pulled down the musty covers, and crawled between cool sheets scented wonderfully by sun and wind and the musky tang of male.

But not the scent of Jon.

Winn pulled off his dripping coat and hung it on a peg beside the one that held his hat, letting the water puddle outside his room. Graves would air it out as soon as the weather allowed. He unlocked the door and entered his cabin as quietly as possible, boots squishing with each step he took.

The room was dark as pitch with the lamps extinguished, making it damnably difficult to see. He bumped into furniture twice before finding his chair. After tugging off his sodden boots, he removed his damp clothing, folding each garment before placing it atop his trunk.

Tired. He was so bloody, bone-weary tired.

He slid between the sheets, smelling the enticing scent of woman a moment before his skin met hers—her velvety-soft, floral-scented, warm, bare skin.

The woman was naked.

Something his hardened shaft knew well before his brain did.

Desire licked up his belly like a flame, encompassing him in a fine heat. He hadn't felt this way in a very long time. Gently he encircled her in his arms, pulling her closer to his body.

So good. She felt so good.

His hands found her breasts and cupped their warm softness. He could hear the altered pattern of her breaths while her nipples tightened beneath his fingers. Her quiet moan filled the night as she pressed into his touch, wiggling her backside closer to his hardness. Winn's fingers grew bolder, sweeping across her sweet flesh, touching every aspect of her body.

Making him grow harder still.

He'd have thought such a response impossible. Not that he didn't function at all—his was a problem of infertility, not impotence—yet he'd never been so stirred, so ready for mating, in the nine years since that hellish day.

He'd quite forgotten how wonderful a person felt in rutting heat. It proved definitely better than any memories.

Holding the woman even closer, he breathed in her sassy scent, drew in the naked warmth of her body. Suffused himself with the absolute power of pure sensation, glutting his senses with all she was—sweet spice, firm softness, incredible heat.

Aye, she was all that and more—enticing, responsive, sensual, and strong—he'd been able to discern that from the first. There was something so tantalizing, so unique about her, it drew him to her despite his reserve.

She snuggled against him while she dreamed, her body melding with his wherever they touched. Turning, she wrapped her arms around him with the artless grace of innocence no doxy could feign, holding him to her gently, as if her actions spoke of love.

It was too soon—surely too soon to think of such things. Yet there was that immediate, inexplicable pull that had him cradling her in his arms as if she belonged to him. He wanted to possess her totally, brand her to him—every inch. He wanted to crow to the heavens that she was his.

And he didn't understand a damn thing about it— not how he felt this way, certainly not why. It was a ridiculous reaction, premature. Absolutely absurd.

And so damn true a feeling, his heart practically sang with the rightness of it all. The happy contentment that filled his being lulled him as surely as the rhythm of the ship, settling his tired body at the edges of sleep while his fingers softly stroked the woman beside him, coaxing her closer to his soul.

3

"Get your filthy hands off me, you damn pervert. Or I'll take a knife to your genitals and perform a sex-change operation."

The hollow roar reverberating in his head had Winn up and racing to the door before he had a chance to think much beyond, Thank God she isn't talking to me. Pulling the door so hard the hinges bent, he charged into the corridor, cutlass in hand, intent on rescuing his lady.

He had to rescue his man instead.

The woman was kneeling atop Grizzard, the most dangerous and depraved of all his men, a true pirate in every sense of the word. Winn had rescued him from a cruel captain, earning his startling, undying devotion. The man's name combined grisly and gizzard—an apt description—from his favorite way of attacking with a lethal slash to his enemy's throat.

Winn's heart pounded in his chest when he noted the deadly blade his man gripped. But he stopped his charge when the eerie stillness of the tableau registered upon his mind.

Grizzard's grip was tight but his arms relaxed, as he looked up at the woman in total horror. One of her knees dug into his stomach, the other into his groin, while she held a pocket knife against his shriveled masculinity.

Winn waited for her next movement, fascinated by the bizarre scene. But Grizzard regained his senses first and lashed at the woman with his tongue.

"Why, ye're a bleedin' tart, ya are. I'd have naught to do with the likes of you."

"Call me a tart, eh?" she asked, a wicked light burning in her green eyes. "Say it again and you'll be singing soprano."

Grizzard's face paled as he inched back against the wall, hoisting himself to a sitting position with the woman now firmly atop his lap. Taking command of his senses and his formidable strength, he swept her aside, clicking his tongue while he adjusted his pants. Disgust covered his face as he watched her rise, her little knife still in hand.

"Tart . . . woman . . . they're one'n the same. Ain't no such bloody thing as a lady. Sell ya to the Grim Reaper for a farthing." He spat on the floor as he stood. "Thought you was a new boy per'aps looking for a mate. Wouldn't bugger me no woman. Trouble, they are." He gave her one last menacing glare before stalking away. "Nothin' but trouble."

Her eyes practically popped from her head at mention of Grizzard's amorous preferences. It would be in terribly bad form to laugh, Winn thought, so he suppressed his amusement for the moment, calling to his man instead.

"Mr. Grizzard. You will clean that up immediately." His voice was pure command, cloaked in steel.

Grizzard stopped short, whipping his head around to face his captain. Embarrassment covered his coarse features.

"Aye, Captain." He saluted smartly.

"And you are to apologize to my lady." Winn's tone brooked no disobedience.

"*Yer* lady?" Grizzard asked, appalled.

Winn nodded and shifted his gaze from the stunned look on the fierce man's face to the equally stunned face of the woman. So, she wanted no master, he thought. Or could it be the fact he was leaning against the wall, cutlass in hand—completely nude—that had her mouth gaping like that of a beached fish?

Winn's best gunner gave her a respectful, if not courtly, bow. "Beggin' yer pardon, ma'am." Then he scooted down the corridor and out of sight faster than the rats in the hold.

Winn's gaze returned to the woman. Her tongue darted out to moisten her full, dry lips, and his manhood sprang to attention as smartly as Grizzard's salute. Her gaze caught the movement, shifting to rest on his proud anatomy so intently, he practically blushed.

He continued to watch as her breathing grew shallow, her emerald eyes glazed. She seemed as confused as he felt.

Taking pity on her, Winn pushed away from the wall. He advanced slowly, extending his hand—she grabbed it as though it were a lifeline. But he saw no logic in the words she mumbled as they retreated to his cabin.

"And Little Red Riding Hood said to the Wolf, 'My, Granny. What a big, uh . . . uh . . . '"

Had his cock always been that big?

My God, it was all she could think of as she watched him casually throw on a shirt and attempt to tug up those tight breeches. Unfortunately for him, they didn't fit. Not over *that*.

He gave up on the pants, leaving his shirt untucked, and covered the object of her fascination. Had she been blind all those years with Jon? A man could pump up his muscles, but . . .

Well, he couldn't pump up that much, could he?

Quite disturbed at the direction of her thoughts and the subsequent throb of her body, Zoe looked up at him from where she sat on the bed. The emotions that flitted so openly across his face ranged from lust to chagrin, laced with pure masculine pride. Yet they were tempered with a twinkle of amusement.

This was a Jon she didn't know.

Jon could control his lust and genitals as easily as he controlled his temper, keeping his emotions in check at all times. If he had any emotions, that is. She often wondered about that.

Here was a man who embraced emotion. Naturally. Freely. Quite a refreshing character trait. One she'd tried to foster in him for years.

She decided that schizophrenia was highly underrated.

Realizing she'd been staring and, from his merry crinkles, that he'd been watching her stare, her gaze dropped. The opened Swiss Army knife lay in her hand. That deadly blade she'd used for protection turned out to be the nail file.

She heard his deep chuckle but wouldn't look up. Let him laugh if he wanted, it had done the job. Now all she needed to do was close it.

Struggling against the knife's stiffness, she managed to shut it without any help—though not without snapping it on her finger. A tiny trickle of blood oozed from her flesh.

"Stubborn woman. You've hurt yourself."

Black Jack Junior sat beside her and took her hand gently in his. She smiled to herself as he bent to examine it.

"I thought you were the scourge of the seven seas. Pirates don't play nursemaid."

"Don't they?"

A smoldering fire lit his eye as, lifting her hand, he placed her injured finger in his mouth. His full lips closed around it, one corner of their sculpted fullness drawn up in a crooked grin.

Raw sensation flooded her, intimately linking her body to his through the mere tip of a finger. Heat flashed through her blood as his tongue caressed her—his gaze never leaving her face—hypnotizing her with his sultry look, the press of his warm body.

Such primitive pleasure washed over his features, she groaned—reality filtering to her brain when she realized she'd been the one to make the sound. Zoe pulled back her hand as if her face had been slapped and confronted him with a tart tongue.

"Enough of this nonsense pretending to be your rapacious, thieving ancestor."

"Thieving?" His brow puckered. She noticed he didn't question "rapacious."

"Yes, thieving. What else was Black Jack, but a pirate—"

"Privateer."

"Privateer, whatever. Just another name for a glorified thief."

The man whipped around faster than the wind, pinning her between his arms. It wasn't the Jonathan she knew who pressed against her, flooding her body in desire, warming her with his own heat, stirring her senses.

No. The man was pure pirate.

A proper heir to Black Jack Alexander.

"It seems Grizzard was right." He pressed closer, voice low, arms rubbing against the sides of her breasts. Her nipples hardened immediately. "You certainly are a handful, woman."

He reached up, on cue, to cup one breast. She slapped at his hands even as she stifled a groan.

"And stop calling me woman," she snapped.

Her finger started throbbing, so she popped it in her mouth. The taste of him lingered, overwhelming her senses, a clean cinnamon spice. Her heart did somersaults in her chest.

"What else should I call you?" His head dipped toward hers.

"Zoe." The word trailed away on a sigh.

He brushed her cheek with butterfly kisses, the warmth of his breath branding her skin. "And you may call me Winn," he whispered, his mouth sweeping across her like velvet, his tongue painting a moist trail to her lips.

Zoe swallowed audibly, feeling as though the air had been sucked from her lungs.

"Winn," she murmured, caught in his spell.

More like Errol Flynn, she thought. The way he handled her like the finest of treasures bespoke the gentleman as well as the pirate.

"Short for Jonathan Winnthrop Alexander Dunham, ninth earl of Ravenscourt. Alias Black Jack Alexander."

Those words released her from his spell like a key to a lock. She'd finally broken free from Jonathan. She wouldn't be reeled in by an alter ego or his long-lost twin.

Pushing against him with all her might, Zoe managed to duck under his arm. Then she scrambled back upon the bed till she thumped against the headboard. Jon remained where he was, his dark eyebrows furrowed with confusion as Zoe tried to control her breathing.

She kept her eyes on him, wary now, having learned the pull of him to be more deadly than a knife and neary able to cut out her soul.

"Okay." She held up her hand in surrender. "I give in. As long as we're on this ocean adventure you can be Winn, Flynn, whoever you want." He eyed her speculatively. "But then I get to be Princess Di."

"Princess Di?"

"*You* may call me Princess."

He flashed a rakish grin, pure pirate persona. "I much prefer Zoe," he said, seducing her with the sound of her own name.

Zoe shook her head, mouth gone dry, unable to speak, watching a range of emotions sweep over his darkly dangerous face. He seemed to come to a decision, standing to full height before bowing deeply before her.

"Your wish is my command . . . Princess." He spun around and strode to the door, but turned to her before he opened it. "Right now *my* wish is that you sit tight and stay out of trouble. The storm has picked up and the waves grow higher. I don't need to worry about you while I'm up on deck."

She nodded, watching as he adjusted his pants before leaving. The click of the door marked his departure.

Zoe's head buzzed with a rush of blood, loud as the roaring wind and as erratic as the slap of the sea that battered the hull of the ship. The waves continued to dip as wildly as Jon's assault to her senses.

Funny—she'd completely forgotten about the storm.

"Well, Adam. I've about had it."

Zoe glared at the boy like the worst sort of poor sport, but hell, it was natural after losing ten rounds of old maid and eleven of go fish. Especially since she'd been the one to teach him how to play.

"You sure you don't want to try one more hand?" he asked with the enthusiasm of a gambler on a hot streak. She'd already lost twenty sticks of gum and her remaining Yodel to the little monster she'd created.

"I'd rather have my teeth pulled out one by one."

The boy put away the deck. "We could play charades again—"

"Not on your life. I'm breaking out of this joint before I'm as insane as your erstwhile captain."

"Wouldn't want to cross the captain, ma'am. His temper can be terrible frightful, and he did give us orders to stay—"

"I don't take orders from Black Jack Junior. Besides, we've been in this cabin all day. I need some fresh air before my lungs shrivel up and die, not to mention my nose. The smells around here are horrendous. Why anyone enjoys boats—"

"Ships," he corrected. They'd been over this earlier.

"Whatever. I need air, Adam, and I need it now, before the sun goes down and I'm cooped up for another night. It seems quite a bit calmer to me, don't you think?" Zoe flashed her most engaging smile, a sure sign that she was close to breaking.

"Well. . . "

"Great, that settles it."

She was out the door before the boy could dissuade her. He followed her on deck like a puppy, guarding her from the shocked and speculative stares of the crew. She ruffled his silky blond curls, thinking he deserved more affection than that, the way he stuck so loyally by her side. The mite seemed lonely, in need of nurturing and motherly attention. She decided to temporarily apply for the job, having had plenty of practice with Alexa and Alex.

Too bad they're not here, she thought, wondering if she'd been wrong to leave them in boarding school until she moved back to the States. Then she quickly dismissed her guilty reflections. With their term ending within the month, it was no time for vacations. A shame, really—they'd have enjoyed their father's new personality, even though his mind was a bit short-circuited. Jon had always been too rigid to bend, too staid to stoop as low as playing with the children.

This was a Jon they would love—provided he stayed this way—not the one who had scarred them with his distance.

Zoe sought the object of her musings, catching sight of his silver-laced obsidian mane high in the rigging. The thought of him up there sent her heart into palpitations, but she didn't call out to him, for fear he'd lose his grip and crash to the deck below. Bedlam was preferable to death, after all. And how would she explain it to the kids?

She watched him climb like a monkey along the ropes, with a young man following right behind. Jon seemed to be explaining something as he led the way. Satisfied, he clapped the young man on the back, then shimmied to the deck below.

She never knew Jonathan could shimmy.

Heart thudding back in place, she stalked up to him in a rage and stomped her foot for effect. "How dare you scare the hell out of me! Errol Flynn you are not."

"You're right, Princess. The name is Winn." He almost disarmed her with his rakish grin, but she would have none of it.

"Well, Winn, you have a damn brick for a brain."

Both of those dark eyebrows shot upward in amazement while he absorbed her with his midnight gaze. His grin turned into a brilliant smile, the white flash of teeth reminding her of the predatory wolf she'd likened him to earlier. And that triggered the memory of his magnificent hardness, weighing down her retort with awful, wonderful sensations to her body.

"Ah, frig it," Zoe cursed the lure of the man.

"Frigate?" he asked, grabbing his glass.

"Aye, sir. Got a glimpse through the fog," the lookout shouted from above. "Coming at a steady clip off larboard bows."

Winn clapped Zoe on the back, nearly knocking her off balance with his strength. "Good work, Princess." He turned away, putting the spy glass to his eye.

"Looks like she flies the Union Jack, mates. Raise our own Jack—we'll try to brazen her out. But be prepared for action."

Zoe observed the efficiency of the men with quiet awe as they scrambled up the rigging, threw sand on the deck, and prepared the cannons for a fight. She could almost believe the show was real. It must've cost Jon a fortune for this scheme.

He turned to her then, a frown marring his wind-swept face.

"Best to get below now—it's safer than on deck. And make sure Adam's with you, I'd hate to have anything happen to the boy."

She started to turn away, piqued by the way he ordered her about. But he stopped her with another command.

"And for God's sake, Princess, take off that bloody jacket. We don't have to spell it out that we're Yankees."

In an instant he was gone, shouting commands in his wake. Pretty impressive for a guy whose future consisted of a long stint in the loony bin.

Having no intention of going along with his nonsense, Zoe zipped up her baseball jacket and found a place at the rail. If the show was for her benefit, she'd damn well watch. The cool mist swept through her hair. Looking at the tempest-tossed waves around her, she lost herself in the majesty of the sea. She'd needed a vacation before she started her new life— how ironic it was provided compliments of Jon.

She had to hand it to him, everything seemed so real, every aspect of his fantasy had definitely pleased. If he'd been like this during their marriage, she certainly wouldn't have left him. It was too late to go back now, though. His personality change was probably no more real than this dramatic scenario he'd wrought.

Zoe returned her attention to the water, surprised to see a gray shape in the mist. Like the *Flying Dutchman*, the ship took form, a ghostly intruder on their flank. Another ship loomed beyond it, and an eerie tingle crept down her spine. She blinked her eyes, almost expecting the image to disappear in a puff of smoke.

But the ship veered closer, on a course that would surely cut through theirs. She didn't like this twist to Jon's fantasy, not one bit. Something was definitely wrong. Unless Black Jack's treasure was a veritable fortune, Jon would never have been able to afford the scenery. She didn't think there were this many old ships left in England.

The second ship had turned, marking her course toward the stern of Jon's ship. What were they trying to do, the damn nuts? They'd cut her off, block her path. Surely they were about to collide.

And then she heard it—a splintering crash. Yet the ship hadn't been jarred by a collision. Shouting, coming from the mast above her, called Zoe's attention to a group of men on a wide platform. They motioned to the stern with rifles as authentic looking as their costumes.

The big sail's yardarm had broken like a toothpick.

The young man Jon had been training earlier hung from its ropes by his foot, blood covering his leg and dripping to the deck below. Another thunderous clap, and shot ripped through the sails.

Zoe's mouth went totally dry as Jon scrambled up the rigging to keep the young man from further damage. He held him secure until more of the crew could reach him.

"Mr. Leetch!" Jon called down to his helmsman. "Turn to larboard. We'll brake by backing the main and mizzen tops'ls."

"Aye, Captain." He saluted as Jon picked his way back down the ropes, shouting orders to his men.

"I want the artillery engaged on both sides as soon as they draw in. Continue to man the fighting tops. We'll follow the cannons with rifles and swivel fire."

Zoe watched in dumb fascination as the fantastic scene unfolded before her. Their ship braked as Jon had ordered, sails billowing in the wind. The enemy ships sailed by on either side while the roar of Jon's cannons split the air. Even she knew a broadside when she saw one, and they were engaging the ships on both sides at once.

A return blast of enemy fire knocked her to the deck. Acrid smoke hung in the air, obscuring her view as something warm and wet trickled down her arm. Unbearable pain ripped through her, blackness swam before her eyes. For the second time in her life, she was going to faint.

But not before she realized the fantasy was real.

There was no Jonathan.

He was a creature of the future.

And the man scooping her close in his arms was indeed a pirate thief named Winn.

4

The crash of waves beat an angry rhythm inside his head as Jonathan stirred to aching consciousness. Patiently awaiting his perusal stood a surreal-looking landscape of twilight gray. His gaze met nothing more than a silent mist that wove around the scattered boulders that littered the deserted strand.

He tried to lift his head, but hot arrows of pain pierced his skull. Ever-widening circles of agony assailed him, lacerating his stiffened muscles. His gut burned as cramps gripped him and stirred his stomach into nausea.

Then the heavens opened with a saturating rain that played a cold tattoo upon his body.

What the bloody hell had happened?

This certainly wasn't the hidden passage he'd discovered. Perhaps he'd fallen through a secret tunnel that led to the beach below the estate. . . .

He'd never heard tale of such a thing at Ravenscourt—he'd seen no mark of one on the original estate plans in the archives. Nor was there mention of it in the family records. Yet his explorations had turned up a few hidden panels he'd never been aware of. Why not a bolt hole?

The family history was riddled with intrigue, and the manor could hide an army within. Anything was possible. It could even provide a clue to the whereabouts of Black Jack's treasure. He'd bet his last pound this had something to do with his scapegrace ancestor.

Ah, what a rascal that rogue had been. A man to admire for his rakish appeal and swashbuckling demeanor. What he wouldn't give to have inherited but a bit of the old boy's adventurous manner.

Ah, hell. It was too late now for regrets. He'd dug his own hole with his stodgy precautions and had needed to dig for old Jack's treasure instead. The business was in shambles. His marriage was defunct.

At least the children weren't here to pester him—a good move, despite Zoe's protests. He needed time to himself to straighten things out, not a zoo full of kids to take up his attention.

He shifted slowly to his side and pushed himself to a sitting position. His hands felt cold and gritty, lined with sand. He brushed them together briskly, trying to warm them before he stood.

He had to find the treasure soon.

Either that or run away.

The idea had appeal. It wasn't the first time it had crossed his mind. In fact, it had become a major theme in all his fantasies—leaving the ruins of his life for adventures and intrigue all his own.

Perhaps he had a bit of pirate in him, after all.

Jonathan smiled as renewed vigor coursed through him, lightening his load. Zoe would be worried if he didn't return soon, and he had work to do. By God, he'd find that damned treasure yet!

He pushed to his feet, intent to get out of the rain and back to his digging, but his leg buckled under, slamming him to the ground in a shout of agony. While he rubbed his injured ankle, he heard harsh whispers and the dull pound of running feet.

Sand sprayed across his lap as a burly figure stopped short beside him. Before he had a chance to protest, the brigand hauled him up by the collar in one meaty fist.

Jonathan groaned with renewed pain. His ankle threatened to collapse beneath him. Only the hoodlum's strength kept him from falling face first in wet sand.

He steeled himself and turned his gaze on the assailant. The big man's face became a study in comedy. It was all Jon could do not to laugh as shock turned a fierce, pitted mug into the frightened embarrassment of a child.

"Lor', Cap'n. Didn't know it be you—Mr. Gartner says to quiet the intruder. What happened? Been set upon by the king's men?"

Jon looked at him blankly, not having a clue to what the creature had said. Still, the man seemed to be waiting for an answer, and he was in no position to defend himself from the brute. Not that it was anyone's business but his own what he was doing there.

"I have no idea what happened or how I came to be on the shore. I awoke but a few moments ago, with a knot on my head and the realization that my ankle is at the minimal twisted, and quite possibly broken."

He wondered if the man understood anything he

had said—from his atrocious accent, he'd clearly had little schooling. Jonathan was totally unprepared for the look of concern that crinkled the big man's face.

"I knew it, Cap'n. Lor', I knew it. No good comin' from a night the likes of this." He wrapped an arm around Jon and hoisted him closer. "I'll be helpin' ya back to the ship, er, the *Blackbird,* that is. The *Raven* set sail upon the tide. Not to worry, though—Cap'n Messier will take things in hand."

The man dragged Jonathan down the shore, calling to his fellows to give a hand.

"Who is Captain Messier?" Jon asked as haughtily as he could with his bones being crushed in the man's massive grip. "And who in bloody hell are you?"

"Larmer, Cap'n." The man turned his astonished gaze to Jon.

"I am not your captain, nor have I ever been. I am Jonathan Alexander Dunham, earl of Ravenscourt. And I warn you, Larmer—if you don't unhand me posthaste, the queen herself will have your head."

Jon saw panic fill the man's dark gray eyes. Good. Despite the lack of help at Ravenscourt, he hadn't lost his touch with the serving class. But instead of letting him go, the fool pulled him closer and hurried his steps.

"I demand you release me!" Jonathan shouted.

"Beggin' yer pard'n, Cap'n, but I can't do that. You forgot to say Winnthrop."

The loon seemed to think that explanation enough.

"What in bloody hell does Winnthrop have to do with this?"

"Why, it's yer name. Jonathan Winnthrop Alexander Dunham."

"That was my great-great . . . Damn. I seem to have forgotten how many greats he was—"

"Not the only thing you forgot," Larmer mumbled.

"Anyway, he was one of my great-grandfathers."

"Lor'. It's worse than I thought. Not soon enough I can get ya to the ship. Don't know yer own name, and blatherin' about the queen—"

"What does the queen have to do with this?" Jon demanded, puffing with the effort it took to hobble along.

"Nothin'. Ain't no queen. Ain't no king, for a fact. Just that fat prig Prinny."

"Prinny?" Loon was too good a word for the man. Demented was a better one.

"Aye, sir. The prince regent." Larmer gave him a worried glance.

"This is absolutely ridiculous. Now let me go, I have to get back to my wife before she leaves."

"Wife?" Larmer hastened his steps. "Don't fret, sir. That knock on the head has ya a bit barmy. We'll get the sawbones to look at ya, and you'll soon be feelin' right as rain."

Jonathan shook away the frigid droplets streaming down his face and cursed.

"That's what the bloody hell I'm afraid of."

"Dammit, Princess. Wake up."

Winn's voice was one of command while all the while his heart silently begged Zoe to respond. He wet a cloth in a basin of cool water, wrung it out, and placed it gently across her burning forehead.

It was all his fault.

He should have had Grizzard escort her down to the hold the minute the fighting began. From all he'd seen in the short time he knew her, trouble followed closer on her heels than a pet hound.

Winn dipped the cloth again and patted it over Zoe's flushed cheeks. Why hadn't the little termagant listened? Women were supposed to be obedient. Pliable. His own men would have rushed to do his bidding.

But not Zoe.

Oh, no.

His little princess would obey nothing less than a royal command. If she was awake, he'd wring her neck. That wasn't an option, however. She'd been unconscious since the piece of shot had ripped through her upper arm.

Winn fought the urge to gather the feverish woman in his embrace and give her a good shake. He'd do it, too, if he thought that would help revive her. For the better part of a week he'd been nursing her, as Doc McCairn was up to his armpits with injured men.

Thank God most of the men had suffered only mild injuries. There'd been but one death—and a tragic one it was. A newlywed boy had been blown to bits, leaving his young wife behind and a child on the way. He still had to write to her—a hellish job—one he always dreaded.

Winn pushed his fingers through his disheveled hair, then scratched at his beard, feeling old and unkempt. The new growth itched like the devil, but he'd been too busy, too worried, to shave.

Ah, if Decatur could only see him now. His friend's dashing good looks had the ladies swooning wherever he went, yet Stephen never failed to tease him about his own fastidious grooming and dark appeal, delighting at the telltale blush that would stain Winn's face.

It had been a long time since he'd indulged in such vanity regarding his looks. He kept clean and groomed for comfort alone, caring not a whit what the ladies thought. Until he'd met Zoe, that is. For the first time in years he'd looked in the mirror—really looked at himself. And he'd noticed every gray hair, every timeworn wrinkle, each weathered crease that lined his face.

Hell. He'd even discovered a pure white hair. In his ear, no less!

He'd plucked it out immediately. But he couldn't pluck all the silver hairs from his head or chest, else he'd see his scalp. And to add insult to injury, the hairs on his chest seemed more abundant than ever while he suspected a bit of thinning on his head.

What did the damn things do? he wondered. Migrate?

Oh, well. What was there to worry about? The woman had seemed only mildly interested. Surely with her beauty and her engaging personality she could find a more virile partner, a younger man. Someone like Leetch, perhaps.

But, no. Leetch was too young, too tame, for a woman like Zoe. She needed a sure hand, a firm but loving touch—the mature attention of a man, not a boy. No, Leetch wouldn't do.

Although several times he had caught the stripling eyeing Zoe in quite a mature way. It had made his own blood boil, he admitted it freely . . . at least to himself. The thought of Zoe turning her attentions elsewhere made his innards flip-flop violently in a way not unlike a bout of seasickness.

It was an awful feeling . . . one he felt every time he wiped her hot brow or touched her parchment-dry skin. In little over a week the woman had stood him upon his head and neatly tied him into more intricate knots than the saltiest old sea dogs could ever untangle.

Zoe suddenly moaned and looked up at him with

bloodshot eyes. For a moment Winn held his breath, trying to calm his erratic pulse as she finally came to. He swept a tendril of hair from her face, and Zoe gave him a crooked, heart-wrenching smile before falling back to a restless sleep.

Winn's heart took a minute or two to steady its cadence. That simple smile had pierced his soul. Any more like it, and he'd be leaky as a sieve. The blood seemed to rush from him even now, leaving him drained of energy. Each day she continued like this, her chances grew worse. Winn felt as if the sand from the deck were in his eye as a hot tear dripped on his hand. He ignored it.

But he couldn't ignore the quiet sniffle that sounded behind him as Adam shuffled to his side. He'd been so deep in thought, he hadn't heard the scrape of the door. The boy carried a bowl of steaming oatmeal, which he held out to Winn with quivering hands.

"She isn't able to eat yet, lad." Winn's voice cracked midway through the explanation, and he bit his cheek, striving for control. The iron taste of blood filled his mouth.

"It ain't for the princess, Captain. Thought you'd like a bite. Me and Cookie, that is." The boy thrust the bowl into Winn's hands, then lowered his head, shyly scuffing his shoes against the floor. "You should eat regular-like to keep up your strength, what with yer lady needin' you to care for her, and all."

The little boy's lower lip trembled as he stole a glance at the unconscious Zoe. He swiped at his teary eyes with the back of his sleeve, and Winn's heart twisted. The boy was like a son to him. It hurt to see the lad suffer any more than he already had in his short life.

"There now, Adam." He ruffled the boy's windswept hair and drew him close for a quick hug—he smelled like sunshine and youth. The mite buried his face into the crook of Winn's neck and let out a heartfelt sob.

"She taught me how to play cards, she did, sir. I'm the best man on ship at go fish. But I know Miz Zoe let me beat her a'purpose a time or two. Let me win all her sticks of chewing gum and the most heavenly chocolate cake. Please, Cap'n, don't let her die," he choked out.

Winn looked down at the small flushed features of his patient. The taste of fear filled his mouth and mingled with the flavor of blood. Struggling to control long forgotten emotions, he shifted his gaze to the row of windows at the stern of the ship. The dying sun shot a last defiant shaft of golden light across the somber pewter sky.

"She won't die, lad," he whispered. "Not if I can help it."

Winn took a spoonful of oatmeal and shoved it into his mouth. Although it smelled richly of brown sugar and cinnamon, it tasted like paste and sank in his stomach like a rock. He ran his hand through the silken tangle of curls that framed Zoe's porcelain face before forcing another spoonful down for nourishment, determined to maintain his strength to see her through this. . . .

Winn remained anchored to the spot—not only through a sense of duty, but because of the invisible chains that led directly to his heart and soul.

Squish, squish, sssss. Squish, squish, sssss.

Zoe heard the sound again, just on the other side of consciousness. She could almost reach it, pulled by its mystery as well as by the sharp tang of vinegar and the aromatic scent of coffee. She couldn't pinpoint the strangely familiar noise. But it had been going on for a good five minutes before she felt strong enough to flutter eyelids that seemed to weigh a thousand pounds each.

Slowly lifting one lid, she peered through a bleary eye. At the foot of the bed sat Winn, his loose dark hair shielding his face from her gaze as he bent over an object in his lap.

Squish, squish, sssss.

Her attention shifted to the source of his fascination—her pump-up sneakers. Why are men so engrossed with gadgets? she wondered. It seemed they hadn't changed much through the centuries.

Well, at least it wasn't a power tool. Even Jon had played enthusiastically with the gardener's electric shears. She wondered what Winn would think if he could get his hands on a chain saw.

Oh, my God.

Winn. She tried the name out in her mind. This wasn't Jonathan, she realized. Yet they looked so much alike, they could be twins. Zoe felt as if the air had been squeezed from her body as she struggled for both breath and sanity.

Her sudden gasp drew Winn's attention. The look of awe and delight that covered his face was quickly supplanted by one of concern and awkward embarrassment. He looked like a wreck. The dark circles under his eyes brought to mind a raccoon. His hair stood on end where his fingers had swept through it, and his face had taken on a grayish cast.

"You look like hell," she whispered through a raw throat. Her mouth tasted as if something had died in it.

"That's because I missed you like hell," Winn murmured in a voice as rough as hers.

He came to her then, kneeling by her side. Brushing a stray hair from her eyes, he rained kisses over her face. Zoe's body turned languorous as she drowned in a sea of sensations.

Emotions overwhelmed her—confusion, disbelief. Wonder. Memories of the last week flashed across her consciousness, reminding her of Winn's gentle devotion throughout the days and nights when she was sure she was going to die.

She owed him her life . . . whoever he was.

It was only due to the man's relentless pestering that she'd fought her way back. She couldn't die fast enough to avoid his haranguing—the only way to shut him up had been to reach for the light. A wise choice, she thought, pleased with the way his response had stirred her blood.

Still stirred her.

Zoe tingled to the tips of her toes, relaxed if not refreshed, relishing each soft brush of his mouth and the gentle fingers that stroked her hands. Those same fingers had cooled her warm brow with a soothing touch, had held her chilled body close to his. And they were not the hands of Jonathan, she could see that now. The blunt tips lacked the refinement of Jon's tapered fingers, and the wide palms and thick calluses spoke of a life outdoors, at sea. Such wonderful hands, really. . . .

Her errant thoughts brought a flush of excitement, and Winn pressed his lips to her forehead. "Feverish, Princess?" he asked. His concern melted her to her bones like warm butter, penetrating her soul like a soothing balm.

Zoe raised her shaky hand to his beautiful obsidian-

and-starlight hair, but the motion hurt her and she groaned with the pain. Damn, she'd been hit by that Mack truck again. Her stiffened muscles screamed in protest, her left shoulder ached, and her head began to pound.

"You haven't been hitting me with a hammer, now, have you?" she grated out, looking up into his pain-darkened eye. He shook his head, unable to speak. "And you aren't Jonathan, either." It was more a statement than a question. Zoe concentrated hard on his face, recalling her last lucid thoughts. "Your name is Winn."

He bent down to kiss her full on the mouth, lingering there for a moment. "Aye, Princess, the name is Winn. And it sounds beautiful upon your lips."

"Winn," she said again, testing the sound of it, relishing the way his eyelid lowered seductively each time she said his name. To the bottom of her soul, she knew him for a pirate. But was he actually Black Jack Alexander?

Zoe sighed and closed her eyes, drifting on the edge of sleep while Winn held her hands in his. He couldn't be, she thought. Yet what other explanation did she have? She'd sort it out sooner or later. Right now she could barely keep her eyes open, and her arm throbbed something awful. Her last thought was that time travel was so Orwellian. . . .

She woke up with a start after what seemed only a few minutes, to discover Winn curled up at her side beneath the covers. He looked younger in his sleep, boyish despite the silver shining at his temples. The dark circles below his lashes were proof enough of sleepless nights, constant care, and his stubborn devotion.

She instinctively knew he'd earned his rest.

And knew they belonged together, side by side.

Zoe snuggled up to Winn's warmth and fell back to a sweet, dream-filled sleep.

Winn paced the deck restlessly, pondering the mystery of Zoe. His heart had stopped beating when he'd found her on the deck, covered with blood.

The battle had waged around him, but no more so than the battle that raged within him. It was all he could do to place one foot in front of the other as he had made his way to the lower decks.

Poor Adam, he thought, remembering that awful day.

The boy had followed him to the cabin, tears streaming down his pinched little face, and had thrown himself on Zoe's still form the minute he'd lowered her to his bed. Then Winn had gone in search of the doctor, leaving Zoe to Adam's care.

McCairn had been busy with injuries but had already treated the worst of them. Winn had practically carried the man back to his cabin, demanding immediate attention for Zoe. While the doctor had dug into her arm for pieces of shot, he'd felt as if his heart were being cut out.

Not till Zoe was resting as comfortably as she could, and he had pulled a protesting Adam from her side to sleep someplace other than the floor, did Winn realize he'd abandoned his command for a stubborn, independent wisp of a woman he hardly knew.

No, that wasn't entirely true.

He knew everything that mattered about the woman. How she valued honesty, cherished loving, craved the same intimacy he wanted to share. He knew her as thoroughly as he knew himself. And knew they were meant for each other as surely as he knew there was a divine hand dipping into their lives.

Fate? Destiny? The hand of God himself?

Hell, he hadn't a bloody clue. He just understood to the marrow in his bones that this woman was his and he was hers. But who was she? From whence had she come?

Aye. The puzzle remained, though he'd put it aside in the days since her precipitous arrival. So much had happened in so little time, it was no wonder he hadn't pondered the situation more carefully.

There had to be a logical reason for her arrival. He wouldn't believe otherwise.

Winn stopped his pacing and surveyed the ship with his keen eye. The men worked in a natural harmony, with a precision that was the envy of his other fellows who captained the budding American Navy. He'd chosen to command as a privateer, in charge of his own ship as he saw fit. Many of the crew were navy issue, but they'd been with him for two years now, since the start of the war in 1812.

His own men filled in the gaps—a mixture of hardened seamen, young scamps, starry-eyed dreamers, and reformed pirates. He'd never truly been a pirate himself. That rumor had sprung from his forays into English waters against her profitable merchantmen. The regent had been a close friend, after all, and was loath to call the Ravenscourt heir traitor.

So Prinny had opted for pirate instead, securing Winn's fierce reputation with that one word. Winn chuckled to himself and directed a change in sails with a flick of his hand, so well were his men trained.

Already he'd amassed a fortune, as had his crew,

compliments of the rich prizes taken from the hapless merchantmen. He easily had enough to pay the debts on his American estate, with money left over to send to his grandmother and the few of his relatives who remained in England.

He sent it via secret messenger, of course. It wouldn't do for a captain representing the United States Navy to have direct intercourse with patriots of an enemy nation. It had taken blackmail to force his meeting with the regent's man. Despite the way it galled him, Winn would comply with the terms set forth in order to maintain his English holdings and thereby provide his relatives with a secure future.

No. Prinny's request would not alter his duty or his plans. It was a debt of honor, not an act of treason. He wouldn't jeopardize his mission for personal matters. And he would never betray or abandon the country of his heart, preferring American citizenship to any title conferred on him elsewhere.

He did remember Zoe saying something about returning to America. He hoped it was true—it would be another secure layer added to the foundation of their future. But come what may, he'd have a future with her. He'd decided that in a heartbeat when he'd found her inert form on deck.

The only questions remaining in his mind were linked to the mystery that had brought her to him. Winn looked around, pleased with the smooth running of the ship, and nodded to the ever-energetic Mr. Leetch. The young man bobbed his own sandy head in acknowledgment.

It was amazing how easily the boy took to command. He would be a good leader for the men to follow when Winn returned home to a new life on his own land.

Zoe by his side, God willing.

Winn's feet took him automatically in her direction at the same time his thoughts did. Perhaps there was a way to get to the root of her puzzle. He'd already planned to ask her himself, when she finally awakened—she was presently catching up on a recuperative sleep. But there was another way he might be able to put together the pieces of the puzzle.

Winn stepped into his cabin and went to his desk. He cleared the top of clutter and slid onto his chair before hoisting Zoe's bag from the floor. The bloody thing felt like forty-two-pound shot. The woman was evidently stronger than he'd thought to carry such weight.

He found the clasp that held it closed and, with a flick of the wrist, pried it open. Then, feeling like a true pirate, he turned the bag over to study his plunder. The array of items proved mind-boggling. Many of them were foreign to him—objects he'd never seen before. And the woman still had a healthy stash of food, despite her losses to Adam.

Flying must demand much energy, he thought, for such a slim person to require such large amounts of nourishment. The woman carried not an extra ounce on her lean frame. He'd noticed as much over the days he'd cared for her and cooled down her fevered body.

He stole a glance at Zoe, and his mouth went dry. The covers had tangled beneath her long legs as she tossed and turned upon the bed and now rode sinfully high upon her thigh. Winn's groin tightened immediately. He prayed that his princess wasn't a spy, for she controlled his mind and body even when asleep. It was a sobering thought, bringing Winn's attention back to his booty.

He shifted the contents around on his desk, determined to find a clue to Zoe's identity and past. And to find out just who the bloody hell this Jonathan was.

It proved an easy enough task to separate the food into a pile. Some of it was foreign, and others—like the well-ripened banana—were exotic treats that he'd seen only in the tropics. How she'd managed to preserve them was a mystery.

But what amazed him most were the intricate wrappings made from materials surely wrought with magic, a conclusion he knew to be patently illogical and one that tested his beliefs. What he would have scoffed at as absurdity mere moments before seemed as logical an answer as any he could conjure. . . .

A poor choice of words, he thought.

After snapping the clear paper for several minutes, stretching it till it tore, then wadding it into a cushiony ball, Winn played with the metallic wrapping. It was not capable of stretching like the clear one but had excellent properties when it came to folding and retaining its shape.

Clearly a miracle.

The possibilities it brought to mind—the application to shipping alone—made his mouth water with anticipation. The copper sheathing below the water line had a tendency to rot the lead bolts of the ship's frame. A new metal with the tensile abilities of copper, but without its corrosive action, could revolutionize the entire shipping industry.

Perhaps Zoe was an inventor.

Aye, he thought. Inventor seemed a more logical conclusion than magician or witch, and also pleased his practical nature. He couldn't wait to discuss her findings. They could work together, form a partnership in business as well as in life. What a wonderful thought.

He'd always been attracted to intelligent women and didn't adhere to the rubbish about the inferior minds of the fairer sex. While his profligate father had gambled enough money to reduce the estate to a pitiful condition, his mum had held the family together with her own forays into a profitable cottage industry with the servants.

Yes, men who claimed that women were of lesser intelligence were stupid themselves, insecure . . . or both.

Winn sifted further through the objects on his desk and found an amazing pen with ink located within a slim, elongated barrel. A wind-up ruler curled into its own metal box, much like the insides of the clock he'd taken apart as a child. He played with clever folding pins and scissors with remarkable blades, thinking he'd like a cutlass with such a fine edge.

The remaining objects were mechanical by nature and would require weeks to figure out their intricate functions, which was fine by him—days often passed slowly at sea. Although he practically drooled in anticipation, he had the self-discipline to sweep the items aside to explore another time.

He always had been fascinated by mechanical devices, the lure of the new—the quest for buried treasures.

Perhaps the word *pirate* suited him better than privateer, after all.

Winn shook his head, amused at the thought. Then he turned his attention to the remaining devices—two intricate mechanical items that had immediately tugged at his attention. He'd purposely saved them to study last.

One had numbers inscribed across a foreign material unlike metal or wood. Another of Zoe's inventions, he supposed. When he pressed the inscriptions, numbers flashed across the top. But the numerals appeared erratic in the dim light he worked by, and he hadn't the patience to tarry with it.

The other item was rectangular, with gears and dials marked "LOUDNESS" and "BASS." A musical instrument of great wonder, he discovered as a sudden blast of sound rang forth. Winn's fingers flew over the gears and depressions until the music subsided, fortunately before Zoe could wake.

An entire orchestra housed within a little box.

Amazing.

Winn's gaze shifted to the final items he'd gleaned from Zoe's full bag, and his mouth watered. A stack of magnificent books made from the finest paper, with imaginative titles and equally colorful and scandalous illustrations wrapped around cover and bindings. Half-naked men and women in intimate embraces.

Quite titillating, actually.

Winn grabbed the book with the most enigmatic title and relocated to his cushioned chair. Then he sat back into its downy softness, consumed the ripe banana, and, utterly fascinated, began to read what was lauded as a romance.

5

"*For God's sake, Winn.* Turn down the lamp and get to bed." Zoe blinked at the flickering light. Winn's profile was haloed, giving an angelic cast to his devilishly appealing features. "You're going to need two eye patches if you don't shut that book—you'll go blind reading in such awful light."

"Just a little more, Zo," he mumbled.

Besides the ever-present slap of the sea, all she heard was the soft rustle of a page turning.

"That's what you said the last two times I awoke. What on earth are you reading, anyway? Nothing can be that engrossing."

Winn lifted his gaze, taking a moment to focus on her. A lock of dark hair swept over his forehead, making him look like a mischievous boy. Only the flicker of silver betrayed his age. There it was again— her heart doing gymnastics.

"Actually, they're some of your books. Quite fascinating," he said. "Didn't know which to read first, so I've been switching between them."

Zoe rolled to her side, pillowing her head with her hands. "And exactly what books would those be?" she asked.

"*Bride of the Devil, Love's Flaming Conflagration,* and my personal favorite"—his smile widened to devastating proportions—"*Pagan Pirate's Perpetual Passion.*"

Zoe stifled the laugh that bubbled up to her throat. "And what makes that one so special?" As if she didn't know its appeal.

"Why," he drawled, "because everyone knows that a pirate lover is ever so much more virile than other men." His dark eye positively gleamed with self-satisfaction.

A pirate lover.

It held some interesting possibilities—ones that skipped through Zoe's head and heart and had her body singing. What would he be like as a lover?

The man intrigued her no end. Even now, watching that familiar, devilish smile twitch at his lips, her emotions were pulled inside out. She met his gaze, finding a pool of fire lighting his eye. Seduction in a glance, she thought.

"By the way, did I hear correctly before, Princess? Were you asking me to join you in bed?" He raised a questioning brow.

"No, Winn. I didn't ask you to join me in bed." She paused, and his grin crumpled. "Nor am I asking you now. I'm demanding it." She was enjoying this—the camaraderie, the teasing—it was great fun watching his frown turn to a heavenly smile. "Of course, all we'll do is sleep," she added sweetly, not trusting his expression.

"Of course. Sleep. We wouldn't want to compromise you, now, would we?"

He rose from the chair, marking the page of his pirate saga before placing the book on the desk. Then he stretched his arms, working out the kinks in his neck. A sudden groan drew Zoe's attention.

"What is it?"

"Nothing."

She noticed the grim line of his lips. "Since when does nothing elicit a groan?"

Zoe watched as Winn drew closer and bent to drop a kiss on her nose. "If you haven't noticed, my dear, I am not the man I used to be."

"Since I never knew the man you used to be, what difference could it possibly make?"

Unease flickered across his expressive face.

"I've had my share of injuries, and the subsequent aches and pains that accompany them." He paused significantly, holding her gaze. "I'm not a young man anymore."

She looked him up and down, liking what she saw. "You're not in your dotage, either."

"I'm thirty-five years old, Zoe. Are you sure you don't mind sharing your bed with an old man?"

Zoe saw doubt still etched into his face and heard his sigh of defeat, as soft as the wind. Her heart tumbled over at his sad perception of himself.

"I don't mind, as long as you don't. I'm thirty-eight, Winn. Three years your senior."

He raised an imperious brow. "I'm being serious, Zoe."

"So am I. I'm just better preserved. Must be all that good food and vitamins we have in the future. Come here, Errol Flynn, and warm my tired old body with yours."

Winn looked at her searchingly, as if trying to decipher what she'd said. But she didn't have enough energy for explanations. Coming to some inner conclusion, he stepped over to the lamp and doused the wick. She could hear him fumbling with his clothes in the dark and imagined him folding the garments and placing them neatly on his trunk.

So different from Jonathan, she thought. And so alike.

Chalk another aspect up to genetics. For all his faults, Jonathan had been an excellent—if methodical—lover. Had he also inherited his prowess from Winn's genes?

The squeak of the bed ropes marked Winn's arrival. He slid beneath the crisp sheets, smelling of sea and sun. . . and Winn. A heady fragrance, she thought, one that would make a best-selling after-shave. She could imagine the advertisements with her virile pirate. With his enticing patch and windswept face, dressed in boots and tight breeches and unbuttoned silk shirt, he'd bring modern-day women to their knees. She stifled the feelings of jealousy that image brought.

She snuggled up to him, pressing against his back, and noticed they were both modestly wearing loose shirts. Bless the man—he owned a conscience. Unfortunately, she didn't. Character makes the man, she thought, and Winn's character rivaled the depths of the sea. Ironic that so humble a quality only enhanced his sensual appeal.

Zoe drew her hand along Winn's jawline, feeling the sharpness of his beard. Sifted her fingers through his hair, the thick silky waves she always longed to touch. Then stroked down his wide shoulder and muscled arm, till she caught his hand.

She twined her fingers through his.

Warmth radiated from him. Soothing. Comforting. Better than an electric blanket. Their joined hands brushed against his lower torso, and she could feel the muscles tense, his shaft spring to life.

"Oh, my," she whispered as Winn rolled on his side to face her. She shifted closer and winced.

Winn drew his arm over his eyes. "Ah, Princess. You'll be the death of me yet."

"And how's that?" she whispered, imagining the bemused look upon his face. Skimming her fingers over his lips, she detected his quirky grin.

"Heart failure."

"Funny"—Zoe drew her hand down Winn's sculpted chest and pressed her palm to his heart—"it seems to be doing fine." Her fingers skittered over his body to his hardened masculinity. "But other parts are throbbing."

"Exactly," Winn hissed through gritted teeth. He grabbed her wandering hand and pulled it away. Zoe's sharp breath betrayed the pain that slight movement brought. "And with your wound far from healed, those parts will have to keep on throbbing. I'll not hurt you, Princess."

Zoe shifted to a more comfortable position. Damn, but he was right. If a gentle caress could stir up this much pain, she'd be dead after a night of loveplay.

"Then hold me, Flynn." She waited in silence for his response. She heard a soft sigh, then his gentle curse.

"It's Winn, dammit."

He drew her against him, careful of her injury, snuggling close. Again she smelled the clean enticing scent of him, so unique. A medley of the elements—

wind, and sun, and rain—with a touch of. . . banana?
She needed her rest more than she'd thought.

"Keep on holding me, Winn Dammit," she murmured.
And he did just that.

She had once read that the first step toward insanity was smelling things that weren't there, and the second step was hearing things. Well, she'd been smelling
the vinegary aroma of salad dressing for days and had
even detected the sweet, ripe tang of bananas. Yet she
knew the one in her bag was gone—she'd checked.

And now she could swear she heard chickens.

It wasn't a good omen.

Zoe crossed the deck with a tentative step, still
weak and unsure of her footing. She'd never been a
good sailor. The few cruises she'd taken with
Jonathan were disasters. She'd spent most of each
voyage in bed, nauseated, until discovering medica-
tion for motion sickness. But her affinity with the sea
had already been soured.

Luckily she'd packed two boxes of pills for her flight
home. Rough weather in the air affected her as much
as the dips and crests of the sea. The second pack had
been thrown in as a backup—she had a tendency to
lose things.

The combination of her trip through time, the
knock on her head, and her injured arm had made her
viciously ill. She popped a pill as soon as she awoke,
praying they'd reach land soon.

Zoe turned with a start at the distinct squawk of
chickens. This far out at sea she could imagine an
occasional migratory bird, perhaps a seagull roaming
afar. It wouldn't have bothered her in the least.

But . . . chickens?

She surveyed the deck and saw nothing unusual. All around her the sailors were hard at work—men spliced ropes together, boys stitched sails—everything was being scrubbed, polished, and well attended to.

In fact, amid the bustle of so much activity Zoe felt oddly invisible.

It was clear the men wouldn't bother her or hinder her explorations. So she continued to stroll the deck, surreptitiously eyeing every nook and cranny for the mystery chickens. It was like a game of hide-and-seek—she'd hear a squawk and sidle over to it. But the noise stopped when she drew close.

After half an hour of this game, she grew tired and irritated, so she parked herself on the side of the deck and leaned against a lifeboat. She had closed her eyes, resting her head back to catch the warmth of the sun, and was just drifting off when she heard a loud squawk directly behind her.

Zoe jumped up, steadying herself before turning to the boat. Gingerly she pulled back a flap of canvas and peered into the shadowed interior. A foul smell assailed her. Well, not foul.

Fowl.

The whole damn boat was filled with chickens.

She couldn't believe her eyes—cage upon cage of chickens were stuffed in the lifeboats. It was straight out of a Monty Python movie. But at least her brainbox wasn't faulty.

Imagine, all those pirate romances she'd read, and not once had they mentioned chickens. Granted, chickens were loud and smelly and not very romantic, yet she thought their presence both logical and interesting. And it solved the mystery of the endless bowls of chicken soup Winn and Adam had been shoving down her.

Cookie must have had a Jewish mother.

Zoe straightened the canvas, wondering what other surprises the ship held, when a *clip-clop* sounded directly behind her and something smacked her in the butt. She banged against the lifeboat before falling to the deck. If this was someone's idea of a joke, she wasn't laughing.

As she pushed herself to her hands and knees, evil ideas for retribution crossed her mind. But before she could confront the prankster, she was whacked again. This time she rolled to her side, keeping her vulnerable anatomy behind her, so to speak. As she lay on the deck a raspy tongue slobbered across her face like wet sandpaper.

"Yuck!"

She practically gagged at the awful smell that accompanied it. "Dog breath" was too good a description. It was foul. She squinted her eyes against the sun as she focused on the perpetrator.

Goat breath.

She'd never smelled anything so rank in her life. It was worse than the stink of chickens. High on the scale of utterly gross.

And the damn thing continued to stand over her, fanning her face with its warm nastiness. She tried to scramble to a sitting position, but the goat closed in and licked her each time. If she didn't get away soon, someone would have to scrub the deck again, for she'd surely be sick.

Zoe heard a chuckle but was not amused to find Winn standing beside her, a wicked grin upon his face.

"Get this damn thing off of me now, Flynn. Or

you'll be eating raw goat meat in three seconds flat."
She couldn't say another word without risking a goat
tongue in her mouth.

"It's Winn, dammit. How many times must I tell
you that?"

"I don't care if it's Old MacDonald and you're a
gentleman farmer, or if you're Noah, and this is the
freakin' Ark. Suburban women do not let goats drool
on them—young or old."

She managed a sitting position by batting the goat
on the nose. Winn grabbed a tuft of fur on the
offender's neck and pulled until the animal backed
up. Zoe shot to her feet like a rocket, not chancing
another assault. She straightened her drool-dampened
T-shirt and cast an icy stare at Winn.

"This place is a damn zoo. A menagerie."

"Something bothering you, Princess?" Winn looked
at her straight-faced, but she'd swear a dirty gleam
sparkled in his eye. "Pray, don't hold back. It isn't
good for your spleen. Tell me what you really think."

She stuck her tongue out at him, and his facade
began to crack. Soon the hint of a smile became a
downright belly laugh. Zoe placed her hands on her
hips and scowled. It did nothing to stop the tears that
ran from Winn's eye.

The man was incorrigible. Hell, he could afford to
laugh. He wasn't the one who reeked of goat.

Zoe gave him one last killer glare before turning to
the gangway in search of Adam, leaving Winn doubled over with laughter. She heard the chuckles as his
men joined in.

Sure doesn't take much to amuse these louts.

Zoe ignored the idiots, heading for the lower decks
as she followed the scent of vinegar, determined to

filch some salad from Cookie. And to hell with the chicken soup.

"Excuse me." Zoe tapped the shoulder of a young sailor. "Could you point the way to the kitchen?" The sooner she got there, the better—her stomach was beginning to growl.

The young man blushed when her belly gurgled and nodded his head. "Seems you're a bit turned around, ma'am. The galley's back a ways and on a different deck. I'll take you there if you can wait a moment while I finish my task."

Zoe looked at him oddly as the smell of salad dressing wafted by stronger than ever. "Thanks, but I think I'll pass. There's something else I need to do now." Like figure out whether she was at step two on the route to insanity.

The man bobbed his head, and Zoe continued following her nose and the increasingly strong scent of vinegar. The fumes nearly overwhelmed her by the time she found the source. She stepped into the room, eyes watering not from the acrid aroma of vinegar, but from the putrid odors of stale sweat, old blood, and the gut-wrenching stench of decaying flesh. Hammocks hanging from the ceiling of the close quarters held a number of severely injured men in varying states of consciousness.

"Someone open a window," she groaned. She managed to pull one side of her jacket over her nose the moment she started to gag. Another straight breath and she'd be puking all over the floor instead of being racked with dry heaves.

She made her way to a porthole and opened it

wide, fanning some of the foul air outside. She'd opened another before she heard a roar of outrage directly behind her.

"And precisely what are ya doin' in my sickbay, mistress?"

Zoe turned to see the mottled red face of a very angry, very large man. His shoulders blocked the entire doorway.

"Looking for a bowl of salad," she said through her jacket.

"Well, ya won't be findin' it here."

"Thank God."

The big man eyed her. "I'll kindly thank ya to mind yer own business, mistress, and leave the doctorin' ta me." He crossed his arms in a belligerent manner that irked her no end. "And that includes keepin' the air out so my men can recover."

"If you don't let the air in, your men will die, from the stench alone."

He scowled. "I'll have ya know the vinegar's used as a disinfectant."

"And I'll have ya know it's not the smell of vinegar that'll kill them. Haven't you bathed these men, doctor?" Zoe looked him up and down. "It *is* doctor, isn't it? You wouldn't happen to be the local butcher, would you?"

"Why, ya sassy bitch," he growled, and took a menacing step forward. Zoe held her position, despite a slight quiver to her knees. The man was as big as a house. "I'll not take this insubordination. You'll shut that fiery mouth and hie your wee tail outa here." He loomed over her quite effectively.

"You and what army are gonna accomplish that?" she asked in her softest tone.

The man paused—her self-assurance seemed to draw him up short.

Probably used to mindless servitude from women, she thought. Well, welcome to the world of women's lib.

"I don't need no army to toss ya out on yer little bum."

"Since your captain is mighty fond of my little bum, I'd suggest you rethink your plans. That is, if you're capable of intelligent thought. . . ."

Yes, she detected it again. A definite growl that matched his hairy demeanor. The image of a fuzzy red bear came to mind, sending her into sudden fits of laughter. The doctor looked at her askance, taking a long step backward. If she wasn't mistaken, fear had supplanted his angry glare.

The bear was afraid of her!

That revelation did nothing to halt her peals of laughter. She was doubled over, tears streaming from her eyes, when she heard a shuffle behind her.

"What, may I ask, is going on?"

Winn's dark tones didn't stop her amusement, but lack of air did. She gulped in as much as her lungs could hold while the Bear turned to his captain.

"The woman's a bloody lunatic. Stark ravin' mad. Comes into m' sickbay thrustin' open the port'ls, then keels over in hysterical laughter."

Winn turned to Zoe. "Is that true?"

She nodded, managing to catch her breath, and answered. "At least the part about opening the windows and laughing."

Zoe looked up from her bent position, noticing for the first time the attention they were drawing from the patients who were awake. She also noticed how the doctor's bristling brows resembled fuzzy caterpillars. . . . To her credit, only a fraction of a chuckle escaped.

Winn held out a hand to her, helping her to stand upright—a good belly laugh was tough on the back. She accepted it gracefully, giving the doctor a pointed glance. He turned to Winn with a scowl.

"Ach, I can see yer rod's been doin' yer thinkin' for ya. No use in statin' m' case fer nothin'. The mistress here'll be wheedlin' ya to her side with a mere swish o' her tail," the Bear growled. He shook his head in disgust and did an about-face out the door.

"Zoe?"

"Now, Winn. You know I don't swish my tail." She watched his brow raise over his good eye. "Well, not on purpose, anyway. I had to open a window. The air in here was unfit to breathe." She crossed her arms in front of her, waiting for an argument. There wasn't any.

"Now that you mention it," Winn said, nostrils curling, "there is a bit of a stink to the place."

"A bit?"

"Quite a bit."

"Exactly."

"You still had no right to open those port'ls without the doctor's permission."

"I didn't think beyond getting some clean air in here, let alone know there was a doctor to confer with first. Recycling germs is not healthy, Winn. Neither is the filthy state these men are in."

She swept a glance at the occupants of the gloomy quarters, took note of their dirty, discolored bandages, and winced. With no sunlight or air, and filthy bodies, the place was a breeding ground for germs. Something had to be done or, having survived their wounds, the men would die from infection. She wished she had a medical degree.

Well, she thought, you don't have to be a doctor to know about first aid and the importance of cleanliness. Zoe took off her jacket and tossed it to Winn, who had been watching her.

"Here ya go," she said as she rolled up her sleeves. "When you put that away, send down Adam to help me. Oh, and some muscled men with the cleanest linen you can find, strong soap, boiling water, and lots of alcohol in whatever form you have it."

She turned away, intent on opening the other windows, uh, port'ls. Winn's deep rasp echoed behind her.

"Have you any other orders, Princess?"

She spun around, catching a fleeting twitch of amusement on that stern, angular face. Yet a second later the man looked as if his features were carved from stone. She started to explain, but the "doctor" chose that moment to reenter the room.

"So. The sassy baggage is now givin' orders to the cap'n as if he were a lowly cabin boy."

Zoe had the grace to blush. She did sound a bit of the boss—all for a good reason, of course.

"Nay, leave her be, McCairn. Zoe is a famous inventor. I gather she has knowledge that can help the men."

Inventor? Famous? She hadn't a clue to what he meant. But he could call her whatever he chose if she could help these poor souls.

McCairn looked at her again, eyeing her slowly up and down. He didn't appear a bit impressed, but the menace in his eyes changed to interest.

"An inventor, ya say? And what does that have to do with doctorin'?" He kept his gaze upon her while Winn answered.

"I imagine she's discovered new methods that might save these men's lives. Is that it, Princess?"

Zoe gulped, amazed at the confidence Winn showed in her. She managed a "Yes" while crossing her fingers behind her back. McCairn's steady gaze didn't waver. Goose bumps marched up and down her spine while she waited for God knew what. Then the bear of a doctor nodded, and Winn slipped out the door.

"Fresh air, ya say?" The doctor's booming voice jerked her spine. "And boilin' water?"

She nodded.

He shook his head back and forth. "What'll they be thinkin' of next?"

Zoe remained glued to the spot, praying she could actually make a difference. She'd hate like hell if her efforts failed. In any case, it wouldn't do any harm to instill some good old twentieth-century cleanliness into the habits of the nineteenth-century doctor.

If it *was* the nineteenth century. . . .

McCairn's formidable growl drew her from her introspection and spun her around. He had pried open another porthole.

"Well. Aren't ya gonna get started, girl? Or are ya gonna leave me guessin' as to your methods?"

Zoe squared her shoulders, approaching her new charges just as Adam zoomed into the room. The boy skidded to a halt by her side, chest plumped out with self-importance.

"Water's comin' down soon, Princess. Cap'n says you need my help." Wonder shone in his eyes.

"Sure do, Adam. Couldn't get a thing done without an assistant."

Zoe smiled at the boy's sudden speechlessness— she'd never encountered it in Adam before. And she really did need his presence beside her—if only as an ally. She pulled him to her side in a quick hug before she began her ministrations.

Looking up, she caught the Bear's assessing gaze. His features seemed to have softened somewhat. Whether it was due to her ideas or the close relationship she'd developed with Adam, she didn't know. And she didn't care, as long as it was a good sign. Putting her worries aside, she cleared her mind for the task at hand.

But not before adding a mental note to ask Winn exactly what century it was, anyway.

6

Zoe rubbed the small of her back, then moved on to her tender arm—after four days of nursing the injured, her entire body ached like hell. Her hair oozed oil, her scalp itched, and the tips of her fingers had cracked from the harsh soap and alcohol she'd wielded. The one good consequence was that she'd finally grown immune to the overpowering stench. Her nose would never be the same again.

She stretched the kinks out of her shoulders, then shuffled down the planks with a pan of hot water. One man had died despite their efforts—an old salt with a gut wound—too weak to fight the rapid infection that fired through his belly like a furnace. His death had been a blessing, but his cries of agony still echoed in her head.

There'd been a brief service above deck—a touching eulogy for a well-loved friend. He'd been a favorite among the crew, and not a dry eye could be found on board as he met his final resting place in the sea he so loved.

Winn had withdrawn after the ceremony, and she'd avoided the cabin for privacy's sake. But he'd come looking for her deep in the night, insisting she get a few hours' sleep, even if he could not. Ignoring her protests, he'd swept her up, carrying her to his cabin.

She'd fallen asleep against his shoulder long before they arrived. And had wakened in Winn's arms shortly before dawn.

He'd held her there all night.

A tousled black curl had fallen across his forehead. She'd brushed it back gently, not wanting to disturb his sleep, noting the wings of silver that framed his face. A rush of tenderness coursed through her at the memory.

Even rumpled and weary, in the depths of sleep, with dark circles beneath the fan of his lashes, she thought him the handsomest man she'd ever seen. And wondered how she could have mistaken him for Jon.

Yes, she thought as she carefully crossed the uneven floor, there was no mistake about it. The man was a definite rogue. Look how he affected her.

He made her heart do terrible things. . . .

Flip within her like a circus dog. Ache like a teenager's in the first throes of love. Thump at a pace so hard and strong, she feared it would explode inside her chest.

Everything about him drew her to him. The way he walked. His dimpled cheek. His gentle teasing and frequent laughter. The strong, easy way he commanded his men, keeping a quiet dignity about him.

And his ebony voice—as dark as his black velvet patch and the licorice depths of his eye. Even in the dark of night his voice could stroke her senses with its raspy edge until she felt her very soul afire.

He controlled her heart without a thought, wringing an unwanted desire in her. Making her think of insane possibilities and yearn for entanglements she'd meant to avoid. Winn made the impossible come to life, accomplished merely by who and what he was. Just by being Winn.

Zoe pulled herself atop a stool, balancing the pan of sterile water in her lap. Slowly she cut through the crusted bandages and pulled them back from Turcotte's knee. Thankfully, the swelling had subsided and the lacerations from the ropes appeared to be clean, but the calf below it was still ripe with pus. McCairn would take off the leg at the first sight of gangrene.

It would be the leg or his life. Maybe both.

McCairn had spelled it out plainly.

It wasn't fair, she thought, how cruel life could be. He was such a young man, not yet in his prime. He was the one Winn had been instructing in the rigging, who'd been blasted with shot but a moment later.

She remembered seeing him caught in the ropes high above her, his lifeblood dripping to the deck. He'd been through so much. . . . She imagined him, broken in spirit as well as body, unable to climb any rigging again, returning home to his young wife. Or worse, she thought, would be his shrouded body, sliding like the old salt's, into the cold, deep sea.

Zoe dipped a cloth into the boiled water, then into the jar she held in her hand. It had to work; she had nothing else for him—only her antibacterial face wash and the antibiotics she kept for her ears. Every time she flew they became blocked, and she always wound up with a sinus infection.

It was a sure thing she wouldn't be flying again soon.

She finished a thorough washing of his leg, leaving a generous amount of cream upon the wound before binding it in boiled cloths. Then she fished in her pocket for one of her pills and opened the capsule onto Turcotte's tongue. She coaxed a few swallows of water past his cracked lips, having learned from McCairn the trick of keeping an unconscious man from dehydration.

And she smoothed a dark curl from the young man's brow, with a prayer it would one day show strands of the same silver that threaded through the glorious black curls of her Winn.

"By the way. I am, you know."

"This is becoming a familiar scene. Too familiar," Zoe mumbled, thoroughly annoyed at being awakened to cryptic comments. "You are *what*?"

"Mighty fond of your little bum."

Zoe cracked open an eye at Winn's announcement. "I didn't think you had heard that."

"Not only heard it, but wholeheartedly agree," he answered between self-satisfied chuckles.

A feeling of tension plucked at her belly. It always amazed her how those rough, uneven tones floated down her spine like a velvet touch. They were the complete opposite of Jon's smooth, modulated notes, but never had her ex-husband's voice affected her so.

And it was such a welcome relief after Angus McCairn's constant bellow. . . .

Both eyes snapped open, and she pushed to her elbows. A crack of sunlight filtered through the shutters. What time was it? She'd left sickbay for a much needed nap, but that was late last night and she'd been so tired. She hadn't meant to sleep this long.

Zoe pushed back the covers and struggled to sit up. But a pair of strong, gentle hands held her firmly in place.

"Easy, Princess. What's the hurry?"

"I'm late for sickbay, and the Bear will be growling. You know how testy he gets." She fumbled with the blankets, to no avail. Winn had her pinned to the spot. "Let me up, Flynn. I have to get dressed."

"And spoil the pretty picture you present?"

She looked down at her tangled nightshirt to find the rosy tip of one breast poking its way into view. The smile Winn flashed her was purely rakish. Butterflies began to dance in her chest. She started to tug the nightshirt in place, but Winn halted her efforts by capturing her hands in his.

"I think not, Princess. I enjoy the view too much."

"But, McCairn—"

"But, McCairn, nothing. It was the Bear who ordered you to rest." Amusement played over his lips before turning into an outright laugh. "I'm merely complying with the butcher's orders."

A hot stain flooded Zoe's face. She'd long since regretted those words. McCairn was a caring, if gruff, doctor. She'd realized that as soon as she'd seen him attend the men in sickbay. He'd cared for them as best he could—the medicine and practices of the time were at fault. Even a simple wound could prove fatal, despite the doctor's skill at surgery.

Zoe shivered, realizing in that moment that only Winn—and luck—had kept her alive.

Still, she had to hand it to McCairn. As soon as he'd seen the results of her simple changes, he'd implemented them even better himself. He wasn't so rigid that he couldn't, or wouldn't, change his methods. A person willing to learn always earned her respect; it was one of the highest forms of intelligence on her personal list. One aspect at which Jonathan had failed.

No, McCairn wasn't what she'd first thought. Not at all. And, on closer inspection, she'd noted how neat his stitches were, how thorough his care. They'd come to a comfortable truce a few days before. She even suspected the Bear of liking her.

"Were you?"

Winn's question interrupted her thoughts.

"Hmm?"

"Ah, Zoe. Your mind's been wandering. Your thoughts wouldn't still be on those scathing comments you first made about the dear doctor, now, would they?" He released her hands, sweeping his fingers against her hot cheeks.

"Was I what, Winn?" she asked.

"Were you actually hunting for lettuce in sickbay?" The corners of Winn's mouth twitched in merriment.

Zoe rolled her eyes. "Salad, Winn. I was on the trail of salad."

"Oh, salad. Beg pardon. That makes all the difference—"

"It was the vinegar, you see. I'd been getting whiffs of it from my bandages for days. How was I to know McCairn uses it as a disinfectant?"

Winn let out a belly laugh. She ignored it, focusing on a question she'd meant to ask days ago.

"Winn?"

"So now it's Winn, not Flynn. Is there something you want from me, my dear?"

She scowled at him. "Stop teasing. I'm being serious."

Which was a hard thing to do with him looming above her so closely that she'd long since slumped back to the bed, cushioning her head on her cotton-filled pillow. She'd abandoned the feather one as soon as she'd discovered her sneezing and sniffles were due to allergies and not a cold.

Winn had the cotton one made up especially for her from the bales he'd acquired intercepting an unscrupulous American merchantman. It warmed her heart to know the depths of his loyalties to his adopted country. Remembering his comments at the time he'd presented it to her—about patriotism on the high seas—prompted Zoe's questions.

"Where exactly are we?" she asked.

Winn looked at her with concern. "Why, in my cabin."

"I know that." He seemed to relax. "But where?" The relaxed mood lasted but a moment.

"On my ship, of course." He placed his palm to her forehead as he answered. "Are you feeling ill, Princess?"

Zoe batted his hand away. "I know I'm on your ship, dammit."

"You forgot the 'Winn.'"

She disregarded his silly grin. "Where the hell is your ship? And don't tell me at sea, 'cause I swear I'll smack you one."

"Why, we're out on the Atlantic a ways, closing in on the northwest coast of Africa."

"And this isn't the American Revolution, is it?"

He looked more confused than ever. "Zoe, have you lost a bit of your memory since your unfortunate crash to the deck?"

She tried to fight his probing hands, but he proved too strong . . . and too determined. His fingertips explored every inch of her scalp.

"You can stop your search, Winn. There is not a

hole where my brains leaked out, and my memory is perfectly intact, thank you." She managed to still his probing fingers, immediately missing the delicious feel his touch always had upon her. "Just answer my questions, Winn Dammit, before you drive me insane. Why were those British ships firing upon us?"

He seemed relieved by her feisty manner, the tension leaving his face as his hands escaped her grasp and continued exploring. This time, however, they moved down to her face and neck. And continued to meander lower still.

"Because, Zoe, dear"—his head dipped toward her and kisses rained upon her face; she had to concentrate to hear his answer—"we are at war with mother England. Have been since 1812. Impressment and all. Remember?"

She certainly did. Even if her history grades never wavered above a *C*. "And the year?" she asked, needing to know. Needing much more than that as Winn's mouth closed upon her breast.

"Eighteen fourteen," came his muffled reply.

Zoe relaxed totally into the cushions. "Thank you, Winn."

"Don't thank me yet, Princess. I've only begun."

And so he had. After running a moist trail up her other breast, he laved her nipple with his warm, wet tongue. His body pressed boldly against hers, the hard length of his arousal stirring her senses like heated embers.

Winn shifted above her, easing himself over her body. The path of his assault altered course, slowly dipping down to her navel. Swirling his tongue on the sensitive spot drained all thought from her mind, leaving her only pure sensation as he progressed farther down her belly, closing the distance to his final destination.

Zoe's knees drew up as if in protest but fell to either side of Winn in final surrender. He drew his head up, capturing her gaze with his own, his eye ebony, dark and deep as the night. When he spoke, the rich velvet of his voice drew long shivers from her body.

"You don't know, Princess, how long I've yearned to touch you like this."

"About as long as I've dreamed of you doing it," she said.

"Longer," he whispered, reverence and awe filling the word. "Longer, my love, than you'd guess. I've needed you, Zoe, for so many years."

And with that statement her pirate lover dipped toward her body to claim his prize. Plundering the very recesses of her soul. Stroking her, loving her, with gentleness and fire. Coaxing moans and gasps from her throat and trembling need from within her body.

Raising her response with each swirl of his tongue. Each sensual stroke of his callused fingers. . . .

She spiraled upward, into the sky, touching the stars and heaven itself. So close, so very close, to attaining fulfillment that she heard the heavens open and thunder roar.

"My God. It *is* like fireworks," she moaned, almost at her peak.

Her body arched with each sweep of Winn's tongue, climbing farther than she'd ever been before. She was delirious now, as more thunder roared—so much so that it took a moment to realize she'd lost some height from her ecstasy and was, in fact, plummeting to the ground.

Winn pulled away from her body abruptly, anger

and remorse clear on his face as he tugged upon his loosened pants. Zoe only stared, unable to make head or tail of why he stopped, until an ear-splitting crash rocked the entire ship.

"I'm sorry, Princess. So very sorry." He pulled the covers up over her body. "But it seems that we are under attack."

"Shit."

"The comment suits the situation better than any I can think of. No wonder it's a favorite, my dear." He ruffled her hair fondly and raised a brow. "And now, if you'll excuse me, I think I'd better see to my ship."

He waited for her stunned nod. Mere disappointment could not describe the way she felt. Devastation was more like it. Winn's brows wrinkled as he tucked in his shirt and fastened his pants, his concentration already turned to his duty.

"I'll send Adam down. Get below to McCairn—he'll steer you both to the hold. I don't want you out until you hear my command." A pointed gaze marked his words. "Do you understand, Zoe?"

She did. It was a direct order given by a man who had a reputation for his strength of command. And she realized, seeing him thus, that she'd been privileged by the openness he'd offered her from the start.

Once again she nodded, and he seemed satisfied. But as he opened the door he paused.

"Fireworks, Princess?"

She felt the heat of a blush. "Just an expression. Obviously an exaggeration."

Winn held her gaze intently with his. "I hope to prove you wrong on that. Soon." He flashed a sinful smile. "I promise you fireworks, Zoe. On that you can rely."

And he swept from the room on those final words.

* * *

"Away aloft! Loose all sails and wet them. You, below . . . I want all hands to toss out the dead weight. We'll have to offer our prizes to the sea, but don't worry, lads—there's richer booty ahead." Winn jumped smoothly from the lower ratlines onto the quarterdeck a few feet below and surveyed the activity around him.

A lucky shot, from a ship a mile off, had rent a two-foot hole in the hull—right below the water line. They were taking in water like a sponge, despite the ferocious activity of the carpenters, who tried to patch the gap. He had confidence they'd do it—the problem was when.

Already the English man-o'-war had swung round, following them in rapid pursuit. Two of its fellow ships trailed in the distance. A damnably bad turn of luck for the *Raven*.

Normally the massive ship of the line hadn't a chance to gain on the frigate. Winn knew his ship the way he knew himself. There wasn't another built could outrun her. But crippled like this, she lost speed. It would take all they had to lose the bastards.

Barrels of goods littered the sea behind them as they tossed hard-won treasures over the rail. They'd overtaken an English merchantman or two and had come away with the precious cargo. It would mean a loss of prize money for the crew, but each knew it would save lives if they could escape. There were always more fat merchantmen ripe for the picking, with barely half of their mission complete.

The loud slap of sails drew Winn's attention. The water had done the trick, stopping the wind from flowing through fabric. Canvas crackled as it caught the air, billowing outward on a heavenly breath—the *Raven* ran with the wind in full-rigged glory, leaving her unwieldy pursuers behind.

As soon as the enemy was but a dot on the sea, Winn made his way down to the hold. A series of whacks echoed from inside the room, chilling his spine. He unfastened the lock and threw the bolt, flinging the massive door open. The screech of the hinges grated through his head as the heavy wood crashed against the wall.

"What in hell is going on here?" he bellowed, frightened beyond reason that something was amiss.

Zoe and the boy stood frozen, midstroke, broken boards tight in their fists. Winn's scowl raised a sheepish grin from Zoe.

"Adam was showing me how to bean a rat." She started to lower the board to the floor but suddenly slammed it down instead. "Damn. I missed him."

"Don't worry, Princess. It takes some practice." Adam patted her hand gently. "You have to try not to twist your wrist."

"Adam." Winn's commanding tone spun the boy around. "Where did you learn about killing rats? I gave the rat-boys specific orders to keep you away from the hold." Winn lowered his brows into his fiercest scowl. The boy was so young—at six years, just a baby—he shouldn't be exposed to rats, let alone kill them.

Adam shook his head as he answered. "The boys didn't tell me nothin' about smashing rats, sir. When I was little, it was my job in the coal mines."

Zoe's gasp vibrated in the silence as Winn squatted in front of the boy. He ruffled the golden curls, like silk they were, framing Adam's face. The boy looked so like Zoe, he could be her son. Regret sliced through Winn's heart. No matter the consequences, or how their relationship progressed, children were one thing he was unable to give her.

Except for Adam.

The boy had become like a son to him—more precious than his booty, more loved than the sea. The only thing that eclipsed him was Zoe, no doubt due to his natural need for a mate.

Winn caught the boy's small hand, tugging him closer. How vibrant he looked, how strong and healthy. So unlike that starving waif he'd found lying in the gutter of a coal-dusted street—orphaned—as alone as he.

The memory broke his heart in two.

Winn opened his arms, and the boy stepped in, giving as well as receiving a mighty hug. Looking past Adam, he caught Zoe's gaze. The tears on her face appeared silver in the lamplight.

Winn loosened one arm, beckoning her to join them in a hearty, three-way embrace. Then together they left the shadows of the hold, heading for the deck, fresh air, and the sweet golden warmth of sunlight.

She wanted to bury her face in his chest.

Wanted to run her hands over the well-defined planes of his hard muscles. Wanted to skim over biceps and triceps and all those other delicious muscle groups. Anatomy 1–0–Winn.

Hell. Who was she kidding?

She wanted to toss the man to the deck and have her wicked way with him. What a fantasy, she thought. And it looked as though it would continue to be one—with the crew looking on, it would cramp anyone's style.

Zoe looked around the deck and rigging. The place was busier than Grand Central Station at rush hour. Tanned, tattooed bodies everywhere. Although some of the crew were below deck, there were easily over three hundred men. She knew. She'd counted.

Five times. . . .

While she sat on the deck and fantasized about Winn.

An effective way to curb your more lecherous thoughts—better than counting sheep, she supposed. A hot nasty breeze assaulted her nose as a drool-covered tongue swiped at her cheek.

And anything was better than counting goats.

Yuck.

She batted the offender away, but the damn thing just came back for more.

"Sit," she said in her sternest voice, pointing to the deck in front of her. And by God, he sat. A good thing, too. Her stomach was already queasy—without some distance between her and the beast, she'd lose her lunch with the next foul breath.

Zoe looked away from that eager, furry face and caught Winn eyeing her, wearing a knowing grin.

"She likes you, Princess." He had the audacity to wink.

"She? I figured it was a 'he,' with the way it persists when I'm not interested. Men, you know?" She lifted her nose in the air, and Winn laughed—a low, rough rumble that stroked her nerves in a most pleasant manner.

How beautiful he looked standing at the wheel. The wind blowing his dark locks, the sun kissing his skin. Those magnificent muscles peeking out of his shirt. She noticed his self-satisfied grin and knew he'd caught her staring.

"What on earth would you want with a smelly goat?" she asked. "Is goat meat a delicacy on the Old MacDonald farm?"

There. She could change the subject as neatly as anyone. Unfortunately the goat seemed to recognize the subject matter and protested with a lusty lick on her lips.

Winn's laughter rang through the air as Zoe spluttered and wiped her slimy mouth on her sleeve. She cast him a chilling glare, and he managed to contain his hoots, although deep dimples framed the sides of his mouth, making her rogue even more appealing.

Adam came over to pet the goat, diverting the noxious attention of the animal and sparing her further assault by halitosis.

"She's a good old girl," Adam told her. "And she makes all the milk for the captain's coffee, ma'am. She's just one for motherin', or so the cap'n says."

Mothering?

Did she look in need of mothering?

Well, perhaps, she thought. Everyone needed a bit of loving care. And it had been so long since she'd been on the receiving, rather than the giving, end. She looked at the beast from a new perspective, wondering if there was anything she could do about that breath.

Perhaps her toothbrush . . .

An awful shudder ran through her.

No way. The mere thought nauseated her. But maybe her breath spray would do the trick.

Satisfied with herself for such a creative solution, she leaned back against a bale of hay. The deck really did look like a barnyard, though most of its occupants were stowed up front on the forecastle. Amazing how fast she picked up these nautical terms—pretty soon she'd feel like one of the crew.

Zoe swept the busy deck with her gaze, then let it wander to the men in the rigging. Nah, she decided. She didn't want to feel like the crew. Their jobs were backbreaking and constant. How they managed on so little sleep—only four hours to a shift—hell, she'd collapse in less than a day.

She closed her eyes, lulled by the rhythm of the sea and the drowsy effects of her seasickness pills. She'd remembered to put on sunscreen and her baseball cap so she wouldn't burn in the fierce southern sun. But without her creams and Retin-A, her face felt tight and shriveled.

A fine sight she must present to Winn.

Somehow it just wasn't fair that wrinkles on women were aging, while on men they translated as character. She hadn't looked in a mirror in weeks, content with a splash of water to her face and grateful for each opportunity to wash her hair.

The little things in life had gained importance.

Besides, there wasn't much she could do for her appearance. Her makeup consisted of partially used samples in her effort to avoid excess weight in her handbag. She always packed for emergencies when on a trip, and this one had been no exception. If she hadn't weeded out excess baggage, her carry-on would have weighed two tons instead of one. Her meager supplies had dwindled quickly.

It didn't matter. She wasn't a person obsessed with looks, in any case. It was okay with her if she was less than perfect—as long as she didn't have to look at herself. Her pity fell on those around her, especially on poor Winn.

Zoe winced.

For once she wouldn't mind being a raving beauty—at least from his viewpoint. After all, the man was a specimen sent from the gods. She squinted against the western sun, watching the object of her thoughts and desires.

"What's the problem, Princess?" the object asked.

"Wondering how fast you age aboard ships," she mumbled, hoping he wouldn't hear, but scrupulously honest and terrible at dissembling. "I feel like the wreck of the *Hesperus.*"

"*Hesperus?* Never heard of it."

Of course not, she thought. Didn't that occur in the late 1800s?

What would Winn think about the idea of time travel?

She shook her head, not yet ready to confront that issue. "Never mind."

Winn remained silent for a moment before summoning Leetch to take his spot. Zoe had to smile at the young man. He was so eager, so full of life. Unfortunately that same energy made her feel older.

It must be one of those days, she thought. Hormones on the blink again.

A shadow fell across her, and she looked up to see Winn. He towered above her, the setting sun giving him a golden aura. Squatting, he drew a gentle finger against her cheek.

"Why so glum, Princess?" He eased his long body to the deck, propping his back against the hay.

"Just feeling ancient. It happens at my age." She closed her eyes, tugging the cap down over her face, suddenly embarrassed about her morose mood.

"Nonsense." Winn tugged the cap up, cupped her chin in a callused hand, and turned her face to his.

Zoe refused to open her eyes, feeling vulnerable from his close scrutiny.

"Princess, you're adorable."

"Not something I'd be proud to repeat to my sophisticated friends."

"Sophisticated? You mean those horse-faced crones with the huge teeth?"

She peeked at him through her lashes to see him jutting out his teeth, nose in the air. A perfect imitation of most of the crowd she and Jon had considered friends. Zoe couldn't suppress a chuckle.

Winn smiled. "Or those whey-faced women who appear to be bloodless?"

She opened both eyes, feasting on his own mahogany features. They sent a rush of longing through her. Certainly the familiarity he exuded, the way she felt so comfortable with him, was due to his remarkable resemblance to Jonathan. After all, she'd been married to Jon for sixteen years. A hell of a long time.

Yet resemblance or not, she couldn't help think there was more to the natural compatibility that existed between her and Winn. A similarity existed between the two men, true. But Winn was secure, at ease with himself, where Jonathan was not. Winn was bigger, bolder. More alive.

And to her eyes and heart, downright beautiful.

She'd never had such rapport with a man. She felt things with him that she'd never felt with Jon, despite their long marriage. A thread existed between them, a link forged out of essence—the meeting of two souls that had recognized each other upon first sight.

Their personalities didn't clash, they meshed. As if each were the other half of a puzzle, the two making up a whole. As if they belonged together, were one, and had been that way through all time.

She had known Jonathan for half her life.

Yet it seemed she had known Winn forever.

The object of her desire swept a finger down her nose. She focused on his face—each scar, each windswept wrinkle, had become so dear. More care and longing winked from his one obsidian eye than she'd ever seen.

Winn smiled at her, while she remained silent. "I much prefer pink cheeks and freckles, Princess," he said, catching her off guard.

Oh, Lord. It was worse than she'd thought.

She hadn't had pink cheeks and freckles since she was a kid.

"And your hair. . . ," he continued.

Her hair? Zoe groaned. She'd colored her aging ash-blond curls before her flight, but by now the rinse would have washed away.

Pink cheeks, freckles, and gray hair.

An alluring sight indeed.

Winn ran a hand through her windblown tresses. "Silver and gilt," he said, his voice low and rough. "The moon and the sun and the shine of the stars all reside within your vibrant locks."

Zoe sat, mesmerized by the soulful tones of his words. By the romantic images they evoked. The words painted a beautiful picture, more poetic than she'd ever experienced.

But what drew her to him wasn't poetry or images. It was his intensity, the naked desire and tenderness that had been laced through his words. The feeling that he truly cherished her beyond looks or lust alone.

And with that, she thought, he'd bound her to

him more securely than any ropes, or chains, or lock and key.

Something passed between them as they stared at each other. Something that eclipsed any intimacy she'd known. A connection. A completeness.

The arrival at a longed-for destination.

They'd discovered the treasure buried deep within each other's hearts, and recognized it as the first blossom of love.

Winn's lashes lowered sensuously, enhancing the desire she saw burning in his midnight eye. He bent his head to her, drawing closer. Zoe felt his magnetic pull as she met his face halfway.

Winn brushed his lips across hers. So soft they were, on such a strong, weathered face. Electricity, pure and simple, tingled across her own lips, diving like an arrow to pierce her body with a sweet ache. The feel of Winn's lips pressing against hers heated her blood to boiling.

His tongue swept across the seam of her mouth, pushing past her lips like a tender marauder, making her hotter still. He plundered her moist recesses with ownership and possession, branding her to her very soul with an intimacy that left her breathless.

Somewhere in the back of her mind floated the realization that she sat upon the deck in full view of Winn's crew. But, usually a modest person, for once she didn't care. What she now experienced was so honest, so true—let everyone know this was how she felt.

Zoe cupped Winn's face with utmost care, giving him a gentleness unknown in his hardened life. How could she leave him? For that was what she would have to do, if she ever found a way back to her own world.

Lately she'd felt out of control, adrift—at the mercy

of whatever fates had pulled her through time—much like the flotsam and jetsam the *Raven* stirred in its wake. She'd put all worry about her predicament from her mind, not knowing what to do to change things. Yet deep down she belonged to the future.

A pity—she had so much to give. . . Feelings deeper than desire, which made desire all the richer. Feelings she'd thought long gone, shielded deep within her heart. She would like to share them all with Winn.

Yes, she thought. She'd offer him anything. . . .

Would give him everything.

Zoe pressed closer, wanting to be a part of his body—wanting to be a part of Winn. Her tongue tangled with his, her fingers combed his hair. Her body grew heavy, hot with need, as their passion deepened.

The sound of her heart taking wing burst in her ears, and a loud caw reverberated in her head.

Caw?

A flap of feathers brushed against her cheek while another loud screech assaulted her ears. Zoe pulled back from Winn, listening to his hearty curse. Upon his shoulder sat the biggest, blackest crow she'd ever seen, looking at her intently with its jet black eyes.

The bird cocked its head as it eyed her. It seemed ridiculous, she knew, but the damned thing appeared to be studying her. Sizing her up. Not in a hostile way, but with a curiosity and intelligence that startled her. Zoe shifted nervously, oddly reluctant to come up short in the bird's estimation.

She supposed she was losing her mind.

Winn shrugged a shoulder to dislodge the behemoth—it probably weighed more than her purse. But the intruder remained, perched securely on Winn's broad muscles.

She stifled a laugh as Winn cursed again. He sounded completely disgusted.

"Ah. So now you make your presence known, you rogue. What's the matter? Miss your lady friends?"

The bird dipped his head as if in answer. Now Zoe knew for sure that her imagination had broken through all bounds of control. Where had the bugger come from? she wondered, scanning the ship for an answer.

High above her she found it. On the topmost yardarm of the mizzenmast sat a huge nest of twigs and twine and bits of hay and sail. A creative, unique home befitting such an unusual bird. She'd never noticed it before, not thinking to look for a nest in the rigging.

The crow looked up as if following her gaze. Zoe shook her head to clear her irrational thoughts. The bird actually appeared to preen—as if it knew what she thought and took pride in its domain.

"The crow's-nest, I take it," she said, delighting in the sudden dimples that appeared on Winn's cheeks.

"In a manner of speaking, yes."

Surrendering to the bird's successful intrusion, Winn leaned back on the bale of hay, giving a sigh and a dramatic look of long-suffering. "Curiosity isn't limited to cats," he drawled. The crow bristled its feathers at the mention of felines. Zoe swore it knew exactly what Winn said. "Raven has the curiosity of a mischievous child."

The bird sidled closer to Winn, tweaking a dark hair from his head as if in protest.

"Why, you obstinate beast," he said, thrusting the offender away.

Raven hopped to the bale of hay, sitting there in a nonchalant manner. A definite atmosphere of satisfaction surrounded it. Zoe raised a questioning eyebrow and turned to Winn.

"I thought pirates preferred parrots."

"And so they do."

He didn't elaborate.

"You were saying," Zoe prompted.

Winn sighed again and continued reluctantly.

"I once took the *Raven* to a tropical port, and I swear, practically every man came back with a bird and a cage. The men made a game of it to teach the creatures some expressive language." He turned to her, eyebrow raised. "Imagine the sound of over three hundred parrots squawking the phrase 'Captain's a sod.' "

Zoe clapped a hand over her mouth but was unable to stop her giggles.

"Precisely," Winn said, wearing a scowl. "Banned the damn things on the last southern trip."

"But Raven?" she asked. "I would swear it was a crow."

Winn quickly dropped his scowl and laughed, relaxing against the scratchy hay. "And so he is, Princess. Adam found him with a broken wing, and brought him to the ship to nurse. He gave him to me, saying that the ship should have a mascot, and the *Raven* would now have a raven."

Winn's gaze swept fondly over the towheaded child who had fallen asleep, head pillowed upon the snoring goat. The smile that dimpled his cheeks touched Zoe to her mother's heart.

"I didn't have the heart to correct him," he said, turning to her. He held her gaze as if expecting further comment. When she didn't say anything, he relaxed visibly and with a low, quiet voice confessed, "A sentimental thing for a pirate to do. Some would think me exceedingly soft." His lips drew up in a rueful grin.

Zoe watched, fascinated as ever by the emotions that flitted across his expressive face. They were there for all to see—not stowed away in some deep cavern of his psyche, to be hidden and denied.

Winn didn't cower from his feelings or refuse to accept them. Yet sometimes they seemed to cause him confusion. As if he thought he should tamp them down but couldn't.

Zoe reached out to him, her hand pressing against his cheek. A paradox, he was. Strength and gentleness, discipline and passion. She could explore his moods for the rest of her life.

She saw him look back at Adam and recognized the naked love upon his face. It captured her heart completely, all her qualms about another intimate relationship fading away on the warm breeze around her. It was too late for second-guessing. She and Winn were already involved.

A sudden tug of pain halted Zoe's introspection as it sliced through her scalp. She turned to confront the culprit, but Winn came to her aid.

"Raven, you scoundrel," he shouted as the bird flapped its mighty wings.

It circled them once, as if in defiance. Then it flew like a shot to the safety of its nest, Winn's dark strand of hair and her platinum one still within its beak. As soon as the crow reached the yardarm, it wove the strands into its nest, then proudly let out a triumphant caw.

Winn shook his head, exasperated, but Zoe began to laugh.

"Snoring goats, thieving birds, and a doctor who resembles a bear. . . Oh, Winn. This place *is* a zoo."

Winn joined her laughter till tears streamed from their eyes.

"Ah, Princess. You do me good. Its been so long since I've laughed this much."

Zoe smiled at him and he drew close, catching one of her tears upon his tongue. Her breath grew short at his touch. Drawing her hand across his cheek, she delighted in the loving look he sent her. Before she could speak, a cabin boy a good five years older than Adam appeared at Winn's side, holding a tray.

"Cookie says 'Greetings,' sir, to you and your lady."

The boy placed the pewter tray in Winn's outstretched hands, bowed his head at his captain's nod, then strode away. Winn lifted the pristine white cloth from the tray.

"What have we here, Princess?"

Zoe's favorite ginger cookies had been mounded upon a stoneware plate. She practically drooled as anticipation wet her mouth and made her stomach growl. She'd exchanged recipes with Cookie the day before.

"A snack from heaven," she replied, and grabbed one.

Winn chuckled. "Would you like some coffee, dear?" He poured a cup at her emphatic nod. "Milk? Sugar?" he asked, pointing out that he'd acquired the exotic sugarcane from an unfortunate English merchantman the *Raven* had recently come across.

Zoe took her coffee, light and sweet, blowing on the hot brew so she wouldn't burn her tongue. She'd been smelling the rich scent for days, each time Winn had a mugful in his cabin, and the aroma had teased her into a craving that surpassed her usual preference for tea. Her first sip proved the drink worth her wait.

As she took another sip, she noticed two empty cups remained on the serving tray and wondered if the third belonged to Leetch.

Winn poured his own coffee, putting the steaming brew beside him on the deck, along with a mug that he filled with the remainder of the milk. Then he removed the tray from his lap and settled beside Zoe in companionable silence, sipping his black coffee with relish.

She realized the mug awaited Adam and felt her heart tighten with profound respect. The goat provided milk, it seemed, but not for the captain's coffee.

More sentimentality, Winn would say.

But Zoe preferred to call it love.

7

Zoe looked over the rail of the ship as it crept silently into the hidden cove. Although she had visited the Canary Islands in her own century, she was struck by how dramatically different they now appeared.

Instead of the cultivated fields combing country and mountainside, the area was lush with tropical vegetation. It would be easy to hide here, screened by the jungle. Even the tall masts blended into the trees and slopes that surrounded the cove.

Winn had told her he'd found the secret inlet a few years before, when avoiding pursuit by an unfriendly corsair. It was a bit off their course, he explained, but it would serve their purpose admirably. They needed to repair the damaged hull before continuing their journey. As the frigate dropped anchor in the middle of the cove, all hands worked feverishly in preparation to go ashore.

Several huts stood in a clearing by the beach—friends,

Winn had said, who had helped him in the past. Zoe swept a windblown lock of hair from her face, watching as the first of the crew descended, eager to greet the islanders. Loneliness stabbed through her, giving her chest a hollow feel. There'd be no old friends waiting for her. Outside of Winn and Adam, and her acquaintance with a few of the crew, she had no friends to speak of. Everyone close to her belonged in another time and place.

Where Jonathan was, she had no idea. He could have fallen through time along with her or remained in the future. Even if he had accompanied her through the time tunnel, there was no guarantee he'd landed in the same era. After all, he'd fallen a minute or so before she had.

For all she knew, he could now be a Neolithic man or a Roman gladiator, although the former suited him better. She didn't want to dwell on his possible dilemma—not when she had no solution for her own. Jonathan was resourceful. He could fend for himself as well as she could.

So far her adventures in this time period had been like a dream, a wonderful interlude. Sailing the Atlantic with a pirate tickled her romantic fancy. And meeting Winn certainly had been the highlight of her dream. A fulfillment of every imaginative fantasy she'd ever explored.

But now that she faced the shoreline, she faced her circumstances as well. The reality of her aloneness, being stranded in a different time, slapped her across the face with a brutal, invisible hand. She might never be able to return to her own time. Even if it was possible, she had no idea how.

The thought of Alex and Alexa ripped at her heart.

For now they were safely ensconced in boarding school. But if she couldn't return, who would care for her children and love them in her stead?

The time had come to talk to Winn and assess her situation—if he believed her and didn't think she was nuts.

Zoe gazed out over the inlet, its azure waters sparkling in the sunlight, and surveyed the tiny cottages that dotted the beach. It would be good to go ashore, to feel her feet touch land again. Perhaps her mind would process the situation better than she could upon the rolling waves. Maybe then she'd find a solution to her dilemma.

God, how she hated being at sea.

Yet she did seem to be finally getting her sea legs. She took her motion-sickness pills only once a day now, saving them for dire emergencies. When she'd first arrived on the ship, not only her days but also her sleep had been disturbed by the constant sway.

Now all that disturbed her sleep were dreams of Winn.

And sexual frustration.

After the time they'd spent together yesterday, she'd thought for sure they would have had an exciting evening. Thoughts of him had stirred her, teasing her body as she'd prepared for bed and a wonderfully sleepless night. Wicked fantasies had filled her head, all of them featuring Winn as the clever, erotic hero.

Unfortunately he'd had the evening shift to pilot. Then a problem with the rudder had kept him away the remainder of the night. And this morning's maneuver of slipping into the hidden cove had proved hectic. Right now her hormones were at a feverish pitch—a nasty feeling she'd never experienced before.

She'd enjoyed making love with Jonathan and hadn't been with anyone since their separation. He was charming and handsome and naturally skilled. Their sex life had been the one positive aspect of their marriage, though it had settled down to merely a comfortable habit.

Winn, on the other hand, stirred her senses like quickfire. He was more colorful, more complex, than Jonathan. A larger than life character, both figuratively and literally, she thought, remembering how his proud anatomy had waved to her when he'd stood before her naked.

His penis had appeared as formidable as his cutlass.

Zoe sighed at the delicious memory. On a scale of fantasy figures, she'd rank her pirate number one, for he enticed her heart as much as her libido. She was ready for him as she'd been ready for no other. It seemed she'd been waiting for him all her life.

Yes, she thought. It was as if her trip through time had been her destiny. As if they had always been meant for one another. She had no reservations about their relationship. Only one question remained.

When would the man take her to bed?

This was the time of Regency rakes, and he certainly fit the bill in looks. Yet he acted like a Victorian prude.

Damn frustrating, if you asked her.

Zoe ran her hand through her hair, and held the wispy strands from her eyes. A familiar step echoed on the planks behind her, accelerating the beat of her heart. Winn grabbed her waist, pulling her close.

"Eager to go ashore, Princess?"

She nodded her head. Eager for a lot more, she thought.

"We'll be having a feast in celebration."

"Not roasted goat, I hope." She turned in his arms in time to catch his grin.

"Don't worry, Princess, your goat is safe. We'll only be eating what we bag on shore."

He looked at her with that dark, soulful eye, as filled with tension as she. The day was hot, and her clothes molded to her curves. Winn's possessive touch heightened her temperature to an unbearable heat.

Zoe pulled her T-shirt from her damp body. Although she'd rolled up her jeans and her sleeves, and had shed her bra beneath her opaque top, she was still sweltering. Her clothes disappeared regularly from the cabin—Adam's doing, bless him—and reappeared there clean, but she'd venture that at the moment she smelled as bad as the goat.

"Hot, Princess?" Winn asked, noting her movements.

"Roasting."

"There's a tidal pool on the island that the natives dug. Full of seawater, but without the unfriendly sea life. A nice, private place to cool off . . . if you'd like."

Zoe nodded. "It would be wonderful to take a swim. Will you join me?"

Winn's eye sparkled like a black diamond, flaming seductively as he bent toward her. But he said nothing—only kissed her nose before helping her climb down the ship's ladder to the rowboats bound for the beckoning shore.

* * *

He didn't join her in the pool, despite her sweet invitation. He had work to do, he'd told her, which was true. It was also true his men had been with him for years and were all well versed in their jobs. Things could get done without him.

No, Winn thought. The problem wasn't one linked to duty and command. It lay within him, buried deep—linked to the fear of humiliation.

He hadn't the nerve to follow his princess, despite the continual hardness of his groin. He knew she yearned for more, he saw it in her huge emerald eyes each time they met his. He yearned for more as well.

But it had been so long. . . .

He remembered the day he'd recovered from his injury to find himself but half a man. It hadn't bothered him unduly at the time—he'd been happy just to be alive—and the lust that filled him had been for revenge.

Not until he'd sunk Reis's ship had his thoughts turned to family and desire. McCairn had told him he might yet sire children, but he had instinctively known it to be impossible. The visits to his mistresses in the ports he frequented had shown him the veracity of his beliefs.

For he was not only sterile, he couldn't perform.

Ah, the shame. He could feel it still.

He'd settled a nice sum on each mistress he'd supported, knowing full well they'd not languish for patrons. Then he'd tamped down desire, knowing the folly it would bring, the impotent frustration.

Nine years—no, almost ten.

An eternity since he'd been with a woman, since he'd tried to make love and failed. Rage smoldered within him still whenever he thought of the corsair's wicked deed and how his lifeblood and manhood had spilled to the deck.

His only solace was the fact he'd later found and killed that bastard Reis. He relished the memory of standing upon his quarterdeck, watching the pirate's ship go down in flames. It was an image he dredged up each time his loins began to stir.

For they had stirred on occasion and now teased him ruthlessly. He knew the result of such stirrings, he'd experienced it long ago—he'd been unable to perform, to reach fulfillment. The ardor he had felt had turned to impotence.

At times he longed to kill Reis again.

Winn looked in the direction of the pool. He imagined the water, warm and blue, caressing Zoe's skin the way he wanted to caress her. Turcotte stood guard. The young man had insisted on helping; after all, he'd said, he owed Zoe his life.

Despite the youth's limp, he was guard enough. None of the men would risk touching her. They knew Winn would kill them on the spot.

Ah, what violent emotions assailed him. He was a jaded man, bewitched—stirred up to feverish pitch by a taut little body, moonlit hair, and the most beautiful eyes he ever saw. Yet to say that was all he felt would be a lie.

There had been beautiful women to lure him aplenty, to have him think about trying his prowess again. But he'd turned them down, knowledge of his shortcomings dampening his desire. Not until Zoe had he questioned his actions and played with the idea of making love again.

By damn, he'd been hard from the moment he'd first seen her. But what kept him in that constant

state of erection wasn't her enticing form or lovely
features. It was the woman herself.

She intrigued him, teased him, made him laugh—
rich belly laughs that warmed his soul. She kept him
in a state of flux, his emotions dipping to all extremes
as she constantly surprised him with her actions and
delighted him with her keen wit.

He wanted her as a loving partner, an equal, and
he longed to bury himself deep within her. He needed
her as he'd needed no other woman in his life. She
had touched his heart and had become his soul. She
was his, dammit, and he hadn't told her, couldn't
show her.

Bloody hell.

This wouldn't do. Had he become weak? Turned
coward? Was he afraid to fight for what by rights
should be his?

Winn forced his gaze from the clearing to Turcotte.
The young man remained in place but showed signs
of unsteadiness in his injured leg.

"Mr. Turcotte."

"Sir?"

"You may leave your duty."

"But Miss Zoe, sir. She should be protected. No
tellin' what could happen in the jungle and all."

"Don't worry, lad. I'll keep her from danger."

Seeming somewhat relieved, the young man gave
his captain a salute. Winn waited till Turcotte left
before ambling down the path. Longing grew within
him each step he took, playing havoc with his body. It
seemed his princess needed protection from him.

Before reaching the clearing, he hesitated, gathering
up his courage. Now that he'd made the choice, committed himself to act upon his feelings, his thoughts

turned to Zoe's needs. For consideration of her alone, he should give her a choice. Winn cleared his throat.

"Zoe," he called. "Are you decent?"

A throaty giggle skimmed along the breeze.

"Sometimes I'm positively indecent, Captain. But if you mean am I dressed at the moment, the answer is yes."

Winn took a deep breath, then plunged into the clearing. His heart plunged to his stomach as well. What she wore proved a thousandfold more erotic than being naked. His tongue stuck dryly to the roof of his mouth.

"My God, Princess. You said you were decent."

"I am. I'm wearing a swimsuit."

Swimsuit, he thought. That's what she calls it?

To him it looked like a bit of nothing devised by some devious soul to pluck all sense from a man's brain. A wisp of shimmering red fabric outlined her breasts, scarcely containing their fullness. Bare skin covered her to the top of her drawers—a minuscule swatch of the same red material that clung to her hips tighter than a lover's hands.

"Why don't you come in and join me?" she asked, waiting expectantly. When he didn't answer, couldn't answer, she shook her head. "Don't tell me you're shy? I promise to turn my back while you get down to your skivvies. Unless, of course, you're not wearing them. In which case feel free to skinny-dip."

The minx's eyes sparkled like emeralds in the sunlight. Winn found his voice, but it came out a croak.

"Skinny-dip?" he managed. Yet oh, how hard it was to get out. Almost as hard as the rest of his body.

"You know . . . swim nude."

He gulped audibly.

"What do you call it in this century?"

"Death by desire," he whispered roughly.

Zoe laughed, a sweet rich sound that bounced against the lapis waters of the pool. Winn's manhood strained against his trousers, trying to get out. He had to fight the monster from having its way.

The jungle surrounded them, a verdant green. Zoe's silver hair shimmered against the exotic backdrop. She stood, a water nymph, reedlike, in the pool—her slim legs disappearing beneath the water. The tide lapped at her lanky thighs. Her supple torso gave way to the magnificent curve of her breasts, beckoning him closer.

Winn took a step in her direction, then another, until he stood at the edge of the pool. The sprite looked back at him, eyes wide and expectant, tantalizing, tempting him, stroking his desire.

Ah. But that's not where he wanted to be stroked.

He looked at his princess with naked lust, reading the desire in her own eyes. God help him, for he couldn't help himself. He was beyond fear or embarrassment. His body ached with a desperate need.

Winn fumbled with the buttons of his shirt, tearing it off when his hands proved too clumsy. Then he tugged off his boots and attacked the laces of his trousers. Within a minute he stood nude, poised on the edge of the water.

Zoe's ragged breath reached his ears, stirring his manhood further. He watched as her eyes grew heavy and her breathing turned shallow. When she held out her hand, it proved his undoing.

"Winn. You're beautiful," she whispered.

"Only to you, Princess."

He strode into the water and didn't stop till he held

her pressed against the length of his skin. The feel of her, the scent, invaded his senses like an aphrodisiac. All his worries left him, replaced by a primitive need.

"You're mine, Princess. Now and forever." He claimed her mouth with his.

Zoe melted into Winn's arms, yearning for his touch. She clung to him, ravenous, sampling his lips, his mouth, his tongue. He tasted better than her favorite dessert—a hot-fudge sundae with the works.

Winn's hands swept down her body in a gossamer touch, as if she were made of porcelain. As if he held his heart in his hands and was afraid he'd break it. A profound sense of belonging invaded her, penetrating to her soul.

To mean so much . . . to be loved like this . . .

The heart that shattered was hers.

Zoe pressed closer to Winn's body, absorbing his warmth where their flesh met. Impressed by the hardness that throbbed against her belly, hot and quivering at her touch. Enraptured by the dark glint of passion in his eye when she looked up and caught his gaze.

God, what he did to her.

With a kiss and a touch she was his forever, willing to relinquish the key to her soul. He commanded her senses like a magician, hypnotizing her with a mere glance to willingly do his bidding. She knew what he wanted without a thought—instinct guiding her to explore his body.

His broad shoulders, muscled back, the taut, slim line of his small male derriere—they all served to entice her. She was in his spell, under his dominion, as his tongue took possession of her mouth. Sparring, teasing.

Thrusting with the unerring rhythm of nature.

Winn trailed his finger down her arms before cupping the fullness of her breasts. He ran a finger inside her swimsuit, stroking her nipple to a tight bud. Zoe moaned. God, how she wanted him, yearned for him. How she needed him to continue his sweet assault.

Her breasts puckered under his fingers, her flesh burned wherever he touched. Tenderly he wooed her to submission, the hard length of his penis pulsing with a life of its own. His hips rocked gently against her till she caught the rhythm, returning the action thrust for thrust.

Then Winn groaned—a note so bittersweet, her heart caught in her throat, a sound of both pain and ecstasy. Only fair, she thought, that he felt as she did. She hoped the pain was as sweet as hers.

Zoe slid against Winn's body, slick with sweat, and sea, and sinful lust. She was the devil's own, and he the devil, as she stroked his body with hands and tongue. Totally captivated. Under his spell.

She welcomed the feel of him, the smell. Jon had always smelled good. She'd even come to wonder if a person's scent played a bigger role in mating than was thought, or if her own keen sense of smell left her more susceptible to the erotic lure of a person's aroma.

But while Jon's aroma was appealing, Winn's scent blanketed her, molded to every inch of her body. Covered her with a sensuous male musk that dripped with form and substance. Bathed her nostrils with its spice, filled her lungs with its tang. And coated her tongue with a sharp robust flavor so rich, she could swallow its thick essence.

Zoe's legs grew weak as her seductive explorations

turned on her, enslaving her with growing passion. She was as moved by her ministrations as Winn, her body melting with each soft touch, each stroke of hers upon his skin. She surrendered to the sultry feel of Winn against her.

As her legs gave way, Winn scooped her up, moving into deeper water until Zoe floated in his arms. He made love to her mouth, her eyes, the dimple in her cheek. Then he progressed slowly along her body.

Water lapped at her heated breasts, teased at the juncture of her thighs. But it couldn't cool, or ease, or stop her sweet misery. Only Winn had the power to perform that miracle.

Zoe shifted in Winn's arms, not content only to receive. She wanted—no, needed—to give as well. Pressing against the well-defined muscles of chest and thighs and powerful male hardness, she discovered that his agile fingers had divested her of her swimsuit.

Nothing stood between their flesh but a growing desire . . . and Winn's growing anatomy. The man's proportions were amazing. Surely if his arousal increased, her pirate lover would explode. And that wouldn't do.

Oh, no.

If there was to be any explosion, she would be a part of it.

Zoe rubbed against Winn's hard phallus, then stroked him with gentle fingertips. She used her other hand to hold his shoulder, lifting herself higher in the water. Then she slid back down his body like butter, sheathing his hardness to the hilt.

Heaven. The man was pure heaven.

And pure hell, she thought as Winn sprang to life inside her, triggering a sudden truth in her mind. She and Jon always used protection. Winn's body was as naked as the day he was born. Zoe moaned, gripping Winn's shoulders to fight his first thrust.

"Stop!" she cried, and thought she might actually weep. "We can't, Winn." Her head sagged against his broad chest.

"We can't?" he asked, dumbfounded, tilting her face to his. The eye that looked at her appeared glassy. Zoe shook her head.

"I know that AIDS isn't a consideration, but pregnancy—" She paused as another thought crossed her mind. "Oh, my God. Venereal diseases. Pirates. Women. A snug haven in every port." She looked up at him, horror dawning at the possibilities.

"What is it, Princess?" Winn demanded.

An old saying sprang to her mind. "A hard cock has no conscience."

"Aye," Winn groaned, stirring inside her. "I tend to agree with you on that." He pulled her closer, seating her more firmly upon his throbbing shaft. "But I can assure you I haven't any diseases, and pregnancy is an impossibility."

Winn slowly eased himself from her, stopping short of leaving her body. He reentered her tightness inch by inch, teasing her the full length of his hardness. Teaching her body to respond. Zoe's breath stopped, her heart thundered. All thoughts fled her mind.

Winn continued with unerring ability, filling Zoe's body with his. Withdrawing till she ached with need, then nestling into her once more.

She loved him.

Wanted him.

What beautiful children they would have.

Zoe's eyes snapped open as the image of Winn's

dark-haired son formed in her mind. She couldn't get pregnant, because she knew she would have to leave him. She had her own two children to think of.

"No," she ground out, clinging to Winn's body. He stopped as soon as the command registered. "We mustn't, Winn. We can't."

"Zoe." Winn shook her hard, and she looked up. His dark eye fixed on hers. "I told you it was safe. I'm sure of it, Princess. I haven't been with a woman in years."

Although she was shocked by so unlikely an admission, she saw the honesty on his face, knew the integrity of the man. And she recognized what lay within his heart—the same feelings that beat in hers.

"I believe you, Winn. But you're wrong about pregnancy. This happens to be my most fertile time."

Winn laughed softly. The sound ran down Zoe's spine, making her shiver—such bitterness it encompassed. He held her tight against his body, and she could hear the strong thump of his heart.

"Ah, Princess." He stroked her arms. "That's where you happen to be wrong. It may be your fertile time, but it doesn't happen to be mine."

"What are you saying?" she asked, confused.

Winn took a deep breath. The ragged sigh he exhaled ruffled her hair. "I'm saying, Princess, that I am sterile."

Her mouth formed an "O," but the only sound that came out was a moan, and he took that as a signal to continue.

What sweet torture she was. He'd forgotten the sweet-and-sour sting that occurred when making love. This time with Zoe proved better and worse than any memory he held. The ache hurt tenfold any he'd experienced, and the sweet sensation eclipsed the stars.

Then again, he thought, he'd never really made love

before. He'd merely made lust, had sex—experienced the sensual fulfillment of carnal pleasure. He'd only been familiar with the mundane, knew only the physical aspects of joining. It hadn't mattered before.

He knew he was considered an excellent lover, he'd overheard a tale or two of his prowess in the ports. He had prided himself on the pleasure he gave his women and measured his success by mistresses aplenty. If self-gratification was his main desire, then pleasing his partners followed close behind. But with Zoe it was different.

With Zoe he'd be making love for the first time in his life.

Winn groaned as she shifted closer. "Princess," he whispered through lips gone dry with desire, "you're killing me."

"How, Winn? How do you know?"

The sway of the water moved them up and down.

"Because I'm dying with every shift of your body."

He raised an eyebrow as she thumped his chest and snuggled closer on his shaft, adding to the torture.

"How do you know you're sterile, you fool?"

"Believe me, Zoe. I know."

"But how?"

"Ah, Princess," he rumbled, resting his forehead against hers while he sought to ease his tension. "You do know how to be persistent."

"Persistent is my middle name."

He felt her smile against his chest. "Is it now?"

She nodded her head.

"Princess Zoe Persistent. It has a nice ring to it. Then what, pray tell, is your last name? Is it minx? Or perhaps enchantress?" His voice grew dark as he thought of the enchanting position they were presently in.

"Alas, no," she said, flinging her arm across her eyes in a theatrical manner. "It's Dunham."

"Dunham?" The sound of his own name on her lips sent shivers down his spine, wishes through his head, and longings singing through his blood. "Would that it were so, Princess," he whispered.

"It is. My ex-husband's name was Dunham."

Winn growled with frustration, grinding his hips into hers. He renewed his previous efforts, sliding slowly in and out of her soft, warm body. Zoe gasped.

"Winn. . . ," she moaned, unable to say more.

Good, he thought. It was a hell of a time for talking and a worse time for discussing husbands, dead or otherwise.

"But, Winn—"

He could feel her pull away from him, feel her struggling with the effort to think. He didn't want her to think, he wanted her to feel. His own tongue twisted into a cramping knot, when he thought that she would stop his actions.

"For God's sake, Princess. Trust me," he whispered against the line of her hair, the curve of her cheek—his breath blowing hot across her neck. "I'll never lie to you, or harm you, Zoe. That, I promise."

His shaft grew impossibly harder and heavier, and the tempo of his thrusts increased. The water rushed between their bodies with every in-and-out stroke of the beat. Their rhythm quickened, the water boiled, all sounds around them ceased to exist.

Only the thump of hearts, shallow breaths, and the swish of their movements could be heard. Winn's hands roamed over her body, memorizing the satin of her skin as he finally claimed Zoe as his.

He dipped his head, invading her mouth with a

single thrust. She writhed in his arms, moving with him, tightening, tightening, upon his shaft. Drawing him into her, ever closer, as she helped make their bodies one. He could hear Zoe murmur against his lips.

"Fireworks. You promised me fireworks."

Winn smiled to himself, joy bursting through him like dandelion seeds upon the wind. When he had promised her that, he hadn't been sure of the outcome. Nine years of agony drifted away on the tropical breeze as he spiraled toward his climax. If his princess wanted fireworks, then he vowed to give them to her.

And, by God, he did.

8

Thank you, Lord, Winn's mind whispered to the blue heavens above him. The sun beat warmly upon the sand where he lay. *Thank you for restoring my manhood, for giving me this day, this experience— the most exquisite moment of my life. And mostly, thank you, Lord, for this woman beside me. This gloriously giving, loving, sensitive—*

"Winn, if you don't roll those tree trunks you call legs off of my body in the next two seconds, I swear I'll scream. These sand fleas are biting the skin off my butt."

—delicate, genteel woman, he finished, gazing down upon Zoe's scowl. He rolled over, taking her with him. Her frown turned to a smile as she lay upon his chest, cradled tightly in his arms.

"Better, Princess?" he asked, stroking her softly rounded rump.

"Much." She dropped a kiss upon his nose. A

questioning eyebrow raised, accompanying her next words. "What exactly are you doing?"

Winn looked up at her, the studious expression on his face meant to confuse her. His hands continued their deft exploration of her softly curved buttocks.

"Why, Zoe, dear, I'm checking for flea bites."

Zoe gurgled with laughter, her eyes crinkling merrily at the corners. God, how he loved to look at her.

"And did you find any?" Her voice was sweetness edged with merriment.

"Aye. Several." He grinned, sending her a devilish look as he hoisted himself onto his elbows.

"What are you doing now?" she asked.

Winn slid Zoe to his lap, turning her sideways across his legs while he sat up. The feminine curves of her hips and thighs teased him mercilessly, but the red bites on her enticing derriere caught his attention. He bent over her, stroking his tongue over each mark, following with a kiss on each spot. Zoe moaned.

The sound of her desire had him instantly hard and pressing against her soft stomach. He slipped a finger over her thigh and into the velvet folds of her recesses. She was wet and tight. Another moan escaped her as he continued stroking.

"I'm kissing your bites," he whispered, "and making you feel better."

And making himself feel worse. His hair, his teeth—bloody hell, even his fingernails ached with need. The woman would be the death of him yet.

Zoe sighed. A deep, lustful, satisfied sigh. It warmed the cockles of his heart to hear her so. A woman should always feel thus when in the arms of the man she loved. And she would love him, he'd see to it—like it or not.

"Winn . . ." His name was a sigh upon the breeze.

He trailed his tongue up the shallow dent of her spine, gratified by her shivers. "Winn."

"Madam, has anyone ever told you that you chatter too much?"

Zoe shook her head.

"Well, you do. You must learn that there are both appropriate and inappropriate times for speech. And now is most definitely an inappropriate time."

His tongue traced the outline of the diamond-shaped birthmark on her lower right shoulder.

"Destiny, as marked by birth," he murmured. "You are a diamond, Princess."

"In the rough?" she asked. "Or in the buff?"

She giggled seductively when he pinched her round bottom.

"Aye, in the buff. But I was thinking of a diamond of the first water."

Her giggles stopped when his words faded, and he continued to wet a path to her side. He flipped her over deftly, to lie face up within his arms. He paused a moment, enjoying the sight of her, flushed and eager. Then he bent forward again, continuing with his hot tongue to place his mark upon her body.

God, how he loved her.

His manhood waggled as if in agreement. Zoe arched in his arms, moaning his name as he swirled his tongue over her tautly budded nipple. Now that his manhood was restored, he felt compelled to, er, test its endurance, so to speak.

No. That would be a falsehood, and he wasn't partial to prevarication. The truth of the matter was the damned beast had a mind of its own and had easily forced the rest of him into submission. He couldn't stop if he tried.

Not that he wanted to try, he thought. Hell, nothing could be farther from his mind. But the fact remained that all the good intentions in the world, all the noble thoughts in his head, couldn't have mastered the savage beast.

Ah, he was under her spell.

And it felt so good.

Winn pulled Zoe's sweet nipple into his mouth, sucking at it till she writhed. His ego swelled along with his shaft, delighting in the way she responded to his touch by giving all of herself, withholding nothing. At the same time she made him humble, and hot, and—God knew how she accomplished it—even harder than before.

He wanted everything from her, whatever he could wring out of her delicious body—a whimper, a honeyed sigh, each low moan of desire. Yet he knew that it wasn't enough—would never be enough. For he wanted much more than just the physical passion.

He wanted the joy of life he saw glittering in her eyes, the tenderness he detected in her soul. And he needed the undying love that he knew lay waiting in the vicinity of her rapidly beating heart.

All of her.

He needed all of her.

And needed her to need him as well.

Christ. He'd never needed anyone, wanted anyone, let alone loved anyone the way he loved Zoe. It scared the bejesus out of him, made him a slave. Quite a humbling experience for such a proud man—and one he wouldn't trade for anything short of his own life.

Winn continued his ministrations with tongue and teeth and hands, raising Zoe to grander heights. He wanted to give to her as she had given to him. Wanted to share this inner peace he felt.

He wanted to be a part of her.

So he continued to touch her, to pet and stroke, arousing her to a shattering completion and preparing her for the affirmation of his desire. Winn let loose the needs and emotions he had bottled up for years, trusting Zoe enough to show his own vulnerability and the total power she so innocently wielded over him.

And last, he gave her his silent pledge of commitment and his vow of never-ending love.

Zoe snuggled against the hard planes of Winn's body, delighting in the simple pleasure of skin against skin. The warm breeze enveloped them like a blanket as she buried her nose into the sculpted confines of Winn's chest to inhale the scent that drove her wild—

Eau de Winn.

The ladies of her century would go dotty over his fragrance. She could market it and make a mint. They would have to change the name to something more erotic, though—marketability and all that.

Besides, Winn belonged to her. It wouldn't do to have his name on the lips of thousands of fascinated females in states of high estrogen. Oh, no, she thought, creating her own pangs of jealousy at that image. It wouldn't do at all.

She pictured herself in the role of the quintessential American heroine protecting her man with a vengeance. A wry smile tilted her lips at the surprising image her mind had painted.

She'd be wearing a black Stetson that dipped

provocatively over one eye, a black silk blouse with buttons open to her impressive cleavage and tucked into a tight, short, black denim skirt with sinfully supple, midnight dark, thigh-length boots finishing off the ensemble. Crossing from her waist and encircling her hips would be an ebony gunbelt studded with diamonds. . . .

Why not? she thought. Might as well think big. After all, it was her fantasy to do with as she pleased. Zoe returned to the image.

She'd be toting a six-shooter in each hand, made of sterling silver and onyx like the enticing depths of Winn's hair. And on the barrel would be the notches carved for each woman she'd shot right in the tail for twitching it at her pirate lover and daring to mouth his name.

No. Eau de Winn would not do at all.

She needed something less intimate to describe the scent that ensnared her. Something that wouldn't stir her ire but would stroke her senses. And that spoke of the uniqueness of the man himself.

It had to be perfect, an apt description of how he could plunder her senses and flame her desire. She would want the name of the essence to be an appropriate example of what she felt when Winn held her close, stroked her body, stole her breath . . . murmured her name.

But more than that, it had to mirror what the smell of him represented to her in order to stir the paying public's senses. She required a title that would incite the same needs and desires that Winn conjured in her. Something that spoke not of her own passion, but his.

"That's it!"

She thumped her hand onto his broad chest. Winn

rolled to his side and pressed closer to her, his body rocking slowly but surely against hers. She could feel him hardening and the echoing moistness that gathered between her legs.

"Not now, Winn. I've just had the revelation of a lifetime—a way to capture the perfume market. A lucrative industry, to say the least."

He looked up at her with a sleepy, heavy-lidded eye, and her heart tumbled over in her chest. Damn. The man was too sexy for his own good. Her breathing grew shallow and her pulse rate soared as he ran a lazy finger under the heaviness of her breasts.

"Be you a businesswoman, Princess? I thought you an inventor. Yet I imagine perfumery to be one and the same, what with recipes and distillations, and such."

He continued to tease her with those callused fingers. Zoe looked down at the long brown length of his hands—the neatly squared, clipped nails, the warm strength of those elegant fingers contrasting with the smooth paleness of her skin—and she groaned. What those fingers had done to her. . . .

Hell. What they did to her still.

She took a deep breath, willing control over her body. When he touched her so, she couldn't think. Couldn't remember what he had said.

"And what would this revelation be, Princess? Perhaps a new method for capturing an essence?"

He gazed up at her, eye clear and interested now. His serious look did nothing to stop the throbbing of her body. Not when his fingers continued to work their wonder across her sensitive flesh.

Zoe grabbed at his hands, stilling his questing fingers against her body. He cupped her breasts instead.

She didn't protest. At least she could think again and regain command of her tongue.

"Yes. Capturing an essence. That's it. And I owe it all to you."

"Me?"

"Mm-hmm. It's your scent, you see."

He clearly did not. His brow puckered in confusion. "But I wear no cologne."

"Exactly."

His brows furrowed further. "Are you making sport of me, Princess?"

She relinquished his hand to smooth the wrinkles on his forehead, then skimmed her nails over the hard muscles of his chest. "Not at the moment. But I promise to make sport of you as soon as we finish talking." She watched as beads of sweat popped out upon his brow.

"Then by all means, get on with the discussion."

She almost laughed at his peevish expression. It combined exasperation and chagrin, laced with a healthy dose of impatience. Now where was she?

"I'll bottle your scent and call it A Pirate's Passion."

"Surely you jest."

"Not at all. Pheromones, you know." He didn't. "The subtle scents animals use to attract a mate."

"Are you, by chance, likening me to an animal, my dear?" Winn's gaze narrowed dangerously.

"Only when you growl." He was not mollified. "Humans exude them, too. If we could bottle yours, we'd make a mint."

"A mint?" He shifted to his elbow, resting his head upon his hand.

"A fortune. With the proper marketing, that is."

"And is a fortune so important to you?"

She watched as his eye shuttered, and his face wore a stony mask. It was so unlike Winn. Had the man met up with fortune-hunting women?

Most likely. Society considered it a main requirement for husband material in Regency days—in modern days, for that matter. Perhaps he'd been burned a time or two. There was also his title to consider. Titles had ever been an important commodity in matchmaking.

Poor dear.

Zoe stroked his cheek to soothe him. "Don't worry, Winn. I'm not after your money. Your body, however, is soitanly in danger," she said à la Groucho, and wiggled her eyebrows.

"Then I wish you'd take advantage of it, dear."

Ah. That languid look stole back into his eye, and his hands began to move once more. She had to talk fast while still capable of speech.

"I know Jonathan will provide for me—not all our assets were tied into the business. But I've played the countess for so long that in the future I need to prove my independence and resourcefulness, at least to myself. Jonathan never understood that need."

Zoe sighed. Jonathan had never understood anything about her. But all that lay behind her now. In front of her sprawled a gift from the gods, wrapped up in a beautifully naked male package. A man who touched her soul with his tender giving. Before her was a second chance at love and an opportunity to begin again.

She looked down at her pirate and brushed a silver-edged curl from his tanned, compelling face. All man, she thought, as shivers raced down her spine.

All mine.

She caught him staring at her, his eye darkening to

a black pool. A barely leashed anger seemed to crawl beneath the man's skin.

"What?" she asked.

"Not what, Princess. Who."

"Who?" He'd lost her completely.

"Yes. Who. As in who the bloody hell is Jonathan?"

She flinched at his bellow, unused to seeing him this way.

"Surely I've mentioned Jonathan before. Why, at first I thought you *were* Jonathan. Although how I could have mistaken you for him, I've no idea. There *is* the family resemblance—the dark hair, the angular features, the powerful build—even aspects of your personalities are similar. However, you're much more loving than Jon, and we're better suited. Physically you're infinitely more appealing than him and bigger"—she felt her face heat with a blush—"in all ways, it seems."

His eye narrowed to a slit at her confession. "And how the bloody hell would you know that?"

"Well, I've seen both of you without a stitch on, and—"

Winn placed a hand over her mouth, stifling her prattle. She was glad of it, for she'd been going on like a giddy fool. He was making her nervous with that hard glare.

"Princess," he said through gritted teeth. "I'll ask you one more time. Beyond that, I don't know what I'll do. I only now realize that I'm a possessive man, and I haven't felt this damned hot-tempered in years—not a pretty sight, I'd warrant."

Zoe nodded her head.

"Then pray tell me, if you will. Who exactly is this Jonathan?"

He released her mouth, his muscles coiled into tight springs as he awaited her answer. She was beyond reassurance, beyond diplomacy. Winn was scaring the hell out of her. So she said the first thing that came to her head.

"My husband."

She realized immediately it was the wrong thing to say.

"Your what?"

He didn't shout.

He wouldn't shout.

The words came out a low growl. Maybe he was an animal after all. He didn't care.

Winn shook her when she didn't answer. It seemed she was beyond a response, and he couldn't blame her. He didn't know how he'd managed the question himself.

Her husband.

Her husband!

He glared at her through narrowed eye, rage and hurt boiling within him. Jealousy as he'd never known swelled into a primitive violence.

"You are mine now, Zoe. *Mine.* No one else can have you. I'll kill the bloody bastard if he tries to claim you. Snap his bloody neck in two."

It was too much to contemplate. Too much.

He started to rise, to push off the sand, but Zoe grabbed his arm. He turned to her—all the fury, and hate, and dashed hopes he felt churning inside him, pouring from his eye. It was her sadness that undid him, that got hold of his senses. That, and the secret smile that touched her lips.

"I would prefer you not do that, Winn. Jonathan might be the consummate jackass, but I'm still fond of him. And he is the father of my children. What would I tell them if the love of my life were to kill their dad?"

Words whirred like knives through his brain. Jackass. Father. Children. They were powerful words that superseded ones like love of my life.

Oh, God. It was worse than he thought. He sank to the sand, his head pillowed against his raised knees, and thought he was going to die.

"Children, Zoe?" His mouth felt dry as the sand that clung to his body.

"I thought I had mentioned . . . I know I mentioned them. Whatever did you think I meant?"

He swallowed twice before he could move his lips and force speech past his aching throat. "I never paid much attention, Princess. I thought you referred to the children of your village."

He was dying inside this time for sure. To have been so close to all he desired out of life, and to have it snatched so cruelly away . . .

"Winn, look at me."

He could hear her voice as if from a distance. He turned to her, concentrating on what she said. At first the words were hard to assimilate, as if she spoke a foreign tongue. His brain couldn't function enough for them to make sense.

"You must listen. Jonathan *was* my husband. He is now my ex-husband."

"You're a widow?"

He'd heard her previous answer and knew the one he sought was beyond hope. But he had to ask.

"I don't know."

"For God's sake, Princess. Don't do this to me. I don't know how much more I can take."

Zoe's heart tightened in her throat. Oh, God.

She'd made a botch of it this time. She'd broken his heart with her lack of diplomacy—a fault, Jonathan had always said, that would someday land her in trouble. Perhaps her ex-husband wasn't such a jackass after all, for she was paying for her bald-faced manner now, as surely as the man beside her.

Zoe moved behind Winn and wrapped her hands around his broad back. She pressed her face to his sandy skin and sank her hands into the center valley bisecting his massive chest—so broad, she couldn't reach across it. Yet he was a baby in her arms, despite his age and his breathtaking build.

"Jonathan and I are divorced."

She felt the disbelief, the tightness that constricted his muscles, and willed her love and concern into him. She smiled against his back when he finally drew a deep breath, shuddered, and released some tension. They were so attuned to each other—he would soon realize he could trust her, that she'd come to him in openness, in honesty. Then he would know how she felt about him.

Dammit. He *should* know.

But men seemed universally dense in that area. Did he think she'd make love with him if her feelings weren't involved?

"I love you," she whispered. "I don't know how I could, because I vowed to spare myself further ache from that emotion. I never believed it could happen so fast, but it did." She felt his heartbeat quicken beneath her palm. "I love you, Winn, with my heart and soul and entire being. I love you with my life."

He turned to her upon the sand and cradled her in his arms. A hot tear trickled down his face onto hers, shattering what composure she'd mustered.

"I'm sorry. So sorry," she said. "I thought I had told you. I was very confused after I first smacked my head on the deck, and so much has happened since."

He looked down at her through a reddened eye, such feelings in its depth, her heart turned over with painful joy. She couldn't leave it like this, though—she had to go on. She wouldn't have him living with false hopes.

"I may have my regrets about Jonathan. But never the children, Winn. I love them with my whole heart, just like I love you. That's the nature of hearts, you know. The love expands. There's enough for everyone."

"Ah, Zoe. My sweet, sweet princess." He pulled her to him and buried his face in her hair. "I wouldn't change a thing about you. Jonathan and your children have had a hand in shaping you, creating the person you are. I don't regret a thing except, perhaps, that had I met you first, the children would be ours."

"Oh, damn." Zoe swiped the tears from her eyes, touched by his confession and his complete acceptance. "I've always been a regular watering pot. The children claim I even cry at jokes."

Winn caught a tear on his fingertip. She didn't know if it was hers or his. "Tell me about the children," he said.

"Alex is twelve and Alexa is ten. Jon sent them to boarding school, despite my protests. I know they're not happy there, and I mean to get them back. They're good children, clever and bright. And so beautiful."

She looked at Winn, thinking how much they resembled him. Bittersweet regrets squeezed her heart. He'd be such a wonderful father.

"Have you any children, Winn?"

Pain as she'd never seen flitted over Winn's face. He schooled his features, but she could tell an ache hovered beneath his serene surface. Winn gazed into the azure depths of the tidal pool. For a moment he seemed to forget her. Then he found his voice and started to explain.

"I don't have any children, Zoe. I thought I had all the time in the world—I was an arrogant young man, you see. And then, in my prime, I was rendered sterile."

He didn't look at her but continued to stare at the pristine white sands that lined the pool.

"How?" she asked

"Ah, Princess. I guess you do love me, if you hadn't noticed."

"What, Winn?"

"That I'm half a man."

She'd no idea what he was talking about.

"Nonsense. You may have half a brain, talking this way, but you're certainly not half a man. And I know that from personal experience, and an afternoon of wonderful loving."

Winn shook his head sadly.

What could the fool be thinking of? Zoe wondered. She'd been impressed by his fortitude, for crying out loud. Twice in the pool and then on the shore.

"Winn, you're being ridiculous. Why, you could tunnel your way to China with a single thrust of your mighty shaft."

A warm smile left dimples at the sides of his mouth. Despite the turmoil she knew churned within him, Winn preened with male pride.

"Do you think so?" he asked with smug satisfaction.

"I do. In fact, my pirate lover, your stamina is

astounding—as if you hadn't made love to anyone in years. Wishful thinking on my part, I admit, with a man as virile as you."

Winn's self-satisfied grin turned bittersweet. "Then at least I've fulfilled your wish, Zoe. For it's a fact that I haven't been with a woman in a very long time."

"How long?"

"Almost ten years."

Zoe gasped—she couldn't help it. Winn had no need to lie. But why would he choose to live like a monk? "I don't understand. . . ."

She watched as he stared into the pool, knowing the white sand and blue waters had receded from his vision. What he saw in their depths was a sight his mind recalled, a memory that was the source of his pain.

She longed to touch him, to give him some comfort. But Winn had demons to wrestle with, and she didn't know how to help him. The one kindness she could give him was to listen while he slew his dragons himself. His voice had the singsong quality of a minstrel as he related his tragic tale.

"It was 1805, toward the end of the Tripolitan War. I'd joined the budding American Navy and was one of Preble's boys, a young lieutenant—full of myself and hungry for glory. I loved that life. And I respected my captain, admired him greatly. When a corsair's attack struck him down, I found myself in charge and bent on revenge."

Winn turned to her, his explanation grating roughly through his throat. "You see, I saw it happen. Watched as his head exploded across the deck and spattered its gore upon my uniform. My hands dripped with his brains and blood." He rubbed a hand across his eye. It remained closed as he continued.

"I turned the ship around and lit out after the retreating enemy. I was within hailing distance when her captain stood upon his deck, bold as brass, and hauled an American flag down from the mast—a common practice to fly your enemy's colors, one we've often used ourselves. But it was what the bastard did with the flag that unnerved me, set my blood to boiling even hotter than before."

"What's that?" she asked when he paused.

"Bastard threw it to the deck and pissed on it."

Zoe barely stifled a laugh at so ridiculous a sight. "But, Winn—"

"I know. A silly thing to stake your life on. But I was so young and self-righteous, full of piss and vinegar myself. The bastard had insulted my new homeland and had killed the captain I'd come to love like a father.

"I lost my head, Princess. Thank God no one lost their lives. Like a madman I had the crew strafe their deck, called broadside after broadside till their masts broke and their ship rolled. And still that bastard stood upon the deck of his gaudy, garishly painted ship, the cutlass and stars of his personal flag flapping on what was left of the mast."

Zoe leaned against Winn, catching his hand in hers. She knew worse was to come—she could see it in the tightness of his shoulders, hear it in his constricted voice. An eerie coldness trailed down her spine, and she shivered despite the warmth of the tropics.

"We boarded the ship, what was left of it, to secure such prizes we could find and to gather our prisoners. Yet the captain refused to strike his colors. When I approached him, he finally yielded, holding his sword out in surrender. Like a fool I ignored the hatred in his eyes and stepped within range of the sword. He delivered it to me, a gleam in his eye, across my groin and through my right testicle."

The last words strangled in Winn's throat. Zoe went hot, then cold, then unbearably hot once more. Her stomach rolled harder than it had on the ship, as if a giant hand had clamped it in a vicious grip.

"Oh, my God. Oh, my God."

She rocked back and forth, closing her mind to an image of Winn sprawled bleeding upon a deck—a faceless monster looming over him.

"The last thing I heard before fainting dead away was the utter joy of his laughter."

"I hope someone killed the bastard," Zoe whispered, sick to her soul at what Winn had endured.

"He dove overboard and was picked up by one of his retreating ships. I lay in bed for months, sickened by a brain fever brought on by infection. When I awoke, it was to find I was but half a man. McCairn said I might yet father children, but until you, Princess, I was unable to enjoy the comforts of a woman."

"But you—but we—"

What on earth did he mean?

Winn turned to her, a wry twist to his mouth. "It was a lesson in love that saved my manhood, Princess."

He stroked a finger down her cheek, then over the fullness of her lips. Zoe kissed his fingertip, waiting for him to continue. A dark flush of embarrassment crawled up his face.

"I felt desire before, but couldn't perform. It took love, true love for a woman—you, Princess—to overcome my shame. In the past I had only had sex with a woman. Evidently it wasn't enough. I needed more, Zoe. I needed love. But I never realized that, until you."

He pulled her into his arms and absorbed her, skin to skin, melting together where they touched. It was so right to be with him like this. Winn's mouth captured hers, caressed hers, drawing on her strength, sharing his pain. Zoe broke away from him, looking straight into his eye.

"I want to kill him, Winn. I want to wipe that evil bastard from the face of the earth."

"So fierce, Princess. You make me believe you do love me." His brief glance held raw, naked hope.

"I do," she answered.

Zoe saw his mood change, his load lighten, and was glad she'd helped bring it about. It was true—she did love him with all of her being. Winn held her chin in his hand.

"You're too late for retribution, Zoe. For years revenge was my sole passion, my reason for living. I became a privateer, turning my merchant runs into a more lucrative business. With my spoils I bought the *Raven* and the *Blackbird,* two of the finest frigates that sailed the seas. They were designed by Humphreys, you know." He paused to wipe a tendril of hair from her face.

"What happened, Winn?"

"Combed the seas till I found the bastard. Took close to six years from the day I recovered. I recognized his tawdry green-and-yellow colors decorating a stolen brig, and knew that whoreson was captaining the ship. I laid her low after a vicious fight, not wanting to taint my hands with the blackguard's spoils. And I watched it sink into the sea, aflame, with the cur bleeding upon its deck."

"Shit."

Winn chuckled. Her disappointment warmed his

being. "If I knew you'd one day appear on my own deck, by God, Princess, I would have saved him for you."

And he would have, he thought, watching the clouds of color in her eyes as they shifted hue with her moods. Shock, lust, revenge, love—he'd seen them all within her expressive gaze. Her openness humbled him, her honesty undid him, and the gift of love she had given him remade his soul.

The shame he'd carried all those years lifted from his being and winged to the sky. She freed him with her acceptance, held him with her love. And somehow, when he wasn't watching, when he'd lowered the barriers to his heart, she'd crept in and had become his life.

He looked at her, aware of a playfulness in her eyes, a deviltry about her lips. She held him spellbound in her hot gaze, a lustful dart of tongue over her lips creating havoc with his body. His tired manhood sprang to life, much to his amazement.

By damn, if anything, his performance had improved. A small boon after years of deprivation. More likely it was Zoe and her deft handling that had wrought such eager responses, even though she hadn't touched him physically till today.

He watched as she studied his body, looking him over from head to heel. Wherever her gaze moved an invisible caress seemed to graze his skin, and he delighted in that unseen touch. But he wanted and needed something more.

Zoe's hand skittered across his chest, leaving a path of white hot lust in its trail. She soothed the heat with her tongue, nibbling gently as she followed her hand. He gloried in the pure sensation of desire, delighted in the feel of her fingers and tongue as they skimmed across his stomach and over his leg.

Then Zoe shifted her attention to the juncture of his thighs and cupped his mangled sack in her hand. Her expression shifted from shock to anger but, thankfully, not disgust. In fact, when she looked up, she gave him a toothy grin, a sensual gurgle escaping her throat.

Oh, she was up to something, no doubt. He could see it in those witchy emerald eyes. For the first time that day, he grew nervous.

"What are you planning, Zoe? Something wicked, I'll deem, by that devilish look about you."

"Worried, Winn?" she teased, tracing the length of his engorged phallus with a finger. She gently caressed his damaged body, putting him through a heavenly hell.

"Should I be worried?"

"Absolutely not."

"The suspense is killing me," he said, but thought her touch and closeness more apt to do the deed. He felt as though he were about to burst. He saw her lean closer, inspecting the softness she held in her hand. He couldn't breathe while awaiting her answer.

"Why, Winn." That secret smile returned to her lips, and the throb in his groin spread clear to his toenails. "I plan to reciprocate. It was generous of you to soothe my injuries, and now I plan to do the same for you."

She winked at him before lowering her head to his vulnerable anatomy. He hadn't the heart or strength to tell her that what she did to him was nothing short of sweet torture. . . .

And worth any amount of vicious flea bites he'd get upon his bare butt.

*   *   *

They awoke to whistles. A whole series of warbles that trilled high and low in contrasting melody. A song, made by people, that resembled the call of birds.

"Our hosts, my dear," Winn explained at her puzzled look. "They have an entire language of whistles. Quite fascinating. I thought to return and study it further one day."

She watched as he pursed his mouth, returning the haunting melody. Zoe scrambled to cover herself, thinking they would soon be discovered. But the whistles changed direction, fading away toward the clearing.

Winn stood, pulling her with him, and began to don his clothing. Zoe followed suit, longing for another dip in the pool before putting on her thoroughly wrinkled clothes. The sand upon her skin itched like the devil, but it looked like Winn's flea bites itched worse. He continued to scratch and rub his buns. She doubted he was aware of his actions.

"Why the smile, Princess?"

"Thinking about sand fleas, that's all."

He rubbed his bottom and frowned. "Damned nuisance, if you ask me. Pesky buggers got a whole meal off my left cheek, and dessert from the right."

Zoe laughed out loud, feeling freer than she'd felt in years. And it was all due to the man who stood beside her.

"Regency rakes are supposed to be wicked, but a bit stiff," she said as she openly studied him.

"Oh," he drawled. "And you are an expert on Regency rakes?"

"Hey, you read my books. Am I right, or what?"

"Seems to me I've been plenty stiff today." He grinned at her, teeth blazing white in the sun.

Oh, that smile.

It had been her undoing from the start. It had recently become her weakness when it came to men, this man in particular. After years of propriety as the countess, she'd become a sucker for smiles.

Not a bad vice, if you asked her. After all, it had attracted her to Winn, and had opened her heart to happiness once more. Zoe sighed a contented sigh.

The world was her oyster, and she was going to eat like a glutton.

Winn's low voice broke into her thoughts.

"You'll need a bath, Princess. Or you'll itch like the dickens all night, and I do want you to enjoy the feast."

"It seems I need clean clothes as well," she muttered, looking down at the now disreputable outfit she wore.

Winn offered her his arm. "I'll see what I can do." Then he led her back to the clearing, chuckling at her blushes when the men glanced slyly their way. She wasn't ashamed of what she and Winn did. But she remained a private person.

Winn, on the other hand, positively gloated as he left her at their hut.

Zoe relished the cool privacy, falling asleep on the soft bed as soon as her head touched the mattress. When she awoke she discovered a hip bath had been brought in, along with clean towels and a simple cotton gown.

Bless him, she thought, pleased by Winn's consideration. She hadn't had so much lusty exercise in years and felt quite sore. She shed her clothes as fast as she could and sank into the fragranced warmth of the bath. Exotic flower petals floated on the surface, perfuming her body, and a mild soap scented her freshly washed hair.

She was hoping Winn would return before she finished soaking—she always did love those tub scenes in her romance novels. But she started to shrivel the longer she sat there. It wasn't until she'd dried off and had fastened nearly half the buttons up her back that the object of her fantasies waltzed into the tiny room.

He filled the small space with his impressively wide shoulders and nearly hit his head on the thatched roof. There was nothing lacking in his build or in his looks. The sheer perfection of the man always stunned her into tongue-tied stupidity and fostered feelings of inferiority. Tonight was no exception.

She looked like a witch while he was a god.

It was hell to be in love with a man more beautiful than yourself. At times like this she felt particularly awkward. A goddess should have been by his side, not her.

She must have blurted out the words, for he slowly approached her, tilting her chin up till she faced him. He regarded her with a thoroughness she found unnerving, and held her gaze captive in his.

"No. You are not a goddess."

Her heart sank at his words and she lowered her eyes. She knew she was far from perfection, but he didn't have to rub it into her already fragile ego.

"You are a princess, Zoe. My Princess."

She glanced up through her lashes. The beauty of him stunned her anew. But what held her attention wasn't his beauty, it was the warm radiance of total love that poured out from him to her.

"A goddess is cold perfection but you, Zoe, are not only flesh and blood, you are my joy. My life. I prefer your warm imperfect body and your hot lusty looks to some paragon of icy perfection. Always, Zoe. I'll always want you."

He took her mouth, plundering it with his own. *Hot,* she thought. Hell, she was about to incinerate with the heat she generated at his touch. She began to melt against him, her hand sneaking under his shirt to caress the hard planes of his chest, when a tiny voice broke into her thoughts and took her mind off Winn.

"Princess! Princess! Come out and join the feast. Cookie says the food is heavenly."

Adam skidded to a halt inside the hut, oblivious of Zoe and Winn's dishabille. He tugged on their arms, propelling them forward. Winn managed to button the rest of Zoe's gown before she reached the fire-lit beach. He bowed to her, every inch the Earl.

"Princess, the food may well be heavenly, but tonight you are manna from the gods."

She watched, satisfied with the way his eye darkened to a midnight pool of desire. Zoe slowly raised a brow.

"In that case, I promise to save myself for dessert as long as you behave before the men."

"It'll be hard, Princess. Damn hard."

Zoe looked down at his straining pants, and winked.

"That's precisely what I'm counting on."

9

"Damn him."

Zoe paced the small confines of the hut, unable to take out her vengeance on Winn and unable to find proper release for her anger. Amazing how drastically emotions could shift in little more than a week.

"The stubborn ass. I'd like to truss him up like a turkey and throw him in the brig. I'd like to see how he feels when a woman gives the orders and smiles condescendingly in his smug face."

"I'd like to see that too, Mizz Zoe. Would be quite a sight to see, what with the cap'n's temper, and all."

"Oh, pooh, Adam. The man's bark is far worse than his bite."

Adam looked up at her with wide, speculative eyes. She'd forgotten the little dear was there. Then again, they were in this together, both of them being foisted upon the indulgent islanders while Winn risked his lovely hide and silvered hair for God, duty, and country.

Well, rot his duties. This was her life he was toying with, not some idyllic interlude. She would not be left behind like forgotten baggage. She would not.

She'd gone over it with the stubborn man, insisting she wasn't frightened about his trip to Algiers. Yes, she knew the danger, she'd be willing to take it. And yes, she knew the rigors as well.

It wasn't that she was a masochist or anything, but she had to get home, and she wouldn't accomplish that by parking her butt on a sandy beach while she waited for him to return from his adventure. That was all well and good for dear Mr. Turcotte, who was also being left behind. The young man continued to recover from his terrible injuries but would suffer with aches and pains for the rest of his life.

Yet Turcotte was a good sport about it all. He knew he'd be no help on the mission and perhaps would prove a hindrance. So with Winn's blessings he would take a boat around the island to a well-known port on the other side and join one of the whalers that frequented it.

Mr. Turcotte may have needed a respite, but Zoe most definitely did not. What she needed was to get home. She had tried to tell Winn about her precarious circumstances, that she actually had come from the future. But he'd cut off her protests each time she tried to explain.

He'd even admitted that once his mind was made up, there was no changing it.

"Damn him," she muttered, and continued her pacing. "I have to stay with him on the *Raven*. It's my only chance of returning to the children. What if something happens? If he doesn't come back for me? I'll have lost not only him, but my only chance of going home."

"You have children, Princess?" Adam asked.

"Yes," she nodded. "A boy and a girl."

"Are they a prince and a princess, too?"

Wistfulness laced his sweet voice, and Zoe's heart filled with tenderness for him.

"Adam, I am not a princess. I was once a countess, but no longer, and if I have anything to say about it, my children will never hold formal titles. I've seen too many pompous asses wearing coronets. You, sweetheart, are every bit as important as any queen, or king, or duke, or lord."

The little boy's eyes lit up in wonder. "Do you mean that?"

"Of course I do. You must never think of yourself as less than anyone's equal. That, Adam, is the American way."

"Cap'n told me something about that. Said he was proud to be a Yank, and that I should be proud, too." He nodded his golden head for emphasis.

"Well, I guess he isn't a total jackass," Zoe muttered.

"No, Princess. Perhaps he's only half."

Zoe laughed at Adam's solemn answer, her mood lightening to a degree. The little boy had stolen her heart long ago. She didn't want to burden him with her anger, even if she continued to relish the idea of hitting Winn's hard head with something harder—but the only thing that she could think of in that category was a rock or a cannonball.

"Adam, this just won't do." She spun around and faced him, mind racing with plans she dismissed summarily. "There must be a way to change Winn's mind. There has to be."

She flopped down on the bed next to him. At this very moment Winn was on the ship, preparing it for sailing. And the stubborn fool was adamant about leaving her and Adam behind.

The little boy looked up at her, wide-eyed. "Ain't no changin' the cap'n's mind, ma'am. He can be one stubborn cuss—or so Cookie says."

Zoe sprang up from the bed and started pacing. "Well, stubborn cuss or not, I'm not being left behind. If I can't convince that thief to take me with him, I'll—" She paused, racking her brain for an answer to her problems. And then she saw it, right before her face. "Well, if he won't take me with him, then I'll have to stow aboard. Yes, Adam. That's exactly what I'll do."

She turned to him, a wicked smile curving her lips, and was shocked by the boy's reaction. His cherubic face crumpled beneath his halo of golden curls, and he flung himself against her legs, hugging her as though he'd never let go.

"Oh, no, Princess. You can't mean to do that," the boy sobbed into her skirts. His face turned stark white, having drained of all its natural rosy color. "Please, ma'am, you can't leave me behind. Please, oh, please, Princess, take me with you."

The boy's sobs wrenched at her heart. What was she to do? Winn had insisted they stay. He'd even brought the damn goat ashore to provide fresh milk for Adam, saying he didn't want to put his milk supply in jeopardy, he loved his coffee far too much for that. She was sure not a man in the crew believed his motives when he'd sent the damn goat ashore.

Would that he were only half so solicitous to her needs. He had a mission to accomplish, he'd told her, and she and the boy would be a distraction. He needed to keep his wits about him, after all.

When she had asked him to postpone his mission until his other ship could rendezvous, he had discarded all her notions of danger. It was to be a simple diplomatic mission, and he had the necessary passes and letters of marque to keep him and his crew quite safe.

Well, if it wasn't a dangerous mission, then what kind of distraction could she and Adam be? She didn't buy into his explanation at all. And if it was dangerous, she'd share the danger with him.

She'd be damned if she'd be stuck on this island, no matter how beautiful or how friendly the natives. She didn't belong here. She belonged home with her children. And the only way she'd accomplish that would be to stick to her stubborn pirate like glue.

Zoe patted Adam's silky head, feeling the desperate fear and loneliness that surrounded him like a mist. She hadn't thought about the boy's plight. If she were to leave him, too, she imagined his heart would break.

They'd become so much like a family, the three of them, these past few weeks. The boy had been attached to Winn long before she'd landed so precipitously on the ship. But he was in desperate need of the type of nurturing only a mother could give him and had grown close to her as well.

Pretty convenient for Winn and his plans.

Zoe sighed and pulled the boy closer. Poor dear. Like her, he had no one to turn to except Winn. And that damned idiot was planning to leave both of them. She ruffled the boy's hair, placing a kiss on his forehead as she wiped away his tears.

"Don't worry, Adam. I won't leave you behind. You can count on it."

* * *

Winn looked back in the direction of the island, seeing it only in his mind's eye. Two days out and well on their way to Algiers, he knew no one on God's earth could detect the strip of land they'd recently left. Yet he tried to conjure the image anyway, despite the pain it brought. God knew he'd see it behind his lids for months.

Zoe hadn't seen him off; she'd been sleeping in the hut with a distraught Adam when he had left. It was better that way, he thought. No teary good-byes or maudlin pleas. He'd done the right thing, taking off at dawn in the tender. And he'd done the right thing by leaving them behind.

Because he had lied.

Straight to Adam's and Zoe's faces, he had lied. The mission reeked of danger. There was no love lost among corsairs themselves, let alone among ships of infidel nations. He'd learned long ago that Mediterranean pirates were fond of the excuse provided by holy wars.

Barbary pirates didn't consider themselves marauders or thieves, nor did they plunder or pillage. Oh, no. They were corsairs, the weapons of Allah, teaching the infidels about the might of Islam. A holy excuse. Winn shook his head in disgust.

If they fight a holy war, then I'm the queen of England, he thought.

Good God. Where did that come from? Everyone knew the regent was upon the throne. A wry smile curved the corners of his lips. Who else could such a ridiculous epithet come from but Zoe.

Ah, he missed her and the boy. They'd wormed

their way into his heart and wouldn't leave, no matter how he tried to ignore the tender feelings there. But this wasn't the time or place to be distracted by sentiments he'd forgone for so long—they would have to wait. He needed his wits about him in the days to come, for he knew, if no one else did, that this was to be a mission to hell.

Winn swayed upon the deck, a sudden bout of nausea assailing him. Damn, if this didn't happen every time after putting out from port. It always took several days for him to regain his sea legs. He'd come on deck thinking the fresh air would relieve his misery, but evidently not. The salty air served only to heighten his nausea, and the flap of sails and creaking of the masts had left him with an aching head.

Winn motioned to the ever-present Leetch, leaving the wheel and the quarterdeck to the young man. Then he headed for his cabin, intent on a rest and sweet dreams of the warm days and hot nights of the weeks he had spent with Zoe.

Outside his cabin he paused, knowing his head hurt too bloody much to get any rest. He turned on his heels, descending the swaying stairs to the depths of the ship and McCairn's ministrations. Perhaps the good doctor had a potion that would cure either his stomach or his aches.

Winn strode toward the direction of sickbay, the closeness of the corridor making his stomach worse. He paused a moment outside the door and rested his head against the jamb, willing down the bile that had risen in his throat. A spatter of tinkling laughter reached his ears, and he immediately thought of Zoe.

Lord, now I'm hearing her, he thought.

He cursed his fanciful imagination beneath his breath. He was acting like a lovesick swain, for God's sake. This wouldn't do at all. He had a ship to run, a crew to manage. He hadn't the time for romantic folly.

But there it was again—a distinct peal of feminine laughter with Zoe's rich warm tones. Perhaps insanity ran in the family. He could remember an odd uncle or two, and his grandmother had been an original. But no, dammit, he heard it once more—he'd swear it.

Winn strode through the door to sickbay and couldn't believe his eyes. At the far corner of the room sat Zoe, Adam, and that traitorous McCairn, laughing together around a rickety table.

"What in bloody hell do you think you're doing?" he bellowed. He could feel the blood bulging the veins in his neck, and his head now thumped to the beat of a drum.

All motion at the table stopped, to his satisfaction. While McCairn appeared sheepish, Adam looked clearly afraid. But Zoe—ah, his sweet princess—she gave him a triumphant smile as she answered: "Why, Winn. Can't you see? We're playing go fish."

He saw nothing but red. She could tell by the way the blood pounded at his temples and how his grin stretched ghoulishly across his tightened jaw.

Oh, Lord. She was in for it now.

Somehow she'd never quite thought of this moment, of what would happen when Winn discovered them on the *Raven*. Now she realized it had been a subconscious act on her part—that if she had thought of it, she'd have damn well changed her mind about stowing aboard.

It was obviously too late now. The only thing to do would be to brazen it out. But so far that hadn't seemed to work very well. She could tell by the tic at Winn's jaw.

Amazing. She would never have thought the man possessed so formidable a temper. Then again, Adam had warned her. Why hadn't she listened?

She turned toward the boy, suddenly remembering his presence along with that of the doctor. A wave of guilt swept through her when she saw the fear upon the little mite's face and the confusion upon McCairn's. Evidently Adam had known better than she what they were getting into—she realized he must have seen his captain's temper before.

But McCairn—that poor man hadn't a clue to what was going on. She never happened to mention they didn't belong there and had, in fact, stolen aboard. Why drag the doctor in on their nefarious plans?

Zoe shivered as Winn's gaze shifted and he turned his wrath upon McCairn. She tried to speak up but couldn't. The pirate's scowl had rendered her speechless.

"So, doctor. This is how you reward my friendship— by going against my wishes . . . behind my back." His features hardened to sculpted stone.

"Now see here—"

"No. You see here. We need you upon this ship, that's a fact. Else I'd tie you to the rigging and take long thin strips off your traitorous hide."

"Try it," the burly doctor growled as he stood.

"Now wait just a minute." Zoe sprang up between them. "I will not have you at each other's throats. This is my fault, all of it." She turned to Winn. "The doctor has no idea what you're talking about. I didn't tell him a damned thing, you thick-headed boob."

Winn's gaze shifted to her. "Boob?" he asked.

"Idiot!" she shouted.

"Well, Princess." Winn's voice lowered to a dangerous edge. "If what you say is true, then I owe my apologies to the good doctor." He nodded in McCairn's direction, and the bear nodded back, despite his own formidable scowl.

I'm really, really in for it now, she thought, watching with trepidation as Winn ignored her and placed Adam in the doctor's temporary care.

Then, that taken care of, Winn grabbed her arm and dragged her to him, a wicked gleam in the center of his dark, jet bead of an eye. Adam whimpered a protest, but Zoe sought to ease the boy.

"Don't worry, Adam. I'm perfectly safe. The captain wouldn't do anything that he'd regret later."

It seemed to mollify the boy, but Zoe had her own doubts. Especially when she caught the gist of Winn's muttering while he dragged her toward his cabin.

"Don't count on it," he said.

The damn idiot had locked her in!

Zoe paced the edges of Winn's cabin, her tension mounting with every step. Where on earth had he gone? She didn't like this stubborn streak in him, not one bit. And every extra minute he stayed away heightened her apprehension.

The devil had possessed him with a vengeance. He had dragged her down the corridors to his room, muttering epithets that shocked even her. She'd never seen the man in such a snit, nor experienced his vile temper before. What had gotten into him?

Oh, she knew he was angry at her. And, in truth, she had it coming. She had disobeyed the captain's orders, and he remained king of his ship. Adam often remarked on the captain's vicious temper, but not having faced it herself, she had pooh-poohed it as a child's greater sensitivity and overactive imagination.

She should have listened to Adam. He was an honest boy and bright. Evidently she wasn't as bright as the little squirt. Ouch. The admission stung.

She'd worked so hard on bolstering her self-esteem that she'd become cocky, self-inflated instead. The truth of the matter was she had thought herself special enough to Winn to expect that her stowing aboard wouldn't matter. She had actually believed she meant more to him than ironclad rules and military regulations.

She'd been wrong.

Underneath all of his deceptively quiet ranting and raving as he propelled her here, she'd felt the tremors of an explosive anger—far more than her deed warranted, in her opinion. One look at Winn when they had entered the cabin confirmed all her worst suspicions. His eye had narrowed to an angry slit, and his voice had darkened to the depths of hell.

"I know I'm going to regret this in the morning, Princess," he'd practically growled. "But you leave me no alternative course of action."

And with those words he had spun on his heels, locking the door as he'd left the cabin. She hadn't seen tawny hide nor silver hair of him for the better part of an hour.

Who the hell did he think he was, anyway?

Zoe shook her head. Not content to voice her opinions silently, she began to mutter aloud. The more she muttered, the better she felt.

"I'm not one of his crew, dammit, or under his charge. I'm not even from his century. Jonathan had his faults, true. But overbearing, high-handed male chauvinism was not one of them. That's something for downtrodden, weak-kneed females with feathers for brains."

Boy, this is more like it, she thought, beginning to warm up to her own ranting. It didn't make up for confronting the man in person, but it sure felt a heck of a lot better than keeping it to herself. She paced angrily to the back of the wardroom, muttering louder, on a roll.

"Who appointed him my guardian? Who put him in charge? The man has no claim to me. I'm a free, independent, modern woman. And I'm certainly my own person to live my life however I please."

So there, she thought.

"Oh, but I beg to differ, madam."

The oily tones of Winn's voice sent shivers down her spine. Zoe spun around, hands on hips, to confront the devil who stood before her in such a wonderfully appealing, well-packaged disguise.

He had swept his long onyx-and-silver hair into a low ponytail, the sides escaping to curl seductively upon his neck. His windswept face had recently been washed and his beard shaved clean—she could see a bit of foamy soap lingering upon his tight jaw.

Damn the man.

He could entice her even when she wanted to wring his neck. Some things in life just weren't fair, she thought. But then she'd come to that conclusion long ago.

"Keep on begging," she said. "You can differ with me all you want and it will get you nowhere. Unless you flog me, I won't give in."

"Then I guess I'll have to flog you," he answered, his voice as low as a winter wind.

Zoe glared at him before answering. "Then, Captain, I guess you will."

She wasn't one to bow down. She'd be damned if she started now. Let the man stew in his own juices and try to find a way around this dilemma. He'd never harm her, in any case. Winn wasn't a man prone to violence. In fact, he was too soft a touch for his own good.

"Whatever it takes, Princess. But you *will* do my bidding—one way or another."

He smiled at her, a smugly evil smile. No. This side of him was not at all alluring.

"Why should I do a damn thing you tell me? You don't care for me a whit. If you did, you would never have left me on that island. I told you how important it is that I return to your manor house. I begged you to take me with you."

She took a deep breath in order to continue. "But I won't stoop so low to ever beg you for anything again. A cruel heart lies under your handsome exterior, Winn. For Adam's sake I won't have you going on about this episode. Besides, unless my calculations are wrong, it's far too late to turn back."

Winn broke out in a beatific smile that transformed the devilish dips and hollows of his face into angelic beauty. Zoe had to close down tight on her jaw so it wouldn't gape open at the sudden change in the man. Something slippery was going on, she knew it as surely as she recognized that triumphant gleam in his soot-dark eye.

"You're right, my dear. Although your words resemble the sentimental songs in your clever music box, it *is* too late to turn back." Winn swept his hand into the top drawer of his desk and dangled her Walkman from his fingers. "As for my cruel heart," he said, "I have only acted with your best interests in mind, out of my deep, abiding concern for you. You see, Princess, I seem to have fallen in love."

Her jaw did gape open now—she imagined she resembled a very large, dim-witted fish. The man was demented. First he threatened to get his way by any means possible, then, with a corny line befitting golden oldies beebop from the twentieth century, he told her he loved her as plainly as the weatherman related the weather. A unique way of learning someone loved you. Or at least she *thought* that was what he was saying.

"What are you doing with my cassette player, and what exactly are you rambling about?" she demanded.

"Why, Zoe, dear, you do have a very modern sort of temper, don't you? It could be a trial to deal with long term, but I think I'll manage."

"A minute ago you were about to throw me to the sharks, or make me walk the plank like you were Captain Hook."

"Hook? Never heard of him." He paused a moment, pondering the question of Hook's identity. "But as for your imaginative comments—I'm afraid you are stuck with me, Princess. You see, you've become an annoyingly endearing habit."

"Habit!"

Habit?

She'd show him habit.

Zoe edged past Winn, stalking through his cabin to the door. She stopped before it, spinning back dramatically to face him. Good. She could see by his scowl she had him worried now.

"I refuse to be anyone's habit. I do not accept charity—never have, never will." She grabbed the knob. "And I will not be sharing this cabin with you, sir."

With that flourishing exit line Zoe twisted the handle and pushed, intent on leaving—but banged into the closed door instead. She twisted it again and again, to no avail. When she started to slam her shoulder against the door, Winn sidled up to her, keys dangling from his fingers much like her recorder had.

"Looking for these, Princess?" One of his brows raised into a cynical arc.

"Give me those, dammit."

She jumped for the keys, falling against Winn and knocking him onto his bunk.

"Ah, so eager, Princess." He pulled her up to straddle his thighs. "I take it you've changed your mind about staying with me."

"Absolutely not," she hissed. "No man will be my master. No man will dictate to me or run my life. No man—"

Winn cut off her angry protest by pulling her to his chest and planting a silencing kiss upon her mouth. Zoe struggled against the sinful lure of the man but found herself melting as disgustingly quick as always. She fell into his hands like a ripe peach.

When would she ever learn?

She couldn't afford to be under his spell—she had to keep her wits about her. She wasn't ready for so intense an affair, nor strong enough to go through the pain caused by another doomed relationship. There were things she had to accomplish, priorities to keep.

Her children needed her.

And she needed to get back.

There was no room in her twentieth-century life for a romance with a nineteenth-century pirate. She must have been insane to get trapped by his come-hither looks. Damn. Her hormones had always been her downfall.

Zoe struggled against Winn, trying to get loose. He only held her closer, plundering her mouth so thoroughly that she couldn't tell where she ended and he began. If he probed any farther, he'd reach her tonsils.

Their tastes met, mingled, blended into one, distracting her once again. Zoe moaned from both pleasure and frustration as she pushed away from her pirate lover.

But Winn flipped her over smoothly to her back, continuing the assault upon her senses. She tried not to respond, to go totally still, but determination was, indeed, his strong suit. So she did the only thing she could think of.

She bit his tongue.

Didn't sever it—that would be an awful waste of an exceptionally good tongue—only nipped at it. But enough for Winn to jump off the bed, wiping a trickle of blood from the corner of his mouth.

His brows drew together in an angry vee, and his lips thinned ominously. A dangerous gleam was in his eye as he turned his piercing gaze upon her. The deep resonance of his voice roared more loudly than any bellow.

"Well met, Princess. I see you have not as yet been tamed, and I applaud you for a formidable foe—it makes the game far more interesting. You see, I look forward to the future and our time together."

Zoe stared at over six feet of defiance glaring down at her in challenge. Thick-headedness was evidently another family trait. Zoe stood upon the bed, preferring the added height it offered. Let the idiot look up at her for a change. She was tired of getting a crick in her neck.

"I have tried to tell you again and again that I do not belong here, but you've been too stubborn a jackass to listen to my story, or believe the few words I've tried to drum into that stainless steel head."

Winn opened his mouth to speak, probably to cut her off. But she wouldn't have it. She drowned him out, stopping the words in his throat.

"There *is* no future for us. There never has been. You are a figment of history, a person from the pages of my past. And I am nothing but a dream, a distant figure on your horizon. From the twentieth century, dammit! Get it through that incredibly thick head of yours."

She stood on the bed, chest heaving as she gulped lungfuls of air, more shaken up by the truth of her words than she would have thought. Winn looked up at her with an assessing gaze. She could see his pulse beat heavily in his neck as he tamped down a barely leashed rage.

"I don't want to hear any more of this nonsense, Zoe. I will do as I please. And you will do as I please, as well."

"But—"

He cut her off. "It's time you got that through your equally thick head. Or is yours truly stuffed with feathers?" He didn't give her time to respond but swept his hand in the direction of his bureau. "I'll give you five minutes to tidy up. I'd suggest you wash your face since it is now quite flushed. Perhaps the water will cool your hot temper."

"*My* hot temper?" she roared.

He ignored her. "If you've a clean dress, you might want to change into it. McCairn will come down to fetch you to the deck. It's the least he can do, considering he had a hand in this deception, ignorant or not."

What was he planning? She knew he wouldn't hurt her, but all this talk of taming left her mouth dry and tasting bitter. He had something up his silky sleeve. Most likely some humiliating public reprimand.

"And suppose I choose not to go?" she asked.

"Did I say anything about a choice?"

Smug bastard—he had her there. She couldn't very well strong-arm the grizzly bear of a doctor.

"If you want to get your jollies by punishing me in front of the men, then go ahead. I'll show you how a real woman faces adversity."

Winn snorted, barely keeping his laughter under control. "Ah, Princess. You are never dull. Of a certainty, I will get my jollies tonight, but not from punishing you. In fact, I'm sure my crew to a man will debate whether you or I will suffer the greater punishment in the long run."

He walked to the door—a scene that had become all too familiar.

"Five minutes, Princess. Or I'll come down, fetch

you myself, and carry you up to the quarterdeck like a sack of booty." He gave her a nod and strode out the door.

Damn, but the man had the best exit lines.

A timid knock tapped against the door, followed by a meaty thud. Zoe straightened the extra dress the islanders had given her—a simple affair of cotton gauze that fit her long slim lines to a tee. She wore it with the pair of sandals she'd stuffed into her bag, so long ago, in anticipation of a fun-in-the-sun island vacation.

Well, she'd had her fun in the sun and her island vacation, though in a way she could never have anticipated or believed so many weeks before. Zoe sighed, tucking an errant strand of hair behind her ear, then calmly pulled open the door.

Adam flung himself at her, pressing his tear-smudged face against her legs while McCairn stood behind him, smiling. She smoothed back the boy's hair and bent to give him a kiss.

"There now, sweetheart. I'm okay."

Zoe looked up at McCairn, wearing a wry smile, and shrugged. "Sorry to get you in trouble, doctor. But I had to stay on this ship."

"I don't understand why you need to be here, mistress. But I do believe you have to." He nodded. "No need to apologize. There's nothing to be sorry about. Yet."

Zoe straightened, searching his face for an insight to her dilemma. "Do you know what Winn is planning?"

"Nary a clue."

"Then it's worse than I thought."

She turned to the cabin, grabbing a shawl the

islanders had given her, and screwed up her courage—
the sooner she got the show on the road, the better.
Then she held Adam's hand in hers, looped her arm
through McCairn's, and headed topside to the unknown.

The closing day had turned a stormy gray that
matched her feelings exactly as she stepped onto the
deck. High up on the masts the sails flapped and
crackled as if in protest of this turn of events. She
felt buoyed by an absurd feeling of support, but
then again, sailors swore ships had personalities of
their own.

Good, she thought. If I detect an aura of empathy
around me, then Winn must be uncomfortable as
hell.

A sudden rush of wind stirred her hair, whipping
it into tangles. A loud caw and a brush of feathers
alerted her to Raven a moment before he landed his
surprisingly heavy body upon her shoulder.
Personally she would have preferred to stick with
parakeets—they were a heck of a lot lighter—but the
bird's defection and obvious affection bolstered her
ego and would undermine Winn's better than thumb-
ing her nose.

Zoe glanced around before crossing the deck. The
majority of the crew had gathered to watch. Some of
the men sat in the rigging, and others were plunked
upon the yardarms. They all looked at her sadly, sympathy in their eyes, as if she were going to Madame
Guillotine.

A shiver ran through Zoe. She chastised herself for
having so creative an imagination. Winn wouldn't
slice her scrawny neck or even wring it. Nor would he
do anything to the rest of her body. She knew his lips
would miss gliding along it too damn much.

The men parted silently at the top of the gangway. A knot of officers stood to the left. As a path cleared to Winn, she swept her gaze over his features. You would think he was the one in trouble. He seemed unusually reserved and sterner than ever, even to the point of grim, which was not the Winn she was used to.

It did not make her roiling stomach feel any better to see that stern facade upon his face. Especially when her imagination wandered to another scenario. Oh, he'd never do her any real physical harm.

But he might not be averse to giving her a spanking. Would he?

Now that kind of humiliation she refused to take. She'd fight him tooth and nail if she had to. Let him try to lay a hand on her and she'd rip the hair out of his nostrils. There was no way he'd degrade her like that.

Working herself into a lather, Zoe pasted a sickly sweet smile on her face and marched with determination toward Winn, feeling as formidable as a pirate captain with the crow riding on her shoulder. She took comfort in the admiring glances of the crew, but the worried looks upon some of the faces sent that chill tingling down her spine again. Winn looked her up and down as if inspecting a side of prime beef.

"Here," she said, stretching her mouth into a ghoulishly wide smile.

Winn raised an eyebrow. "What exactly are you doing, Zoe?"

"Making it easier to count my teeth. You were looking at me as if you were buying a racehorse."

Winn rolled his eye while shaking his head with the demeanor of a sorely pressed man. He turned to his left, motioning a small, dark-haired man forward. Zoe recognized the ship's chaplain immediately, as he was all decked out in white, flowing robes.

Winn regarded her for a moment with what she thought was a particularly hot stare.

"You have met Chaplain Amonte?" he asked.

Zoe nodded and acknowledged the man.

"Hello, Chaplain," she said sweetly. "Are you here to give me the last rites?"

10

A hush fell over the crowd. Aside from the regular creaking of the ship and the slap of the waves, silence reigned. Winn took a deep breath, calming his temper as well as his rising pulse. Damned if she didn't look like a real princess with her regal bearing and that ridiculous fat crow preening on her shoulder. Judging her mood, he knew he had his work cut out for him.

"Zoe, dear," he said, "if anyone is to receive their last rites, 'tis I, since I am about to consign my soul to the devil for the rest of my natural life."

He could tell he had spun her thoughts around with his unconventional approach—the woman seemed mightily confused. She stood before him, hands fisted and ready to use if necessary.

He'd never seen a more spirited woman in his life.

Perhaps he *ought* to check her teeth—she had the fire of a racehorse and the energy to match. Lord, how was he to keep up with her? She'd already led him on a merry chase, and the pace had proved close to exhausting.

Yet it had been a pleasant exhaustion, he thought, remembering their idyllic time spent on the island. She'd been the incentive that had restored his manhood, and for that alone he owed her his protection. But he knew, deep down, the true reason why they gathered today.

He couldn't let the woman go.

She was his, dammit, and she'd remain his. Nothing would tear her away from him. Not fate, or time, or God himself. Aye, he'd even bargain with Lucifer if it meant he could keep his princess by his side.

Winn waited till his pause had raised Zoe's unease to a sufficient point. It wouldn't do to give her the upper hand now, not when everything hung in the balance. He meant to begin in the manner he would go on.

"You should not have disobeyed my orders, dear," he said. "Now you've got yourself in one fine mess. The only way to get out of it is to do what you're told, and that means you must answer the chaplain only with a 'Yes' and your honest feelings. Do you understand?"

He watched as her eyes flared in challenge. It would be wonderful taming the woman, though he wouldn't want to douse all of her fire. Perhaps he could channel it into more pleasing venues, such as making love.

He had to admit the idea appealed to him. Good

thing Zoe was not privy to his thoughts, though. The woman looked like one of those furry beasts of burden he'd discovered on a stop during a trip to South America—the ones that spit at you if provoked. He stifled a chuckle, knowing she most assuredly would spit if he pressed her further, and waited while she struggled to speak.

"Yes, you overgrown spoiled brat. I understand." She took a deep breath, then went on. "I understand you're a dominating, male chauv—"

He cut off her words, not wanting to stoke her indignity higher. Control was the key to manipulating this entire scene, and by God, he'd control it.

"Sorry, Princess. But you've spoken a few too many words, and all of them unacceptable. A 'yes' or a 'no' is all that's required." He stared at her intently, hoping to force her into submission, but knew it to be a losing venture before he'd started. "If you find it too difficult to answer as such, or to control that fiery temper, then perhaps you would prefer to nod."

She nodded.

He knew there were at least a score of spicy words trapped within her mouth and burning on her tongue. At that moment she looked damned uncomfortable— her mouth screwed up into a sour purse, the edges of her lips white from the effort to remain silent.

Winn turned to the chaplain and nodded, anxious to have the proceedings over. He imagined Zoe would be astonished by his unique form of punishment. This, of course, would be followed with pleasure and the appropriate gratification she would feel.

But he had been wrong before.

"We have gathered here today to witness the joining of our captain and Mistress Zoe," the chaplain said.

Winn could see Zoe's face turn pale before her cheeks flooded with a crimson flush. "If there are any among you who have an objection, please state it for all to hear."

Zoe looked around frantically, searching the faces of all the men. Poor chit, Winn thought, she'd find no escape there. He had her now, and she damn well knew it. When no one answered, Zoe opened up her mouth to scream—he was sure it was to scream— she'd taken in enough air to blast the topsails into full billow.

"I do!" she shouted.

The cleric ran a finger under his collar, but Winn merely smiled at her passionate response. She seemed more confused than ever. *Good.* It was exactly the response he wanted. A skillful tactician could easily maneuver an opponent's confusion. He focused an indulgent gaze on her.

"No, no, my dear," he said in the tone he would use on a perplexed child. "You are much too anxious. Though I understand your desire to belong to a man such as I, that response comes a bit later."

He glared at the chaplain, sending a silent command to continue, while Zoe remained speechless, foundering like a beached fish, cheeks puffing in and out with air. Even the damn crow looked at her, head cocked as if in amusement, though Winn wouldn't voice his opinion on that, preferring to remain half a man rather than become a eunuch. He found her completely adorable, even if she did resemble a fish at the moment.

"Do you, Jonathan Winnthrop Alexander Dunham, plight your troth to take this woman as your lawfully wedded wife, to have and to cherish, er, et cetera," he stumbled on as Winn waved a hand to hurry it up, "till death you do part?"

Winn raised himself to full height. Now that he would finally get the deed done, a massive load eased from his shoulders. By God, he'd do it right.

"I do," he bellowed, making sure not a man jack among them wasn't sure of his response. The tricky part was yet to come as evidenced by the angry gleam in Zoe's stormy eyes. How he loved her.

But that wouldn't be enough to get them through this if the woman bridled now. Winn sighed, knowing his next actions would send her in a tizzy. He clamped a hand over her mouth and gently forced her to meet his gaze.

"Before you answer, my dear, let me say that you brought yourself to this demise. I can only provide you full protection from the enemy if you are my lawful wife. Otherwise, a single woman, unattached . . ." He paused for the proper effect. "Well, let us merely say that corsairs traffic in human flesh. The prettier the flesh, the more they crave it. And I do say that your flesh is quite the prettiest I've ever seen."

He'd improvised with that last part, having gone over this scene and his speech a hundred times in the hour since finding her in sickbay. Unfortunately the effect it had on her was not the softening he'd anticipated. He could feel the little termagant nipping at his hand!

He gave her a slight shake that Raven didn't like at all. The bloody bird squawked loudly enough to break Zoe's concentration. Winn cursed roundly, waiting for the crow to settle down. When Zoe's attention returned to him, he stared at her till he was sure the importance of his next words would find their way into her highly intelligent but mulishly stubborn brain.

"There is only one question that matters, and I'll have your reply, Zoe. No prevaricating now, I want a truthful answer." Winn paused and took a deep breath. "Do you love me?" He waited for her response, willing her to say yes, but she remained deathly still. "Please, Princess. I need to know."

Winn saw her soften as he spoke, and knew she'd surrendered by the time he had mentioned *need*. He nudged the cleric with his toe, but the daft man didn't acknowledge it, so he kicked him neatly in the shin. The chaplain droned quickly on while Winn pressed his point.

"You know I love you, Zoe, more than life itself, more than the sea and this ship."

His crew murmured in awe at his last confession— he knew it would impress them with the extent of his feelings for her, and it kept her attention from the chaplain. Zoe looked up at him, conflicting emotions warring in her expressive eyes. He saw she needed a further push.

"Do you love me?" he asked again, hand still upon her lips as he held her gaze, all his love for her pouring out of him. To his immense relief, she nodded.

"Then tell me, Princess. Do you love me or don't you?" He gave the chaplain another kick for good measure, and the cleric sped to the finish, then waited quietly for Zoe's reply.

Oh, he had her now, Zoe thought, never completely oblivious of the happenings around her. She'd caught that surreptitious kick Winn had given the chaplain. If the man was so hell-bent on marrying her, who was she to gainsay him? After all, she longed for a happy ending.

The clouds had slowly thinned in the sky, and a

bright arc of sunlight illuminated the deck where they stood. Taking it as a heavenly sign, Zoe plunged into a precarious future with the man she loved with all her heart.

"I do," she said, watching Winn's anxiety sweep from his face as he crowed his triumphant delight to the top of the mizzenmast.

Raven hopped from Zoe's shoulder to McCairn's with a protesting squawk when Winn pulled her into his arms. Her glimpse of the doctor showed him to be highly uncomfortable, especially when the crow swiped several of his hairs. Zoe laughed at McCairn and at the men, who had already broken out the extra barrels of rum. She knew there'd be a drink for all in celebration, but never enough to endanger the running of the ship.

Married or not, Winn was a nineteenth-century captain bound to men and country, to duty and ship. She'd have to share him with all and sundry, but she'd do what she had to while enjoying the haven of his arms and his love.

And she'd worry about the future tomorrow.

"Enough of that," Zoe mumbled from beneath Winn. If he swirled his tongue around her ear or slid it down her neck once more, she'd lose control and they'd be at it again.

Not that she minded being at it.

Winn was an excellent lover, making Jon pale in comparison, and she'd been quite happy with Jon's abilities. But Winn drove her wild with needs and desires she had never thought she possessed, ones that would take a lifetime to explore and even longer to satisfy. Which was the crux of the problem—she couldn't be sure of a lifetime with Winn, and the thought of that crushed her.

She shoved the persistent man from her tingling neck before the vampire in him sucked out her soul. Their situation was precarious enough without falling completely under his sensual spell.

"Winn, we have to talk." She rolled to her side as he insinuated himself closer.

"You definitely talk too much, Princess," he murmured, his low voice a seductive rumble. "And we have much better things to do."

Winn pressed his point by rubbing up against her. Oh, the man definitely had his talents.

"Later, Captain, if you're good." She tried to be stern, but knew she had failed when merry dimples creased his cheeks.

"I thought I *was* good," he whispered smugly, tongue trailing down her neck in the direction of more sensitive parts.

She knew this wouldn't work. She needed the man's attention for the few minutes she could wrest it from his highly active libido. The insatiable devil seemed to want to draw nine years of missed loving out of this one night.

"I'll count myself lucky if I don't walk bowlegged tomorrow," she said.

Winn threw his head back upon the pillows and roared with laughter. Wiping a tear from his eye, he turned to her, brow arched. "That good, eh?"

She wanted to hit him with a pillow but refrained.

"Ah, Princess, I do love you, you know. You bring a freshness to my life that had been sorely missing." An impish twinkle gleamed in his eye. "And I do have a fondness for bowlegged women."

No. She would not hit him in the head—it was too thick and swollen with his male ego to feel a thing—but other equally thick and swollen parts were highly sensitive and had gone so long without a woman's skillful caress.

Zoe surreptitiously slipped her hand under the covers, keeping her gaze on Winn as she sought a more persuasive attention getter. His sudden gasp brought a smile of satisfaction to her face, and nourished her ego as well.

"Ah, Princess . . . "

Winn's voice trailed off to a strangled moan as one of her hands encircled his manly parts. She didn't continue the motion, however, just waited while his point got hers.

Winn wiggled against her palm, but she remained still. She most certainly had him where she wanted him, and she wasn't about to let go.

"I mentioned a talk," she said.

"So you did, Princess." Winn gulped in a fresh breath of air and eyed her painfully when her fingers stilled. "You were saying?"

She enjoyed commanding attention. "It's about us."

"I'm your husband. You're my wife. Enough said." He started rocking his body toward her, and she tightened her hold upon his formidable parts but refused to give him any pleasure. Winn groaned. "I take it that it is *not* enough said."

"How perceptive of you, husband."

"Ah, Zoe, I do so like to hear that word upon your tongue."

At that, the incorrigible man dipped his head quick as a snake and had his own clever tongue darting into her mouth with a thoroughly expert skill that had her wondering if he possessed a forked one.

Oh, to be so lucky.

Zoe gave in to the simmering burn of his intimate touch, until she hit the point of being frazzled. To go beyond that would mean total bewilderment, and she'd never get a chance to have her say. Breaking the connection between them when Winn came up for air, Zoe chose another method to gain his undivided attention.

Torture.

Sweet, sweet, torture.

She stroked a smooth fingernail down his shaft, pressing just enough to incite his desire. As she drew her hand slowly up and down, Winn's eye glazed with rapture. Pleased with the effect, she continued to wield a masterful touch, rubbing him, fondling him, teasing his manhood, till he ached with a need that hung heavily in the now heated space between them.

Then she stopped.

Coldly. Cruelly. Swiftly.

Effectively.

And he looked at her through his dark eye with a new gleam of respect. Sighing, he gave in, waiting impatiently for her to continue. She continued all right, but to his regret it was with words rather than hands.

Zoe arched a brow. "I see that I have to make this short and sweet, or we could continue like this for hours."

Winn flopped back against the pillow in defeat.

"You wouldn't," he groaned.

"I would."

"Then be done with it, witch, else you'll drive me insane."

"Insane?"

"Aye, with lust."

Zoe chuckled, but Winn did not seem amused. Taking pity on the man, she released him and chose her words quickly.

"I am from the future, Winn. I fell through some sort of time tunnel at Ravenscourt in 1995 and found myself crashing to the deck of your ship in 1814. I am not a witch or devil's advocate, nor am I the highly skilled inventor you supposed. Those mechanical items you found in my bag are regular fare for the average twentieth-century person."

She paused, trying to gauge his response, but he had flung a hand over his eye and his face rested in shadow. Not knowing what else to do, she plugged on.

"I don't know how this happened, or why, but I do know that I have to get back—"

"No." His quiet voice commanded more attention than a shout.

"Yes."

"No." He swept his arm from his face and caught her by the back of the neck, pulling her closer. "You are mine now, and you stay with me."

"I can't." She couldn't bear the pain that etched his face.

"You can, and you will. I command it," he said through lips gone white from tension.

"Winn, please," she begged. "I'm trying to explain, but you won't give me a chance."

"I don't want explanations, Zoe." His voice turned rough and raw as he answered. "I only want you."

Zoe leaned her head against his muscled chest, thinking how good, how right, it felt there—what she wouldn't do to be able to stay—but the children beckoned like faded ghosts in her mind.

Zoe smoothed a hand over the tight silver-and-onyx curls of Winn's tanned chest, glad of the moments they had together and the love they shared. She respected him and couldn't mislead him. She owed him the truth, no matter how painful.

"Listen to me, Winn. This is important. Besides not knowing if a sudden wind will whisk me off into another dimension, I have two young children to return to. They are all alone now—orphans for all intents and purposes, until the day I return."

She bent her head to look at his face, loving the strong, firm line of his jaw, the sculpted angles of his profile, the strength of character the man exuded without saying so much as a word. A muscle ticked at his jaw, and the planes of his face hardened into a tight mask in the ensuing silence. Zoe waited for a reply, but there wasn't any.

"I love them, Winn," she whispered, and her voice cracked. "They're my babies."

A single tear ran down her face to splash silently on his chest. It moved him as her words hadn't, like a band tightening across his chest. He turned to her, cradled her face in his huge, rough palms, and let out a deep sigh.

"I'm listening, Zoe," he said, and waited stoically for her words.

"I know you're listening . . . but do you believe me?" she asked, searching his face for the truth.

A raw ache such as she had never heard colored his words. "I believe you."

He pressed his head to hers and ruffled her hair with his hands. She was amazed at his immediate acceptance. She had thought to hear doubt, question, denial . . . and was prepared to convince him if she had to. All she saw was understanding on his face while his body exuded an aura of regret.

"It's why I tried to leave you behind, and the reason why I married you," he went on.

She didn't get it. "Because I'm from the future?" she asked.

He shook his head.

"Because you coveted my tape player?" she teased.

"Your what?"

"My music box."

"In truth it is a wonderful device, but not enough reason, you daft woman, to shackle myself to someone in holy matrimony." He brushed a kiss along her forehead. She could feel the smile on his lips.

"Shackle? I don't think I like the sound of that, Winn."

"Aye, shackle," he said, "but willingly done."

Winn pushed back until he could look at her fully. What she saw in that look had her heart beating double time with sweet expectation.

"I married you, Princess, because I love you."

"And you left me behind because you love me?" she asked, totally perplexed.

"I did." He watched as her brow furrowed, then ran a soothing hand over her now aching forehead.

Talking to the man was easy enough, but to get him to respond was like pulling teeth, or playing twenty questions. It seemed all too common a male response, reinforcing her theory that the male of the species hadn't progressed much over the centuries, their communication skills being but a hair beyond a caveman's grunt.

"Can you say that in English?" she asked.

He winked. "Aye, and I can say it in French."

"English will do, thank you. Or better yet, American."

"You are a patriot, minx, as am I. By the way, I really admire your Yankee jacket, it's just the thing to stir up our British enemies."

"Thank you again. You were saying?"

"I believe you, dear, for many reasons. For one, you are the most honest creature I've ever met. There isn't an emotion you have that doesn't flit across your face long before you utter your brutally honest words." Zoe frowned at "brutally," but Winn pressed a tender kiss to her lips. "I wouldn't have you any other way. Uh-uh," he said as she started to speak. "No more thank-yous are allowed. I only speak the truth."

"But surely that's not the only reason you believe me," she protested.

"No, it isn't."

"I didn't think so. Most people would find this all hard to believe, and rightly so," she admitted. "It's difficult enough for me to believe, and I'm the one who experienced it. At times I still feel like I'm dreaming."

"I know," he said. "I can see it on your face—that faraway look of loneliness and longing—and I can see it by the sad, defeated slump to your shoulders."

"Then why, Winn?"

"Why do I believe you are from the future?" She nodded. "As you might have noticed, Princess, I am a creature of logic. Although you are one of the brightest people I've met and could easily create such objects of wonder, the mechanical devices in your bag didn't intrigue you the way they would a man, er, a woman of science."

Zoe was impressed—he had thought this out thoroughly. Evidently he was a man of logic, as he claimed, and not pure male braggadocio.

"And I recall you cursing a time or two at the musical device, unable to work the thing correctly," he continued. "Certainly you could have come from some clan or colony of other scientists, yet you never mentioned that, and you seemed as dismayed by your appearance upon my deck as I had been."

"No," he went on. "Those facts alone served to heighten my curiosity, but not to satisfy it. Not until I truly studied one of those wonderful romance books did I learn the reality of your situation."

She had no idea how. "What do you mean?"

"I mean, dear Zoe, that when I was studying the fineness of the paper used in your books, I noticed a date printed on one of the first pages. . . ."

So that was how he knew. She could imagine him fondling the pages of one of the books, only to be shocked senseless by a date close to two hundred years in his future—in her future now, also. Remembering Jon's obsessive devotion to details, she chalked up another personality trait to genetics.

"And what did you think?" she asked.

"What could I think? I was incredulous, shaken, and on the scent of the unknown. Research is often akin to a quest, and something I love. I was excited beyond belief, and immediately tore through your bag and studied the other books. All were printed the same year—1995. The rest, my dear, was purely logic."

"More logic?" He had to be kidding. If the circumstances were reversed, she would have thought she was hallucinating. The utter confidence of the man always amazed her.

"Yes," he said. "You see, all the facts added together pointed to one incredible but wonderfully logical conclusion—that you, Princess, had somehow stumbled through time. Imagine my good fortune that out of the endless places you could have traveled to, you bounced against my deck!"

"Destiny?" she asked, fascinated by his train of thought.

"Exactly."

Zoe nodded. In an odd way it made sense. Winn's logic did seem pretty flawless, but she wasn't finished discussing it yet.

"I have my own theory as to how I landed on your ship."

"Tell me, then." He shifted upon the bed, studying her intensely.

"I went to see Jonathan, my ex-husband, for a final time before returning to the States—that's America, by the way. Because of the failing family business, and thinking it would save our already doomed marriage, Jonathan had become obsessed with finding his ancestor's buried treasure." She smiled a wicked smile. "I was cursing his bastard ancestor as I fell through the time tunnel."

"Was he someone well-known?" he asked.

She nodded.

"Someone famous?"

"Yes."

This was becoming amusing.

"Anyone I know?"

Hell, she thought, it was downright funny. However, she didn't laugh.

"Then who, woman? I'm burning with curiosity." He awaited expectantly, as any gossip-monger would.

"Jonathan Winnthrop Alexander Dunham, ninth earl of Ravenscourt, alias Black Jack Alexander, captain, privateer, pirate, and thief."

"Bloody hell."

"Isn't it? I get rid of one Alexander and wind up with another."

"You're mistaken, Princess. The family name is Dunham." He narrowed his eye dramatically and frowned. "And I may be a pirate, if you wish, but I am not a bloody thief."

"Oh, no," she whispered, her extremely capable hands dipping below the covers. They finally rewarded the eager fellow that throbbed against her thigh. "That's where you're wrong."

"I am?" he asked, voice raised an octave higher and cracking on the last note as she continued to stroke him.

"Aye, you are," she murmured, using his words. "For you stole my heart long ago."

"Zoe?"

"Yes?"

"You definitely talk too much." His voice whispered to her in shades of midnight as his own hands slid beneath the covers to prove their worth.

"Winn?"

"Yes?"

"I have to return. That's why I stowed aboard the ship."

Winn pulled her closer and held her tight. She could feel a tremor in his arms.

"I know, Princess." He kissed her forehead. "I knew it the moment you mentioned your children."

"Then you'll help me? Take me back to Ravenscourt?" She could feel him nod. "I have to try, Winn.

I have to try. But, God, how can I leave you when I've just found you? I don't think I can bear the pain."

Winn stroked her arm and drew a deep breath. "You don't have to, Zoe."

"But that's exactly what I've been telling you—I have to return." Her voice tightened around a sob.

"Of course you must. Your children need you." He tilted her head up and gave her a kiss that promised forever. "But you don't have to return alone."

"What do you mean?" Zoe could barely breathe as hope surged in her breast.

"When you go, Princess, I go with you. And if we can't leave by the same methods that brought you here, we'll never stop searching for another way. That I promise. I'll never willingly let you go."

"Did I ever tell you that I love you?" she asked, and he rumbled with sweet laughter.

"A hundred times, Princess, and it's never enough."

"This time, let me show you instead."

Zoe settled over his thighs, straddling his body. Winn sucked in a sharp breath—she could feel his heart tattoo clear to his stomach and watched the blood beat furiously in his engorged shaft. Then she took command of the situation, placing herself over him and welcoming him into her heat.

She sighed, content with her situation at the present, and whispered once more to Winn. "I'll have you know that I'm finished talking."

He uttered one word:

"Amen."

11

"Let me get this straight."

Winn sat on the deck splicing frayed rope and reweaving it into a sturdier line. He concentrated on the recent revelations Zoe and he had discussed concerning her leap through time, but some aspects of it continued to shock him.

"What?" she asked.

"You were married to my great-great—however many greats—grandson?"

She nodded.

The thought of it left a bitter taste in his mouth. It somehow made him feel, well, disgusting. He noticed Zoe's grimace as she eyed him.

"Don't look at me like that, Winn. We are not in some sort of incestuous relationship. Jonathan is a good guy, but not the one for me."

"You married him," he accused. "And I would warrant it wasn't forced upon you on the deck of a ship."

Zoe raised a brow. "Do you really think you pushed me into that? I saw you kicking the good chaplain's shin. I married you because I wanted to." She paused. "As for Jon, that marriage was the biggest mistake of my life."

"But you stayed with him for so many years."

Zoe nodded sadly, a frown upon her quivering lips. "Yes, I did. I stuck with him through the destruction of his business and his descent into his obsession, or whatever you'd like to call his ridiculously persistent interest that revolved around you and your buried treasure. I tried to keep the family together because of the children."

Winn looked up from the ropes to gaze at Zoe. Sunlight caught the sparkle of sea mist in her silver-gilt hair, bringing a tight feel to his throat. Beneath the gently swaying masts and flapping of the rigging, the deck felt sultry, hot, and damp from the sea and the sun. Although the men worked all around them, they were given a wide berth of privacy—it felt as if they were on an island of their own.

He wondered how she was doing with her chore. She sat close by, tapping her foot in obvious frustration as the rope she was trying to splice began to fray. Each attempt made her temper worse, till she muttered a number of salty curses beneath her breath.

"Here," Winn said, motioning her closer, "you need a sharper edge on that."

He pulled the rope from her hand, laid it on the spar beside him, and placed his rigger's knife across its width. With a swift blow of his marlinespike to the head of the knife, he cut the cordage neatly in half. Then he greased the strands with a bit of tallow and showed her a trick or two about weaving in the new line.

Zoe went to work diligently. He could tell she enjoyed being busy and was not one to idle below decks. Such energy as hers could not be contained in their small cabin for long. Unless, he thought, it was contained to the bunk.

He smiled wryly, enjoying Zoe's intense concentration on the ropes. She had dexterous hands, as well he knew, and made easy headway with the task—one it would take others a long time to master. But ever since they had discussed her precarious presence in his century, he'd noticed she embraced life with an even greater zest, as if she knew her days were numbered and time was something to be conquered.

Winn sighed, not liking the turn of his ruminations at all. He gazed back at Zoe and was surprised to find her sniffing at the ropes. He had to admit, he'd never seen anyone do that before.

"Uh, Zoe?"

"Yes, Winn?" she asked in a distracted manner, her full attention on the smell of the rope.

"What precisely are you doing, Princess?"

"Hmm?" She finally turned to him, perplexity written upon her face.

"Why are you sniffing at that rope?" he asked as patiently as he could.

"Oh, the rope." She smiled. "It smelled familiar."

"Familiar? Have you a penchant for sniffing ropes?"

"Only when they smell like dope."

"You're losing me, Princess." He rested his arms upon his upraised knees and waited for what he knew would be a most interesting reply—Zoe's explanations usually were. It was one of her qualities he found endearing. However, she answered with a question instead.

"What is this rope made of?"

"Hemp."

"Hemp. I was right," she said, inspecting the rope with assessing eyes before sniffing it again. "It is dope." She went on when he looked at her blankly. "Marijuana, Mary Jane . . . cannabis," she explained.

"Ah, yes. I do seem to recall the scientific name as being *Cannabis sativa*—quite an exceptional plant."

"You can say that," she mumbled, eyeing the rope as if it were a snake. She didn't seem to know what to do with it.

"Actually," Winn pointed out, "there is no equal to it for sturdy rope and rigging. It can carry tremendous weight and doesn't swell when wet." He decided he quite enjoyed teaching her about the ship.

Zoe glanced around surreptitiously, noting the men at their duties. Seemingly satisfied by their privacy, she leaned over to him and whispered, "Do you ever catch any of your men smoking it?"

"Smoking it?" he repeated, looking askance. "Do you think my men depraved?"

"Absolutely not. But they do it in my time."

"They smoke rope?" The idea was incredible.

"No, silly, they smoke dope." She smiled at him as if what she said were the height of logic.

"Take pity on me, Princess," he pleaded. "My mind seems to have stopped functioning. I keep having these bizarre mental images of my crew puffing on pieces of lit rigging."

Zoe laughed until she grew short of breath. "Oh, Winn," she said, "you are a card."

He wasn't about to ask her what a card was.

She pointed to the heavy rope in her hand and tried

another explanation. He hoped he would understand it this time, or else she'd tie his brain in knots.

"This is made from hemp. Hemp comes from the cannabis plant. And the leaves from the cannabis plant are used unlawfully in my century as a kind of drug—something like liquor," she added.

Or opium, he thought. She was beginning to make some sense.

"Go on," he said, interested in this newfound knowledge. "Tell me, how do they smoke it?"

"They crumble the leaves of the plant and roll it into paper to make cigarettes, or sometimes they place it in a pipe. It's supposed to make you mellow, but all smoking is bad for your health."

"I'll agree with you there, Princess, at least aboard ship. My men do not smoke, er, dope or anything else—I forbid it, although that is not common practice. Saw a ship go down once from a carelessly tamped pipe. Nearly half her crew was lost. Since then, my men do not smoke." He caught her interested gaze and finished in all seriousness, "Fire aboard ship is too dangerous a venture."

If he had expected any reaction, he would have thought it a sober one. Zoe, however, began to giggle, and he looked at her curiously. She placed a hand upon his and patted it, merriment in her gaze.

"It must be bizarre to have a fire aboard ship," she said, practically gagging on the words.

"I assure you, Princess, it is no laughing matter."

"I'm sorry, Winn," she managed before giving a most unladylike snort, "but I wasn't thinking about the consequences of a fire, I was thinking about your men sniffing the fumes of the burning rope."

She broke into peals of musical laughter and

needed to wipe tears from her eyes. Winn shook his head. The woman had the most quirky ideas on what constituted humor.

"Just think, Winn. With the price this stuff commands in my century, your buried treasure could consist of a box filled with ropes. When Jon finds it, he could make a fortune—illegally, of course, but a fortune nonetheless."

"Zoe, I don't have any buried treasure."

Her smile radiated warmth like sunshine as her laughter subsided. "I suspected as much. Jonathan would have found it long ago if you had. He's a very diligent man." She paused and studied how Winn spliced the rope he was working on. He caught the fleeting impishness that suffused her grin. "I think it runs in the family," she said.

He bit his tongue, so intent was he on his own ruminations when she alluded to that damnable Jonathan again. Winn cursed to himself as he dropped the knife on the deck, barely missing his toe. Damn, but this turn of events had disturbed him more than he would have thought. His emotions were definitely gaining the upper hand over his preferred logic.

"What is it, Winn?" Zoe asked, ever sensitive to his changing moods.

He remained silent, not knowing how to broach the annoying subject, unused to the jealousy it provoked. He noticed Zoe waiting expectantly and charged headlong into his embarrassing, but necessary, questions.

"When you first, shall we say, arrived aboard my ship," he paused, screwing up his courage to go on, "you repeatedly called me Jonathan."

"Yes. You look very much alike." She smiled fondly, but it was not the answer he had hoped for.

"How alike?" he asked.

"You could be twins—"

Winn groaned, cutting off her answer. Damn, but it was worse than he'd thought. Far worse. He didn't want to be like anyone. He wanted to be himself, and to bloody hell with this Jonathan fellow.

It was bad enough the man had been Zoe's husband and lover, the father of her children. . . . He couldn't give her children as Jonathan had, couldn't create the miracle that God had provided most men. He evidently couldn't give her a unique face to love, either.

It proved unnerving.

Winn caught her staring at him from the corner of his eye. She seemed amused, not at all disturbed as he was. Well, it might be amusing for her to compare great-grandfather—oh, Lord, it was more than great-grandfather—and some half-wit grandson. He, however, did not find the situation at all amusing.

No one enjoyed being compared to another, especially if the person you were being compared to could be your twin. Everyone wanted to feel unique, special—loved on your own, he thought, and not because you resembled another.

"Winn?"

He ignored her.

"Winn?"

Lord, she was persistent. Princess Persistent, he remembered, and smiled. Then he quickly wiped the smile off his face. He didn't want to be in a good mood, dammit, when there were serious things to think about.

"Winn!" Zoe shouted, garnering his complete

attention. It didn't pay to piss her off, or so she had once told him.

Well, at least she didn't call him Jon anymore.

"Yes?" he said. He knew he sounded surly but couldn't help it.

"You are nothing like him."

Wait a minute—he was missing a thing or two.

"I thought you said we could be twins?"

"I did. At least at first glance, if someone doesn't know you."

Winn fed off of Zoe's sunny smile as though it were a keg of water and rum and he were lost at sea. She had a knack for infecting him with her generous moods.

"How are we alike?" he prodded, needing to know before it killed him.

Zoe appeared thoughtful, as if comparing him to Jonathan. When she spoke her tone remained serious, but he detected a gleam of deviltry twinkling in the depths of her eyes.

"You are both tall," she said matter-of-factly.

"Wonderful. I suppose I now resemble half of my men."

"You have dark black hair."

"That narrows my resemblance with the crew down to one hundred or so." He scowled at this, never having realized how much more similar men were than they were different. Another disturbing thought. "Go on," he growled.

"That's it."

"That's it?"

She nodded.

"We look like twins and that's it—tall and dark hair?" The woman was mad. Perhaps she'd taken too much sun. Her cheeks did look quite rosy. Maybe he was using the wrong tack to get his answers.

"How are we different?"

"Different?" she asked, as if she'd never thought about it, which unnerved him further.

"Yes," he snapped. "How in hell are we different?"

"Oh, different. . . . Well, now that you mention it—"

"Zoe, I ought to take you over my knee."

"—there are a few minor differences."

He did not like the word *minor*. After cutting his finger with the knife, Winn threw the rope to the deck. He'd never made such a wreck of the chore before; in fact, he usually found mending the ropes to be a soothing pastime.

"You were saying, Princess?" He tried to remain calm, truly he did, but a touch of annoyance laced his tone. To his surprise, Zoe didn't seem disturbed by it a whit—some formidable man he turned out to be.

Zoe's descriptions broke into his thoughts, and he listened with bated and jealous breath.

"Jon is tall, but you are very tall."

Oh, Lord, give me patience, he thought. She's at it again.

She narrowed her exquisite stormy eyes as if inspecting him. He bared his teeth much as she had at their marriage ceremony, and Zoe clapped a hand over her mouth to stifle a chuckle. He sniffed, and she went on.

"Jonathan is a lean man, but you are muscular, and quite large."

Ah, her descriptions were rapidly improving.

"Now that I think of it, the hair is all wrong. Jonathan's hair is solid black . . . "

While mine is becoming gray, he finished silently.

". . . while yours is darkest onyx and silver."

Onyx and silver? Now that she mentioned it . . .

"Jon's skin is always pale, but yours is burnished to windswept mahogany."

He always had liked mahogany—a beautiful wood full of life. He supposed her descriptions were acceptable, after all.

"Your hands are rough—"

Uh-oh.

"—and speak of your love of the sea, the sun, and hard work. Jonathan's are sickly smooth in comparison."

Winn relaxed against the rail, leaning his head back to study her. By God, she was beautiful, and she belonged to him and no one else—save for maybe Adam and her children, he thought, feeling magnanimous. His mood swiftly changed for the better.

He closed his eyes, soaking up the sun and the warm tones of Zoe's voice. At first he had dreaded comparisons, but now it appeared to be a stimulating conversation.

"Your neck is like a thick column of marble. Jonathan, alas, has a bit of a chicken neck—you know—with that thingamajig bobbing up and down his throat."

Thingamajig? He chuckled. Must be a twentieth-century description.

"And the lines of your face are sculpted into the most exquisite angles."

She was "on a roll" now, as she was wont to say. He found he liked it immensely. A smile curved his lips as he listened.

"You have nice, neat feet—Jon's are bony, and not very warm."

"Zoe. . . ," he warned. He did not like any mention

of intimacy with another man, however platonic. She nodded, smiling impishly, understanding him as no one else ever could.

"You have long, muscular legs, and the most exquisite thighs—I like the way they caress me when we make love." She sighed.

He did like her sighs—especially when she was thinking of him.

"Your chest is hard and broad, with well-defined muscles like carved stone. I like to glide my tongue over them—"

Winn moaned.

"—they feel so smooth. As smooth as the muscles of your washboard stomach and your sweet, taut, little male butt."

"Butt?" he asked. "As in the butt of a joke?"

"As in buttocks," she said sweetly, a dimple denting the side of her chin.

What was she talking about? "Are you calling me a whore, dear?" he asked.

"What?"

"Buttock is a vulgar term for whore, though whore seems vulgar enough on its own." He fixed her with what he hoped looked like an innocent stare.

"Do you know, Winn, that your English is positively antique?"

"I imagine it would be to someone from the future." He arched a brow, always relishing their passionate repartee. But when Zoe nonchalantly patted his posterior, his words turned to a groan.

"I'm referring to your delicious bottom, sir."

She began to stroke him, her hand roving from derriere to hip, before gliding suggestively over his thighs. Such exquisite torture he had never felt. Like a seductress she went on, stirring his senses into a lather—any more of her words and he'd foam at the mouth.

"But the nicest of all is your mighty shaft."

He prayed her hand wouldn't roam any farther.

On his next breath he begged God that it would.

"It could fell a tree with a single blow," Zoe continued, "or bring a woman to the heights of heaven." She turned her gaze from her stroking fingers to eye him hungrily, and he could feel the spittle forming in his mouth.

"Any woman?" he asked.

"Only one," she replied, pressing into the side of his body till he could feel the heat of her damp skin through her shirt, the thud of her heart next to his, and the soft, round fullness of her oh-so-wonderful breasts rubbing seductively against him.

In another minute he began to pant, unable to clear the image of her naked body from his thoughts. She had turned the tables on him neatly—his worries no longer upon Jonathan, but on how to take advantage of her mood.

"Zoe, I am a lucky man," he murmured, his tongue trailing over the delicate shell of her ear. "But I see our conversation has drifted from the differences between me and Jonathan—"

"Jonathan who?" she asked.

"—to a far more interesting subject."

"Mmmmm."

She stretched her neck to the side, granting better access for his tongue. With one swift move he swept her in his arms and stood upon the rolling deck.

"Whatever are you doing?" she murmured, her eyes grown glazed beneath languorous lids.

"Why, I'm going to explore this new subject," he

said, watching the growing heat in the yellow flecks of her narrowed eyes.

"Hardly a new subject."

"Hard, yes, and still new," he countered, "after nearly ten years of doing without."

Winn didn't waste any more time with words, but strode with a purposeful step to the gangway, cradling Zoe in his arms. As they descended into the coolness below, he could clearly hear the roaring cheers of his men.

"Remind me to tell you about modern toilets," Zoe said, hesitating outside the door that opened onto the quarter gallery off of Winn's stateroom.

"You could always use the head, Princess." Winn looked up from the charts he'd been studying and caught Zoe's grimace. "Do you know that your nose crinkles quite adorably when you're totally disgusted?"

"I love you, too, Winn." He noticed her sweetness had a bark to it. She held his gaze for a long moment, then continued in a more serious vein. "I've thought of one more way you and Jon are alike."

"And what might that be?" he growled, turning his attention back to his charts rather than let on that any comparisons between him and Jon galled him.

"You both have brown eyes." He did look up. "Though of course Jon's is merely an ordinary shade of brown while yours is dark as jet."

He smiled a sly smile and started to speak, thinking how surprised she'd be about the color of his eyes, but she ducked into the quarter gallery, nature—and Grizzard's sudden appearance in the stateroom—delaying his revelation.

"Sorry, sir. Thought you and the missus would still be abed. But I'm glad to see ya still have yer wits about ya, and have come up for air."

Winn glared at Grizzard, but the man didn't even notice—he just went rattling on as he was wont to do. Without so much as a by-your-leave, Grizzard tugged the maps from beneath Winn's gaze and rolled them up methodically. Then he secured them with string, placed them on a shelf, and swiped a polishing rag across the table.

"Surely you could have moved those papers to the other side of the table," Winn said as the pirate began setting the cleared space.

"Think not, Cap'n. This here's hopefully a once-in-a-lifetime occasion, and Cookie says to do the job right."

Winn smelled a rat. "What's Cookie got to do with you barging in here and removing my charts practically from my hands?"

"Orders, sir," Grizzard explained in the manner one would use with a noddy.

"Orders . . ."

Winn took a deep breath. Talking with Grizzard was an act of diplomacy entwined with a foray into insanity. He had to treat the man with kid gloves, else Grizzard would shut his mouth like a giant clam—but Winn found listening without making scathing comments enough to push a saint to sin.

"Yup." Grizzard did not elaborate.

"Whose orders, pray tell?"

I am a man of patience, Winn repeated silently five times while waiting for Grizzard's response.

"Why, Cookie's, of course," the pirate mumbled.

"Of course. Foolish of me to question the cook's

orders, when I am mere captain and owner of this ship. Isn't that right?"

Grizzard nodded emphatically, placing the silver upon the gleaming table with the delicacy of the finest butler. The man was an enigma.

"Don't want to upset the best cook this side of heaven," he said, "no siree."

Yes, Winn thought, that about summed up the hierarchy on his ship. Grizzard continued to speak in face of his silence.

"Ain't had me a bite of a weevil or a maggot these past three years now. Don't mind me the maggots much—though they be cold, at least they're juicy— but weevils, brrr, they be bitter."

Winn rolled his eyes, wondering if Zoe could hear the conversation. Considering the amount of time she was spending in what she had so quaintly called a hellhole, he imagined her ear was pressed to the door while Grizzard rambled on.

"Cookie told the duck-fucker to wring the neck of his fattest goose. Says he weren't about to be caught like an idiot with Sir Reverence upon his face, and whatnot."

He also wondered if Zoe had any clue as to what exactly Grizzard was saying. He prayed the crewman's language would seem to her to be something out of the annals of antiquity. He moaned when he thought of the explanations she would demand.

"What's that? Tired, Cap'n?" Grizzard asked, and Winn nodded, not even thinking about explaining. "Nothin' to worry about, hey. Any man's prick would droop after a full night's playin' with the mother of all saints."

"Oh, Lord," Winn muttered, and heard a giggle filter through the gallery door.

"Face makin' takes a might of fortitude, but I warrant ya think it better'n boxin' the Jesuit, sir." Grizzard flashed Winn his yellowed ivories as if relating the most humorous of jokes. "Heard a few yelps and yowls comin' from this-here way last night."

Winn heard a smothered gasp from Zoe and began to massage his temples. After all, he told himself, I am not only a patient man, I am also a man of logic. And it is not logical that I strangle the most loyal of my men.

"Yup, that glue pot what joined ya together is mighty pleased with 'imself, acting like it was his glib tongue what had the missus sayin' yeah."

Grizzard folded the fine cloth serviette into intricate designs resembling swans and fussed with their position on the table. Winn watched, awestruck to think his most hardened man, the most depraved berserker he had ever seen, the most singularly deadly man with any knife there existed, would know how to make swans out of table linens. He would have staked his life that the man didn't have the foggiest idea what a serviette was.

"So I says," Grizzard continued as he placed the etched crystal glasses at precisely the correct distance from the plates, "'twas most likely you what did the talkin' what convinced her, and most silent-like at that. Like one o' them types what has no voice and needs their hands to do the talkin, if ya get my meanin'. Cu-rat, I says, I place me confidence in the skills o' me cap'n."

Winn cleared his throat. "Thank you, Grizzard, I'm sure."

Actually he didn't know what to think. As far as he could tell, the pirate had given his prowess high regards and had shown the utmost confidence in his captain's abilities. He wondered what Zoe would think of Grizzard's speech.

Grizzard turned to Winn as if reading his thoughts and gave him a wink. "You can tell the lady she can come out o' the head now. I'll be leavin' to help Cookie with the repast."

Winn nodded, a bit dumbfounded with the turn of events, as Grizzard stood back to survey his handiwork. "Mr. Grizzard—"

"Sir?" the pirate asked, fussing with a final fold of a linen.

"Why are you here preparing the table?"

"Cap'n?" he asked distractedly, rearranging the knife and the spoon. For the first time that evening he seemed to be ignoring him, and Winn knew that something was up.

"Where is Adam?" he asked with the voice of command.

"Adam, sir?"

"Yes, Adam. You know—the little towheaded boy who usually sees to my table." He waited expectantly, and Grizzard, in a manner quite unlike his usual brazenness, shifted from foot to foot.

"Oh, aye. That Adam."

Winn waited, but no answer was supplied. "Is there another Adam aboard this ship?"

"Oh, aye, sir, several. There be Adam Green, a topman, and the sawbones's assistant, Adam Hamilton, and I believe there's a middy—"

"Enough," Winn nearly shouted, but caught himself from that rash act. For all his depravity, Grizzard took to heart what he had to say and often proved overly sensitive about it. "Enough with your prevaricating, man. Tell me what has become of the boy."

"Well, it be like this, sir. What with all the celebrating and all, the wee scalawag seems to have gotten himself in a right pickle."

"You may explain this pickle to me, Grizzard," he prodded when the seaman fell silent.

"Oh, right. Well, it seems he had a nip or two."

Grizzard looked down at the floor as if the design stenciled there held his greatest interest. Then again, Winn thought, from all he'd learned about Grizzard's interests and abilities that night, he wouldn't doubt the man could be a master artisan.

"A nip or two . . ." Winn let his voice trail, and Grizzard's expression turned sheepish.

"Well, maybe three or four, or maybe even—"

"Enough," Winn shouted, rubbing at the bridge of his nose, trying to ease his mounting headache. "You are telling me the boy is drunk?"

"Drunk!" Zoe's voice rang out in rage behind the bathroom door.

"Soused." Grizzard nodded his head sadly. "He's been sufferin' for it all day, sir. Be easy on the mite—he's had punishment enough."

With a flick of his wrist, Winn dismissed Grizzard. The old man left with a nod.

"You can come out now, Princess. And make sure you secure that window—last night I went in and nearly froze my, er, parts off."

Zoe popped her head around the door and, seeing that the room was empty save for him, stepped out.

"You really need plumbing, Winn, or at the very least air spray."

"Air spray?"

"Think of it as perfume you spray in the air to ward off bad scents." She smiled and slammed the quarter room door shut.

"How much did you hear?" he asked, hoping for a reprieve but anticipating the worst—and the worst was swiftly presented to him.

"All of it."

Winn groaned and slid onto his chair, awaiting the tirade. He'd seen a volcano once in the South Seas and thought Zoe's temper often worked on the same dynamics—slow to burn, but then explosive.

"I can't believe they let that little boy get drunk," she said, plopping onto the chair opposite him.

Winn fingered his napkin and held her gaze. "Believe it."

"You won't punish anyone, will you?" she asked. He could see worry cloud her eyes.

"No"—he sighed—"though I'd like to bash someone around a bit or two. The men, well, they've had short childhoods and rough lives, most of them. They see nothing wrong in a boy taking his first taste of liquor. And I daresay Grizzard is right that young Adam has seen punishment enough from his overindulgence."

Her eyes softened, and the worry left her. She looked upon him now with amusement.

"So, you're already making a legend for yourself with your sexual prowess, and from your lady's moans," she teased. "I think we should give the crew something further to wonder about." She left her chair to lock the door, then settled comfortably on his lap, chuckling when his manhood saluted her smartly.

"I'm willing to comply if you are, Princess," he said, slipping his hand beneath the buttons of her blouse and gliding his tongue across her neck.

"Now that I have your attention"—she wiggled her bottom against his hardened shaft—"there are a few questions that need answering."

"I knew your compliance was too much to expect," he groaned, head leaning against the high, carved back of his chair. "What are your questions, as if I didn't know?"

"I believe there are only four," she answered sweetly, and he nodded.

"I remember the answers to at least three."

"Go ahead."

"The Duck-fucker is the name used for the chap who tends all the fowl, and Sir Reverence is a reference to dung." She nodded. "A prick—"

"I'm familiar with that one." Her face dimpled into the most wicked of smiles.

"Then you know about the mother of all saints—" It was too much to hope for. She shook her head. "I thought not. Let's say that it is the female equivalent of a man's—"

"Got it."

"Good. We can resume where we left off." His tongue trailed back up her neck.

"Uh-uh," she whispered, a shiver echoing through her to him. "I've one more question left." He continued his ministrations. "Why would you want to box a Jesuit? Chaplain Amonte seemed to be a very nice man."

Winn roared with laughter, jostling Zoe to an upright position.

"What?" she asked.

"Chaplain Amonte is not a Jesuit—wrong religion."

"But—"

"Boxing a Jesuit is a, er . . ." He trailed off. How

could he put this in a delicate way? "Well, it's something a man does to relieve himself when he hasn't been with a woman in a long time." There, he thought, pleased, well said.

Zoe looked at him as if perplexed, but when her hand started fondling his now extremely swollen member, Winn had his doubts.

"You mean when they do something like this?" She dipped her hands beneath the loosened waist of his pants. The minx had clever fingers indeed.

"Precisely like this," he said, sinking lower on the chair.

"Poor Jesuit," she murmured. "Since you already know what happens when you box him, let's see how he responds to a kiss."

Winn slipped beneath the table with Zoe and managed a shaky whisper. "I'm sure this is sacrilege, Princess."

"I'm sure it is. But in my time and by my religion, this isn't even a sin."

"As I've said, I'm a man of logic, a far-thinking man."

"Then you'll have to tell me what you think."

She eased down his pants and a cool draft of air *whoosh*ed over him. Winn sucked in his breath as wet fire scorched up his hardened shaft. His voice came out a rusty squeak.

"You can tell me later," Zoe whispered.

And with a nod, he readily agreed.

"Winn?" Zoe looked up from the card game she was losing to Adam and took in Winn's fine figure at the wheel.

"What is it, Princess?"

"Dessert last night was delicious." She saw a slight smile curve to his lips as he answered.

"I'll be sure to give Cookie your compliments."

"I wasn't talking about the food," she drawled in her best Miss Scarlett manner. Winn turned to her slowly, his satisfied grin sprouting across his lower jaw.

"I didn't think you were," he murmured, voice so low it drew shivers up her spine instead of down. The man had neatly turned the tables on her yet again.

Adam looked up and tugged on her sleeve. "Your turn, Princess."

Zoe shifted her attention back to the boy but could feel Winn's gaze burning through her damp blouse. The sun was fierce, but luckily she'd packed a full tube of suntan lotion in her bag. She used it again on herself and Adam. She knew Winn should use some, too, but she and Adam tended to burn, and she had no idea how long their adventure would last.

Throwing the tube back in her jumbled bag, she resumed the game with Adam. The little scamp had won the last of her gum and now tried to tackle the mound of jellied candy Winn had given her as replenished booty. It wouldn't be long before he'd win it as well.

All about them the men scrambled at their work. Sails were mended and aired to prevent mildew, ropes spliced and tarred, and the decks properly scrubbed. She had never realized the amount of backbreaking work it took to keep a ship safely before the wind and sea. The elements tried their best to worm their way in and wreak havoc, but the constant attention of the crew held the worst damage at bay.

Her nausea had subsided a bit—she experienced it only after sleeping—and Winn's had died down as well. He said he felt worse right after leaving port, something not at all uncommon. Yet there were times his complexion would look absolutely green, and she was sure he hid his malady from the crew.

A sudden cry let loose from high in the rigging, drawing the attention of all the men. Zoe looked to Winn, who stood at the wheel, calling Adam for his glass. He put it to his eye and focused, then handed it to the little boy.

"Right on schedule," he said, bending down close to Adam to help him with the heavy telescope. "See her, son? Off larboard bows, a dot on the horizon."

Adam nodded, and Winn clapped his back.

"You knew she was comin', sir?" the boy asked.

Winn nodded. "Aye, I knew she was comin'. This time she's sooner rather than later." He turned to Leetch, who had sidled up to the wheel. "The *Raven*'s all yours, Mr. Leetch. Keep the course straight and we'll not have our guests worried."

"Aye, Cap'n." Leetch fondled the wheel, a rapturous smile upon his face.

Winn shook his head and sat beside a puzzled Zoe. "Corsairs, Princess," he explained.

"Will there be trouble?"

"Nay . . ." He looked out over the rail at the rapidly approaching ship, then turned back to her. "At least I don't think so. I'm here on a diplomatic mission that involves money, and a personal one that involves rescuing the regent's goddaughter, Catherine. The dey is also a man of logic . . . at least when payment is involved."

"How long will it take? A week? Two?" she asked, and saw a veil drop over his eyes.

"A month or two will be more like it. I have no way to tell, Zoe."

He took her hand up in his, the hard calluses of his palm oddly soothing across her tender skin. A month or two was a very long time if you had two children waiting for you. But it was no time at all if it meant leaving, perhaps forever, the man you loved more than life itself.

She could tell Winn's thoughts echoed her own but didn't want to voice her opinion. She had to believe in the fates that had brought her here, had to cling to the hope that there would be an ending to this fantasy that she could live with.

They sat there a while, soaking up the sun's warmth, playing another losing round with Adam. The activity on the upper decks seemed hushed, as if all waited with bated breath, feeling the turn of the tide around them. A shiver ran through Zoe, and she rubbed her arms. Winn gave her a quick peck on the cheek and returned to his lieutenant's side.

Adam brought him his glass when beckoned, and Winn surveyed the approaching ship. "Damn," he spat out, the word's sharp tone making it into the worst of epithets. "Adam, go get Dr. McCairn and Grizzard, and hightail it, boy. Mr. Leetch, stand fast no matter what."

"Aye, sir." White-knuckled, the young man gripped the wheel, but in his brown eyes Zoe could see the golden gleam of excitement. Another shiver ran down her back, this feeling more prophetic than the last.

"What is it, Winn?" she asked, standing beside him while her heart thudded.

He pulled her close and put his arm around her. "If all goes well, nothing."

"And if all goes wrong?" she whispered.

He drew her before him and met her anxious gaze. "Then we're in for a battle royal."

She felt her throat constrict, all moisture evaporating in the wind. Sawdust seemed to fill her mouth, and for the life of her she couldn't utter a word.

Winn's arm was still about her as McCairn hit the deck at a run. She never would have guessed the man could move so fast, but then grizzly bears were well noted for their impressive speed.

"Winn . . ." the doctor said with a nod, as he took up the glass his captain handed him. "'Tis the Devil himself." He cursed roundly beneath his breath.

"I take it we are not talking about the mother of all saints," she murmured, winning a shocked look from the Bear. "I didn't think so."

"Dammit," Winn said, pushing her into McCairn's arms as he began to pace the deck. "Where is that beetle-headed man?"

"Looking for me, sir?" Grizzard said on cue. The Bear thrust the spy glass into the pirate's hands. "Holy Mother of God."

"At least he didn't mention Sir Reverence," Zoe muttered, and managed to shock both the Bear and Grizzard. "You'd best shut your mouths before the flies land in them." Both men clamped their jaws shut.

"I spy a cloven foot in the business at hand," Winn said.

"What is he talking about?" Zoe whispered to the two men who now flanked her.

Grizzard turned to her, a nasty scowl upon his face. She knew it wasn't meant for her. "If what we see ain't no mirage, missus, then that-there ship belongs to the dey's head fart catcher."

"What?" she asked, thinking Grizzard's colorful descriptions highly creative.

"Follows the poxy pig of an old man day and night. Only yeah-says him, looking for a pet."

"It's the dey's high admiral," McCairn spat as if he had a foul taste in his mouth.

"You know this man?" She turned to the doctor.

McCairn nodded. "But I won't say I've had the pleasure. The only pleasure I'd get is to snap his scrawny neck."

Winn continued to give orders to the men, preparing them for the worst but telling them to hope for the best. With pride, Zoe watched him take command, knowing his worth to be soul deep.

A few of the younger men threw sand upon the deck as they had on the day she'd been injured. Zoe turned to McCairn and asked what it was for. The big man's matter-of-fact manner turned her bones to ice.

"To keep your footing when things get bloody."

12

The Algerian ship approached, a garish parody of the *Raven.*

Where Winn's hull was long and sleek, the approaching brig—as McCairn had called it—had a round, tublike quality about it. The classic lines and black and white paint of the *Raven* outshone the vibrant colors of the corsair's ship. With a white stripe through her yellow hull, and her bow painted an apple green, the brig looked to Zoe like some sickly flower adrift at sea.

Flowers were indeed painted along her stern, with the figure of what appeared to be a rather naked woman under her bowsprit serving as figurehead. The muzzles of her cannons were washed a vibrant red, and she flew a crimson flag of cutlass and stars.

If ships were female, as the men all agreed, then the *Raven* was a lady, while the corsair was a tramp. Along the starboard side Zoe could see a name painted in what appeared to be both Arabic and English. It said *Meshouda*.

With her sailed two smaller brigs.

A hush fell over the crew as the corsair fired a cannon shot over the hull of the *Raven*, catching the end of the mizzenmast's main yardarm in the process. Beneath a three-inch-long splinter of wood, the bright splotch of blood seeping through Leetch's shirt resembled a red carnation. Zoe's breath caught in her throat. They'd already raised a flag of truce, wanting to parlay with the ship's captain.

"McCairn, tend to Leetch," Winn ordered, worry for the young man plain upon his face. McCairn rushed to the lieutenant's side.

"It's only a flea bite, sir," Leetch said.

"Take care of yourself. I need you, boy." Winn smiled at him, but his charcoal eye burned with angry red embers. "Give him the gybe when he boards. The seal will prove the validity of the pass."

Leetch nodded. Another helmsman managed the wheel while the lieutenant took his place by the rail, one hand pressed against his side to stem the flow of blood, the other gripping the roll of parchment. Zoe could see the slight shake to the hand that held the dey's pass, yet Leetch stood there proudly for his captain.

Winn turned to Grizzard.

"If it's him, this changes things a bit." Their gazes locked. McCairn nodded his furry head as well. "You know what to do." He eyed the two men somberly. "Above everything I want her and the boy safe."

He didn't mention Zoe by name, she didn't think he could at the moment. She could hear his dry rasp grow more pronounced. If there was a plan afoot, she wanted to be part of it.

"What's up?" she asked her two compatriots when Winn joined Leetch to wait at the rail. She knew better than to ask Winn; the man wasn't talking—she recognized that hooded look to his eye.

McCairn frowned, and Grizzard spit on the deck again. She was beginning to know their moods, also. The bear of a doctor shuffled his feet, while Grizzard enlightened her with new colloquialisms. She waited them out patiently and was soon rewarded. Surprisingly, crusty old Grizzard was the first to break.

"Met up with the bastard a time or two, we did. Thought we'd killed the turd, but it looks like shit floats." McCairn nodded in agreement.

"Who is he?" she asked.

"The dey's henchman," Grizzard said, followed by the bear's growl.

"Calls himself Reis Hammida." The words sounded foul on the doctor's tongue. He wiped his mouth on his sleeve as if he'd tasted rot.

"By the mother of all saints," Zoe whispered. "He's the bastard who cut down Winn." The blood seemed to drain from her head and settle, frozen, at her feet.

"So, he told you how it happened, Princess." McCairn bobbed his head in approval. "You've worked wonders in that man."

"Aye, she has," Grizzard agreed. "And she deserves to know what we're confrontin' here."

"No time for that now," McCairn whispered, pointing to the side of the ship where Winn stood.

The corsair had drawn close enough to board. Grappling irons had been tossed to the *Raven,* and the men from the *Meshouda* swarmed up the side like a pack of ants sniffing a picnic.

"Motherless bastards," McCairn swore, placing himself in front of Zoe.

Grizzard backed up behind her. "Mind what you say and do now, miss. It could mean your life, or even the cap'n's." He gave her arm a quick squeeze, and she looked at him over her shoulder. Grizzard wore a grim smile. "And remember, Princess, no matter what we say or do, the doctor an' me both would die for the cap'n. . . ." He paused and gave her a wink. "And for his missus, too."

Zoe almost wept, so sincere and unlikely the pledge was coming from so usually stern and bitter a man. But Grizzard gave her a shake and a thumbs-up, as she had taught Adam

"Oh-my-God, Adam—" She searched around frantically for him but couldn't catch a glimpse of blond hair. "Where is he? I have to find him."

"Not now, missus," Grizzard hissed in her ear. "The boy's with Cookie, an' he knows what ta do. Can't have that scurvy Algerine bastard know he be like a son to the cap'n. Best ta have him be but one of the boys. Ya understand?" he asked, his voice laced with sympathy.

Zoe gave a quick nod, heart thumping in her mouth, as the Algerian crew crawled over the ship. Winn stood his ground, waiting for their captain to ascend. A dark face appeared over the rail, and its turbaned owner dropped to the deck.

Zoe gasped, knowing immediately who it was by the rigidness of Winn's body. The man was not quite as tall as Winn, but certainly tall for this day and age. Slighter about the shoulders and more wiry, he wore an evil sneer that had a scar running through it as though someone had tried to cut it off. The scar bisected his full lips, making them pucker even farther when he eyed Winn.

"What good fortune favors me, that we have met again. Surely Mahomet has had a hand in my destiny, that I may yet avenge myself." He fingered his scar slowly with his nut-brown fingers.

Winn remained silent while Leetch held out the dey's pass. Hammida studied it intently, his frown transforming to open hatred on his face.

"Unfortunately, it seems I cannot yet finish the job I started so long ago. Until the dey says otherwise, you will live." Zoe peeked from behind McCairn and caught the makings of that evil smile. "Yet the dey has been known to change his mind on a whim, and on my advice."

Winn's jaw tightened, but he didn't answer. The corsair captain surveyed the *Raven* with an avaricious eye, practically licking his lips. He gave Zoe the creeps. She ducked back behind McCairn, but the motion proved to be her undoing.

"Well, well. What have we here?" The oily smoothness of his voice made her skin crawl. A moment later he was before her, but to her satisfaction, it took three of his henchmen to push the doctor aside.

"And who are you, mistress?" he asked, placing a finger under her chin as he studied her. Zoe slapped his hand away. Anger laced the corsair's laugh. "How amusing, a feisty one. You'll be a pleasure to tame."

Zoe didn't answer. She'd be damned if she fell willingly into his hands. McCairn's grizzly growl turned the corsair in his direction.

"Do you belong to this one? The man wears no rank."

"It's doctor, you miserable pirate," McCairn rumbled.

"How nice. A man of medicine always commands a high price. Perhaps the dey will retain you for his son—a sickly youth, to his regret."

McCairn's eyes narrowed to slits as he struggled with the men who held him. The corsair stared at him steadily, not cowed by the big man's bark. Then again, Zoe thought, with his crew swarming over the decks, there wasn't much he had to be frightened of. She cringed when his attentions turned back to her.

"No. I do not think you belong to this one. The look he gives you speaks not of ownership."

Hammida studied Grizzard and dismissed him with a frown before shifting his gaze to Winn. After a moment he returned to Zoe, a sly, triumphant gleam filling his eyes.

"Yes," he said, his voice sibilant. "I think I know who you belong to. Such a shame for you, my dear, because I'll have to take you from him, and brand you as mine. Do not worry, though"—he rubbed a long finger over the crease in her forehead—"I'll enjoy myself immensely."

Hammida grabbed her hand and started to drag her forward, but Zoe dug her heels into the deck, the soles of the sneakers beneath her skirts pulling her to an abrupt halt. She shook her head emphatically, noting how silent and still Winn stood.

"I will not go with you. I am a free woman and I am already married, thank you. I'm sure the dey would not approve."

There. She had noticed that flashing the dey's name made him nervous. Let him refute what she said; as long as the dey wasn't here to contradict her, she knew the corsair would watch his evil step—which had her wondering how cruel a master the dey was. She could also see that she had made an instant enemy by the murderous glance Hammida cast her way.

"You contradict yourself, madame," he murmured, teeth gleaming like ivory in the afternoon sun. "Marriage and freedom are mutually exclusive."

"Where did you get your degree?" she asked, irked by his excellent grasp of English.

"Eton." He flashed that sickening smile again. She didn't deign to acknowledge him. "I do not see proof that you are married. Have you any?"

"I've the papers we signed."

"Perhaps, but papers can be forged. If you are the good captain's mistress, though, the dey would be forgiving of any slights I may cause you."

The suggestiveness of his words appalled her. Zoe backed up a step into Grizzard, who steadied her.

"Leave her be," Winn drawled, sauntering closer.

Hammida's men drew flank around him, awaiting their captain's command. He waved them away and looked Winn up and down. High above them the sails flapped angrily and a piercing caw rent the air.

A dark shadow swooped low over the corsair captain's head and alighted with a great *whoosh* and flap of feathers upon Zoe's stiff shoulder. She put her hand up to smooth Raven's ruffled feathers.

Hammida drew back a step, shaking in his boots. "Who is this?" he demanded, waving a hand in Zoe's direction.

"This," Winn said slowly, "is my wife."

The corsair ignored him, flapping his arm, looking not unlike a dark crow himself. Zoe felt Raven bristle his feathers as if he had divined her thoughts and taken offense.

"Sorry," she said, patting his feet. The bird dipped his head.

"Not that one," Hammida bellowed, eyes wide with fright. "Who is *he?*" The corsair pointed at Raven. "That one—the spirit in the guise of a bird."

"Ah," Winn said in a smooth, steady voice. "That one happens to be an old friend of mine—the captain your men killed the day you failed to kill me."

Hammida glared at him, then at Zoe, who upped the ante of the game. "Would you like to hold him?" she asked, and the corsair stepped back farther. "He is mine to command, after all." She smiled an evil smile, and the man practically dropped at her feet.

"Aye," Winn said as casually as one would discuss the weather. "Married the devil's daughter, I did," and he began to laugh with hearty abandon.

If the corsair hadn't been so afraid of the damn bird, Zoe knew he would have used his cutlass on Winn's remaining testicle.

They had slipped through Gibraltar in the dead of night several days before, managing to avoid the men-of-war that cruised the water around the edges of the peninsular war. After the Algerians stripped the crew to their underwear and seized all of the men's clothes and belongings, they sent half of Winn's crew onto the *Meshouda* and another brig and sent as many corsairs onto the *Raven*. Under the watchful eyes of Hammida's men, the crew of the *Raven* went about their duties as usual.

They were becalmed for a bit, and it took close to a week before Winn and Zoe caught first sight of the rugged Algerian coast. They had been given a modest room together—Hammida had the fear of both dey and crow to contend with, after all. Outside of the meagerness of their fare and the lack of creativity in its making, they managed easily.

The *Raven's* crew, however, did not fare so well.

By word of Grizzard, who had somehow convinced Hammida that he was Zoe's servant, they had learned the men were placed in a dark, verminous hold, with only bread dipped in olive oil for their sustenance. Some of them had already weakened.

Hammida called Winn and Zoe to the top deck to watch their dramatic arrival in Algiers. Some of his earlier fear had dissipated since first seeing Raven, but he eyed the bird warily nonetheless. Zoe had to admit that at least the man no longer intimated about sexual favors, but she still saw that hateful gleam in his eyes each time his gaze rested on her.

As they sailed through the twisting, rock-studded channel that marked the harbor of Algiers, Zoe could see a long stretch of bare earth that led out to a fortified island. What appeared to be aqueducts rushed down from the mountains, emptying into the fountains of the city squares. The sun sparkled like white diamonds upon the water, giving the Mediterranean city a fairy-tale quality.

By the time they had pulled into port, the picture of loveliness had faded into a tawdry reality. Algiers was a port city like any other, with narrow alleyways and rank smells that Zoe could get a whiff of even from the ship. A terrible foreboding filled her.

Winn stood by her side, not touching her, not wanting Hammida to know her worth. He hadn't touched her in privacy, either, telling her he feared prying eyes. The thought of someone watching them make love made it easier to bear sleeping platonically beside Winn, but he'd grown more silent with each passing day, and she could feel him pulling away from her.

He had a plan, he said, but was unable to say more for fear there were prying ears, as well. She trusted him, truly she did, yet couldn't keep doubts from creeping in. It wasn't his worth she was in doubt of—it was her own. Perhaps he had come to regret their hasty marriage. . . .

When the boat dropped anchor she could see the *Raven* berthed a dock away, her proud lines the envy of the crowds that lined the bay. As Zoe compared the *Meshouda*'s garish facade, Hammida caught her eye and nodded to Grizzard, who spoke on cue.

"It has all come out, mistress. I had to tell him," Grizzard said sadly.

She hadn't a clue to what he meant.

Hammida motioned again for Grizzard to go on.

"Told him you and the cap'n weren't married-like."

"What?"

She couldn't believe this. Just this morning the three of them had agreed that the best course of action was for her to stick as close to Winn's side as possible. She looked at Winn, who raised a thoughtful brow but remained mute, studying Grizzard.

"Don't be ridiculous, Grizzard," she hissed. "You were witness to the ceremony."

"Poor woman's got a maggot in her brain when it comes to men. Sort of a mothering thing, if you catch my meanin'," he said to Hammida.

The corsair shook his head knowingly.

Zoe fumed. She opened her mouth to refute Grizzard, but the pirate pointed to the parchment rolled tightly in Hammida's nut-brown fist.

"Show 'em what ya got there, Mr. Hammida, sir, and they'll know that the game is up."

Hammida held the end of the parchment, letting it unroll dramatically before them. An admirable likeness of Winn's eye-patched face stared back at them boldly. Beneath was written an impressive reward for the infamous Pirate Black Jack Alexander. Hammida waved it triumphantly before Winn's nose.

"I have word that the dey is not in residence." He tapped the broadsheet. "You see, he has gone hunting for pirates. He will be most disappointed that he did not find you himself, but will be well pleased with me when he fetches this English ruler's reward."

Winn cursed under his breath—something about the dirty, traitorous bastard of a regent going back on his word. A muscle ticked in his square jaw, and the cords stood out tightly against his neck, much as the rigging stood out on his ship. Zoe was impressed.

A deep growl alerted her to the good doctor, who was brought from the hold to their side. Grizzard eyed him with disgust.

"Don't think ya can claim the reward, I've already turned him in."

"You turned him in?" Hammida's voice grew dangerous. "Think you to share in the booty, my friend?"

Grizzard flopped to the deck in sickening obeisance. Zoe thought it a tad overdone, but Hammida seemed to take it as his due. He motioned the pirate up.

McCairn's growl rumbled in his chest at Grizzard's unfortunate display. "Why, you weaselly little runt, what do you think you're up to?"

"Just tellin' Mr. Hammida here that it's a tringum-trangum on the cap'n's part to pretend on this here marriage. And the *princess*"—he emphasized the word as if she were truly royalty—"going along with it out o' the goodness of her heart."

Both Zoe and the doctor snorted.

"Well," Grizzard continued, "it ain't like she got anythin' to gain." He pointed a gnarled finger at Winn. "Naught to get from him 'ceptin' his warmth, if ya know what I'm sayin'. Since he lost his twiddle-diddles, he ain't been but piss-proud with the women, having nothin' left to show for him when it comes down to the finish."

Zoe couldn't believe what she had heard. She thought Grizzard was his captain's man, yet he'd just humiliated Winn before half the ship. She could see Winn's face turn gray, but before he said a word, McCairn stepped in.

Unlike Winn's bloodless pallor, the big man's face reddened with rage. "You weasel-faced maggot. Stop your twaddle before I rip your head from your skinny shoulders." He took a menacing step forward, but Grizzard ducked behind Zoe while he yelled back.

"Kiss mine arse, you quack! 'Tain't no twaddle. I was with him on the quarterdeck the day His Highness here aimed his near deadly blow at the cap'n." He tilted his head toward Hammida, who puffed up with self-inflated ego like a rubber raft.

"So what does that have to do with anything, you bloody beggar of a fool?" McCairn snorted at Grizzard like an oncoming train.

"Why, the man's a eunuch, gelded—had his ballocks cut clean off by the sheik." He nodded once more in Hammida's direction. "The princess, here"—again that royal emphasis, she noted—"has gone along with this marriage nonsense for the cap'n's protection just so's she won't be ransomed. But as soon as I saw the proclamation here"—he pointed to Winn's Wanted poster—"I knew it be old Black Jack Alexander what's been meanin' to hold the princess for ransom, and she'll be that much safer without him, she will."

He stood there proudly, almost as puffed up as the despicably oily Hammida. Zoe didn't like this turn of events one bit, and neither did Winn, if she could judge the sour expression on his face. McCairn went for Grizzard's throat, but the old pirate jumped behind Hammida and his men before the burly doctor reached him.

"Take him below with the others," the corsair ordered, pointing to McCairn. "But be gentle with him, if you will"—he smiled benignly—"the doctor may be useful to the dey." A pale assistant repeated the words in their native tongue.

Zoe watched them leave, the hair rising on the back of her neck. Then Hammida turned to Winn, who waited expectantly for the corsair's command as if he already knew the man's course of action.

"You know what we must do with you, do you not?" Hammida's greasy voice slid down her spine like rancid oil.

Winn nodded, then fell in step with the corsair's men, his flashing eye and commanding demeanor daring them to lay a hand on him. They did not. He strode away from Zoe without a word.

"Where are they taking my husband?" Zoe demanded.

Hammida began to answer, but Winn suddenly halted, spinning around to face her, though regarding her silently. All upon the deck waited to see what would happen.

"Winn?" Zoe's voice rose an octave. "Where are they taking you?"

"The ruse is up, madam, don't you see?" he drawled, as if explaining to a country hick. "That ceremony on deck was all a sham. Didn't you hear what Grizzard had to say? I wanted you only for the mounds of money I could wring out of your exceptionally wealthy father."

Her father had never been wealthy, and he'd been dead for years. She smelled a ruse.

He looked at her through a shuttered eye. No emotion could be detected on his usually open face. It gave her the willies even as Hammida nodded in her direction and a hefty guard gave her arm a pull.

"Get your hands off me, lard ass," she growled through bared teeth. "Answer me, Winn."

Silence reigned.

The guard jerked her close and spun her about, propelling her roughly down the gangway. She looked over her shoulder at Winn, receiving no reply. The act he played was a fine one, his performance impeccable, but she still had to know where they would take him. How else could she begin to formulate a plan without knowing where they held the stubborn man?

Zoe began to panic as they neared the dock.

"Winn, for God's sake. What the hell is going on? Where are they taking us? Winn!" she shrieked, not wanting to be separated from him, twisting frantically in the guard's hold. "This is not my idea of a great honeymoon."

Winn took a step to the rail, his smile rakish as he played the Regency scoundrel to perfection. Looking her up and down with a bold, appreciative stare, he shook his head.

"Nonsense, my dear. As you now know, the honeymoon served the ultimate scam. Why don't you think of this as a romantic adventure? After all, I know how the basic romance story works—I've read your books. First you must be given to a sheik and fulfill his every pleasure, whereupon your uniqueness and agility will capture his attention as well as his heart. Unless, of course, he is not the hero. Then you must use your inventiveness to forestall his lusty fulfillment."

He kept a phony smile plastered across his face. If she'd been closer, she'd have smacked it off.

"Don't you dare leave me, Winn."

"Unfortunately, I find I must. You've a fine face and figure, madam, despite being a tad long in the tooth. But I'm afraid you're a bit of the shrew and definitely more trouble than you're worth."

A few of the men who spoke English chuckled. Zoe pulled up short, nearly knocking her guard to the dock. Winn's pretense had gone too far.

"Why, you insufferable bastard—"

"Uh-uh, Princess," Winn called down to her. "You're turning the shrew again. I suggest you hold your tongue—your next master may not be so appreciative of your feisty ways." He winked at her and blew her a kiss. "And remember to stay put, my fantasy bride, and cease your flighty ways. Who knows? A real man might come to your rescue."

He waved at her, a little salute mixed with an okay sign. What cheek! Long in the tooth, eh? She thought he played the part too well. She'd do without him and his insults, real or not, just fine, and she certainly didn't need anyone to rescue her—hell, she was supposed to be the guest of the dey. Who needed an over-the-hill pirate anyway?

"I'll be waiting for that real man, Winn!" she shouted up to him.

He merely nodded. "You do that, Princess. And no unscheduled flights, please. It'll make Flynn's swashbuckling twice as difficult."

And with that he turned once more from the rail, this time disappearing from sight.

13

"*Get back, Jack. Or I'll* cast the evil eye on you."

Zoe took a mean glance at the pudgy gnome the guard had brought her to. Was the whole Barbary Coast made up of midgets? Granted, they made them smaller in the 1800s, and she was above average height for her time, but the majority of the men on Winn's ship had at least been up to her nose. She felt like the Jolly Green Giant without the green makeup.

The gnome walked around her, surveying her features, the pebbles of the courtyard crunching beneath his considerable weight. He checked her out in a way that would have had him up on sexual harassment charges if it had been the twentieth century.

But it wasn't the twentieth century.

Which made the guy's assessment all the more unnerving.

He took a step closer, and she made the sign of the

cross with her fingers. "Listen, baldy. You'd be wise to keep your distance."

"There is nothing to fear, mistress. I am the dey's vizier. It is my duty to inspect you, and determine your worth."

"My worth is more than yours, my little Kojak." She circled away from him each step he took.

"I believe this belongs to you, mistress."

The munchkin stopped a moment, lifting his arm in the air. Zoe's purse dangled from his wrist. She made a grab for it, but the little man stepped neatly away a moment before the guard grabbed her from behind.

"Easy . . ." He motioned to the guard. "We wouldn't want to damage the princess."

"I am not a princess."

"So you say. But I believe otherwise." He peered inside her bag. "There are wondrous things in here befitting none but superior rank. The dey will be most pleased with your gifts."

"The dey can readily have my gifts"—she looked him straight in the eye—"if you will set me free."

"That, mistress, is impossible. For you are a gift as well. Though it is the dey's decision whether you be concubine or wife."

Zoe wiped a bead of sweat from her forehead, not knowing if she perspired from the oppressive heat of the Mediterranean sun or from the heat of lust in the evil midget's eyes.

"Thanks, but no thanks," she said. "I'm already married."

"There has been some question to that, so I've heard, and no proof."

"Listen, you little rodent. I am no virgin to be given to the dey as playmate of the month." She glared at him with all the venom she had, but it didn't faze him one bit.

"We will see soon enough, after you are examined fully."

"What do you mean, 'fully'?" Zoe struggled in the guard's grip, not liking the conclusion she'd come to. "You lay one filthy little finger on me, and you won't walk straight for the rest of your miserable life." Satisfaction surged through her as a look of shock tightened his features.

"Still your concerns, mistress. None but the dey's head eunuch will determine your purity." He clapped his hands and started forward. The guard followed, with Zoe shuffling along behind.

In the quiet of the courtyard she could hear her own ragged breaths with each step she took down the meandering paths. She didn't know which she felt more—fear or rage. Opting for the latter, she let her good old American independence surge to the forefront.

"Listen, Kojak," she said, enunciating clearly. "I've had enough of this craziness. No one inspects me but my husband or a certified gynecologist."

The gnome raised a puzzled brow. "It is necessary, madame."

He led her through a marble arch and into the cool shadows of an opulent hall. The lower temperature was a welcome relief. Zoe looked around. Luxurious carpets covered the floor, and rich tapestries fluttered against the marble walls. In the distance a fountain tinkled along with the soft laughter of women.

"Look." Zoe dug her heels in the carpet and placed her hands on her hips. "The dey's going to be mighty pissed when he finds how you've treated me, an innocent American citizen—political repercussions and all that."

The midget turned to her, the epitome of patience. "Mistress. You will not be an American citizen when you belong to the dey."

Zoe stomped her foot. "The dey will not want me. I'm soiled goods, as they say in this misbegotten century."

"The status of wife may not be yours, but there is also the place of the concubine," he explained. Then he clapped his hands again, and the guard disappeared down a seemingly endless corridor.

She felt like bolting but knew she'd never find her way out. The place was a maze. Already her head was spinning from the turns that had brought her here.

"I'm too old," she said. "Thirty-eight, almost. What the dey needs is a young honey."

"Mistress, surely you exaggerate. You may not have the first bloom of youth, but you are not an old woman. The dey appreciates a mature figure more than a youthful one. It gives a woman character, so he says." He eyed her up and down. "Although you are somewhat thin for his taste—we'll have to fatten you up—and your hips look a bit slim for childbearing."

"Listen, bud, I'm far from anorectic. And as far as my hips go, I've had two kids by natural childbirth with none of that yelling, screaming bullshit you read about in books." She crossed her arms in challenge. Let him dispute that.

It appeared he would try. She watched as his eyes narrowed in thought.

"How may I believe you?" he asked.

Zoe glared at him. "Because I don't lie. And I have the stretch marks to prove it."

"Do the children live?"

"Yes."

"Are they healthy?"

"Yes. And they have gifted minds, besides," she bragged.

"Male or female?"

"One of each."

His eyes lit up. "Excellent. Now show me these stretching marks. Koto is here as witness."

Zoe swung around in the direction of his glance. A huge sucker loomed behind her. In this land of five-foot men, he easily topped six feet. His formidable size would give even Winn a run for his money.

He wore loose gauze trousers in a burgundy hue and a matching embroidered vest that winked with jewels. Real jewels. Diamonds, rubies, emeralds, sapphires. Not a cubic zirconia in sight. A huge diamond stud—three carats, at least—adorned one ear, and his dark, shaved head sported a miniqueue that was wrapped with gold links at its crown.

Mr. Clean must have won the lottery, Zoe thought. An idea so surreal, she almost laughed.

Almost.

Until she saw his face. A huge puckered scar slit across one swarthy cheek to disappear around his neck in an arc. She would not mess around with a man who had survived a slit throat.

"Toto, I presume." Somehow she managed to get the words out. The inside joke did not relieve her tension.

While she stared at the giant's bulging muscles, Kojak Jr. made a grab for her. Zoe slapped his hand away and took a swing, but the weasel dodged her.

"Either you show these marks, or Koto will inspect you fully." The little man held her gaze.

The guy was serious. It took but a moment to make up her mind. Zoe unsnapped her jeans, glad she had worn them instead of her dress, and pulled the zipper down till the thin silver scars of childbearing could be seen. Both Koto and the vizier bent closer for inspection. The vizier seemed satisfied until his gaze dropped lower.

"What is this intriguing piece of finery?" he asked, slipping a finger under the elastic of her silk bikinis.

Zoe slapped his hand, and Koto growled, taking a menacing step between her and the little man.

The vizier jumped back, sweat popping out on his forehead. "Forgive me." He bowed to her. "Forgive me, Koto. The unusual raiment compelled me." He salaamed to the eunuch, who fixed him with a beady stare.

Then Koto spoke, his voice like a low, dry rush of desert wind sweeping through the marble hall.

"The dey would not be pleased to have his wife touched by a servant."

The munchkin bowed lower, head hitting the floor.

"Come," Koto said, grabbing Zoe's purse from the little man before turning from him in dismissal. He beckoned her to follow.

Zoe's stomach twisted into intricate knots that any sailor would be proud of. She held up her hand, stopping the overgrown Toto with the motion. "Wait. You're mistaken. The dey won't want me now."

Koto's dry whisper raised the hairs on her neck. "It is you who are mistaken, madame. A fever swept through the city and harem. It has been a year, and still no children. You are precisely what the dey wants."

Zoe stood rooted to the spot, clicking her heels to the mantra of "There's no place like home," until

Koto lifted her in his arms and strode away, taking her far from the yellow brick road and Kansas.

She came to slowly, the heavy spice of incense tickling her nose, and sneezed—a great "Achoo" that jolted her upright and had her staring at her rich surroundings. The pillows she leaned against were made of silk embroidered with the colors of the rainbow and, from her itching nose, filled with feathers to the point of bursting.

Zoe pinched the end of her nose, avoiding another sneeze, and, for the first time, noticed her outrageous outfit. Someone had dressed her in shirred, rose silk pants that billowed out below a richly embroidered tunic. A pair of matching slippers stood by the open doorway. The last time she'd worn such an outfit had been in belly-dancing class.

No, she thought, the nightmare hasn't ended. She'd read enough novels in the course of her not-too-aged lifetime to realize that the sherbet they'd given her for sustenance after she fainted had most likely been laden with an opiate-based drug. So there—her brain hadn't stopped functioning since hitting that time tunnel, worm-hole, or what have you. It just didn't function at the same rate.

Then again, that could be chalked up to the onset of early senility.

Zoe looked around her with a critical gaze, unable to recall if she was in a zenana, or if she was a banana even to think of escaping. All she knew was that she wanted out of her gilded cage of marbled walls, perfumed air, and the most luxurious accessories she'd ever seen decorating home or hearth. She must have looked as though she were about to bolt, because a gentle voice from the shadows sought to ease her.

"There is nowhere you can run without being caught and then punished. The bastinado hurts wicked hard." A young blond woman slipped from the shadows and continued, "I know, they used it on me once. I did not try to escape again."

Zoe squinted at the girl, thinking something about her was familiar, but she still felt dopey and couldn't put two and two together except to get too much.

"What is your name?" she asked through dry lips, but didn't dare touch the water for fear it was also drugged.

"They call me Yasmine, but my Christian name is Catherine. My friends call me Caty." The young woman brought her the pitcher she'd been eyeing, assuring her they had yet to spike the water.

"It was the sherbet, right?" Zoe asked.

The girl nodded. Zoe realized she couldn't be more than eighteen—closer to Alex's age than her own.

"I knew it," Zoe said, referring to the sherbet. "That's how they always do it."

The girl looked at her with interest. "Are you familiar with Mideastern culture?"

Zoe smiled. "Let's just say I'm a voracious reader. Tell me, Caty, how did you happen to get here?"

"I was kidnapped some months ago, taken right from the strand outside our estate. Bold as brass they made off with me, having spied my early morning walks, determining me to be an important enough personage to bring a high reward."

Zoe whistled. "Holy mother of all the saints."

"I beg your pardon?" Caty asked, cornflower blue eyes wide at the epithet.

"You're the girl that Winn is looking for."

"I am?" she asked, hope filling her beatific smile as she shuffled closer.

Zoe made a mental note to take it easy with her newly acquired curses, no matter how colorfully creative she found them—she wouldn't want to corrupt poor Caty; the girl was as innocent as they came. Zoe would miss the peppery epithets, though. "Sir Reverence" was ever so much more inventive than the modern "shit-for-brains."

She turned her wandering attention back to the girl. Perhaps she really was going senile, and this was one big mixed-up reality. Nah, that would be too easy.

"Are you the regent's goddaughter?"

Caty flung herself at Zoe and started to cry. "Oh, God, I never thought they'd find me. Thank you, ma'am, for coming for me."

Zoe patted the girl tenderly. Another poor mite in need of mothering, she thought, and was immediately racked with fear for Adam.

"Tell me, Caty, do you know what they do with the cabin boys they capture?"

"Why, yes," the girl said, snuffling back her tears and scrubbing at her face with the edge of her long buttercup yellow silk tunic. "They use them for palace servants. It's a hard life for the boys, but not dangerous."

"Thank God," Zoe whispered, relieved. Adam was a good boy and would do what he was told, working hard as always. She didn't need to worry about him for the moment. Just as well, since she required all her wits to figure a solution to everyone's dilemma.

"Are you all right, ma'am?"

"I'm fine," she answered. "And please, call me Zoe. It's so much friendlier than 'ma'am.'"

Caty smiled and sat next to her on the cushions that were spread across one corner of the floor. The girl held out her hands, palm up, her sweet voice blending with the hushed music and daily sounds of life in the harem.

"I'm to tell you your duties," she explained, "and the way things are run. Koto doesn't have much faith in the others who speak English, and for once, I tend to agree."

"There are other Westerners being held hostage?" Zoe asked, and the girl nodded. "I had no idea. Quite frankly, I've only been here a few hours—"

"An entire day has passed since you arrived."

"Boy, when they spike something, they go about it whole hog." Zoe shook her head. "I have to tell you, this entire harem scenario is not what it's cracked up to be."

The girl regarded her blankly.

"Never mind."

Caty nodded. "This is your room," she continued. "We are to share while you become familiar with the routine. Actually, there is a lot of freedom within the harem itself. It ends, however, at the boundaries of these walls."

Zoe frowned at the mention of walls, rapidly developing a hearty case of claustrophobia. "And what do you do for fun?" she drawled, biting off the more sarcastic comments that sprang to mind. She was not in a good mood.

A melodic giggle halted Caty's answer as it floated through the room from the doorway behind them. Zoe turned around to find a trio of women standing at the door. Unlike Caty, they did not seem to be victims of melancholy.

A small, voluptuous woman floated into the room on silent feet and answered Zoe's question in a throaty, upper-class English accent.

"There are many ways to pass the time, and many things to dream of. If you are an imaginative person, nothing is dull, even with a snake like Hadji."

"Hadji?" Zoe asked.

The woman seemed surprised at her ignorance. "Hadji Ali. The dey."

"And what is the dey like?"

As Zoe awaited her answer she sensed a maturity in them that was missing in Caty. They probably would not wind up hollow and broken, as Zoe suspected the girl would be if she stayed in this place much longer. Oh, no. By the meaningful glances she'd detected at the mention of their master, these were women who had grabbed life—and the dey—by the balls.

But it was Caty who answered her question. "He's an awful, lecherous old snake, with beady little eyes and a stomach like a fat pig. A terrible, disgusting stub-faced man."

"Stub-faced?" Zoe asked, hoping for another colorful epithet to add to her repertoire.

Caty nodded. "He looks like the devil ran over his face with his shoes full of horse nails."

"That good-looking?" Zoe raised a brow. "Sounds like quite a catch."

Caty glanced away, confused. Evidently subtle wit wasn't the girl's strong point. But the other women enjoyed a bit of laughter.

"He's every bit the horror she described, yet so much more," the exotic one explained in a British drawl, joining Zoe on the pillows. The other two women followed suit. "You would never think such a crotchety, nasty old man would have such an inventive mind. He's putty in your hands if you know how to tie a good knot."

Oh, my, Zoe thought, this is getting interesting.

Caty shook her head in disgust, looking daggers at the women. "They like to bait me like this, and tell me about their filthy adventures when they all play the role of harlot."

"Oh, I wouldn't be so hard on them, dear," Zoe said, giving the women a wink. "Life hands you some difficult choices, and sometimes you have to pick the least offensive in order to survive."

The women nodded and murmured among themselves, eyeing Zoe with newfound admiration.

"The child doesn't realize that eventually she'll have to make those choices, and it would be better for her to make the most of them," the tall, dark-haired woman said in a soft brogue. "It should be easier for her than it is for us. After all, so many hours pleasing Hadji takes a tremendous amount of vigor, and she has the energy of youth."

Damn, but these women made some sense.

"And," added the chubby one with the lovely voice, "she's ever so much more supple than we are. Why, I couldn't begin to imagine how amusing things could be with that goat Hadji if I could only twist myself into some new positions."

Zoe raised an eyebrow, cocking her head as she looked at the women. These three seemed so familiar. If she could only remember . . .

"Where is my bag?" she asked, an odd thought tugging at her mind. She bet these ladies would enjoy a good modern read.

Caty's brow furrowed. "Your reticule?"

"Have you seen it?"

The girl nodded and dug behind a pile of pillows until she came up with the purse. She scooted closer to Zoe, curious, as were the three other women. While Zoe scrounged through her bag, they told her more about Hadji Ali.

"He may be stout, but so is his Thomas," the tall one cooed. "And it's mighty long for all that he's a short fellow. The man can go on for hours."

"That's completely disgusting," Caty cried, but the dark-haired woman looked at her sadly.

"Girl, you've tongue enough for more than two sets of teeth, and you've no idea what you are talking about."

Zoe chalked up another good put-down but took pity on poor Caty, who turned to her.

"The old man looks like a troll and acts like a veritable satyr. Beware of him, Zoe. My virtue remains intact only because his love of money and thievery outweighs the joy he derives from forcing himself on innocent women."

Zoe brushed the blond curls back from the girl's flushed face, hoping to calm her before she grew hysterical. The others looked on with pity.

"You'll change your song soon enough when you see how wonderfully inventive the man is," the short one said, meaning to soothe the girl.

It was the wrong thing to say. Caty attacked with a verbal vengeance. "You're nothing but a bunch of star-gazing hedge whores who can flop to your backs faster than you can draw a breath!" she cried.

Zoe was shocked.

The women meant well, really they did. She couldn't detect a hint of malice in their collective demeanor. But then a girl wanted to be loved and cherished by a young man, preferably one of her own choosing.

She had a nagging question, though. If Caty was as innocent as she seemed, where in the world had she learned those scathing comments? Zoe was impressed as well as shocked. She hoped the ladies' feelings weren't hurt.

"Uh-oh," said the exotic one with a fancy for ropes. "We're in the suds now."

Out of the corner of her eye Zoe saw Koto sauntering over.

"I'd have a try at old Koto himself," the chubby one said, her laughter sweet as music, "but I prefer my men stocky, and he's a bit too spider shanked for me."

Zoe glanced through the doorway at the approaching man, totally confused. "But I thought he was a eunuch."

The trio giggled in unison as the imaginative, voluptuous one answered. Even Caty's ears perked up.

"Oh, but he *is* a eunuch. The head one, as a matter of fact, and master of the harem. Yet, as long as only his ballocks are missing, a man who's stone can still prove amusing." She winked at a flustered Caty, who gasped.

"Yes," said the one with the incredible stamina, eyes glazed in rapture. "His member works as well as any, and he can go on a-pounding close to forever."

The exotic one smiled slowly at Zoe, who sat, mouth agape, listening in fascination. "They tend to get a bit violent before they find their heavenly release, but a talent with sturdy rope can keep them from doing harm," she confessed. "Downright exciting it be."

Caty took shallow breaths and looked close to fainting as she eyed Koto through the doorway.

"Easy, girl," the tall woman said, fussing with

Catherine's hair till it lay smooth. "Pull yourself together slap dash, and you'll look smart as a newly scraped carrot."

Was being compared to a carrot considered a compliment or an insult? Zoe wondered. She reserved judgment for a later time since Koto had reached the edge of her room.

"Ladies," he commanded in that Mr. Clean voice, "it is time for the *hammam.*"

The chubby one fanned herself, and the tall one giggled, eyeing the eunuch seductively till the big man left. Zoe followed Catherine and the three other women to a large steamy pool. After seeing the others jump in naked, she decided her bikini would be redundant, so she stripped to the buff and dove in.

She came up screaming, having noticed what they'd done to her while she'd slept. "You rotten bastard!" she screamed at the startled Koto, who stood guard like a statue at the lip of the pool, arms crossed over his powerful chest.

"Mistress, control yourself," he hissed. "It is the way of the harem."

"Well, Mr. Clean," she spluttered. "How would you feel if someone shaved off something of yours while you slept?"

"From my experience, none too good, mistress." He raised an amused brow and the corners of his lips twitched. "But at least *your* parts can grow back."

Zoe narrowed her eyes, feeling no sympathy for the irritating man. "Well, at least you'll never itch to death!" she shouted, and splashed the big man with a slap of water.

Koto threw back his head and laughed till tears

ran down his face and mingled with the water that dripped from his soaked clothes. The women looked at Zoe in awe.

"I've been here ten years," the chubby one said, "and I have never seen that man smile, let alone laugh."

The woman's own musical laughter glided like a balm over Zoe's sorely tried soul. She gave the eunuch the evil eye, brain working overtime, imagining scenes of revenge.

A sudden ear-splitting caw rent the warm air of the bath as a dark shape winged into the room and circled beneath the roof. The crowd of women stilled. Some grew frightened, others craned their necks to see. But Zoe stood where she was, waiting for the drop.

Raven spotted her in an instant and dove to her side. Not liking the water, for all he was the ship's mascot, he landed with a squawk upon her head. For the second time in minutes, and the second time in years, the harem rang with Koto's deep laughter.

Zoe stared into the little pool, trailing her fingers idly in the water. She'd been here for several weeks, she thought, but time lost meaning quickly in the harem. The garden was beautiful, all sunlight and flowers set within lustrous pink marble. Yet despite the heavenly setting, she felt as if she were in prison.

She didn't mind the harem itself; the splendor of her surroundings appealed harmoniously to her senses. The company of the other women was pleasant, and they were much impressed by her growing friendship with Koto and the loyal attachment of her magical bird. They meant well, all of them.

Yet young as Caty was, Zoe saw the girl's wisdom—

a harem was a slow death if you couldn't fit within its walls.

Zoe eyed those walls, wondering how fast she could scramble over them. With the latex tubing she always packed for exercising a shoulder injury, she could probably bungee jump her way out, providing Koto didn't catch her first. And then there was the dilemma of finding her way through the maze of corridors without attracting attention.

She sighed, discarding yet another escape plan. So far she had faced neither hardship nor Hadji Ali. The dey still sailed the seas on his adventure. At least she'd made fast friends with the three "Englishes," as Koto called them.

On a whim, she had given them her romance novels to read. Totally enraptured, they'd devoured them, deciding to change their names to those of the authors they loved. Which was just as well, since Zoe couldn't pronounce a syllable of the Algerian names they'd been given.

Each one took on the name of the author whose style best fit her. Appropriately, the tall dark-haired woman with the excellent stamina rechristened herself Virginia. The quiet, exotic-looking one with a penchant for bondage became Johanna. And the intriguingly creative lady with the rounded form and musical voice named herself Bertrice.

Johanna strolled up to her, borrowed tubing in her hand, eyes flashing with merriment. "This bungee rope is wonderful, Zoe. May I borrow it when Hadji returns?"

"Be my guest," Zoe said, smiling at the delighted woman.

"It's time for the next aerobics class," Johanna reminded her, but Zoe's heart wasn't into leading the exercise class she'd devised to stave off boredom. Used to playing passive games for entertainment, the women of the harem had taken up the routines with zeal.

"Why don't you take charge this time, Johanna? I think you'd make an excellent instructor."

"Oh, Zoe. May I?" Johanna's eyes positively sparkled with her newfound power. Zoe nodded, and the woman squeezed her hand. "Thank you, thank you, thank you, dear friend Zoe."

Zoe shook her head in amusement as Johanna strode off with a jaunty air, snapping the bungee cord in her hands. Not a moment had passed when a trill of musical laughter sounded behind Zoe.

"There you are," Bertrice said, Virginia following in her wake. "We've come up with an inventive new twist to the nightly bingo game and wanted to see what you think about it."

"Yes," added Virginia. "We were thinking along the lines of marathon bingo. The last one still able to respond wins the game. What do you think?"

Zoe looked up from her perch on the fountain to the two eager women, who had taken up bingo like Las Vegas gamblers. If she had known the game would be so addictive, she would have thought twice before teaching it. But if any two people could take care of themselves, she knew they could. They did just fine here on their own, in their isolated circumstances. It was Zoe who was desolate without the children and Winn.

"I think your bingo idea is excellent," she replied, as amazed as ever by their stamina and inventiveness. "Why don't you share the idea with the others?"

Bertrice giggled. "I appreciate your opinions, dear. It's nice to have such an imaginative friend."

"And we appreciate your stamina, dear," Virginia

added as they took off in the opposite direction. Zoe
thought they'd left her alone, but Caty's melodic voice
called her attention.

"Why so glum, Zoe, so down in the dumps?" she
asked, sitting beside her upon the stone fountain.

"I miss Winn and the kids," she admitted, swirling
the water in the pool.

The young woman's forehead crinkled in worry.
"But you said this Winn of yours will get us out.
Don't you have confidence in him?"

Zoe looked around the courtyard. Life in the
harem could be beauty itself; the palace rooms spilled
with riches and wonders. Yet the emptiness that filled
her reached to her soul. Perhaps it was time she
thought of a way to save Winn.

A sudden wail screeched through the air and her
thoughts like chalk on a blackboard. Another followed
close behind, and Zoe clapped her hands over her ears.

"What the hell is that?" she shouted to Caty over
the ear-splitting noise.

"That is the dey's first wife. The only one who has
given him a son. Why, the old fussock is dreadful,
lazy, and fat, and ordering the rest of us around to
do her bidding when she deigns to show her face."

"Koto!" Zoe called as the man ran by, face constricted.

Zoe jumped from the fountain's edge to follow
him. She'd grown fond of the lug—he really was a
good guy—and had learned he'd had a wife and
family before they'd caught him for the harem.

She'd never seen him show fear before.

"What's the matter?" she asked, running after him.
"Can I help?"

"It's the young master, Mistress Zoe. He's having

an attack and cannot breathe in the air." He raced before her on his long legs, wet cloths in hand, toward that God-awful wailing.

"Wait up!" she cried, grabbing the purse that Koto had returned to her the first day in the harem. She couldn't take another minute of that terrible sound ringing through her aching head. She followed Koto through a latticed door in the private quarters reserved for the dey's first wife and entered a scene from hell.

A woman she assumed to be the tyrant Caty had mentioned was pounding at her breast and rocking back and forth, shrieking incessantly. Koto pushed her attendants back and placed the cool wet cloth over a red-faced, wheezing boy who was close to Alexa's age.

"What happened?" she asked, bending closer. The boy's lips were turning blue.

"Mistress, you should not be here," Koto said. "The boy grows worse with each seizure. If he were to die, they would not be the ones to accept the blame." He motioned to the women, who eyed Zoe with both speculative and hostile stares. "They would point their accusing fingers at the one with the least status. That, mistress, would be you."

"Where's McCairn?" she asked. "He should be here."

"I gave word, mistress, but he was already fetched to attend an accident at the quarry. I fear his return will take too long."

A frown marred his swarthy face, and worry clouded his dark eyes. Zoe placed a comforting hand upon the big man's arm, ignoring the collective gasps of the onlookers.

"Koto, bless you for the friend you've become, but this boy needs some air. Tell me whatever you know while I try to help him."

Koto looked back and forth from Zoe to the boy. She could see by his drawn face that the boy meant a great deal to him, and by his hesitation, she could also see that she meant something to him as well.

"Please, Koto. I have a son and daughter, too, and this is a familiar scene—" She pointed to the boy. "My son had bouts like this when he was little. I think I can help."

The head eunuch's brows crinkled with worry, but he finally gave in. "I have noticed this often happens after he eats, but the mother will have none of my ideas."

"When he eats what? Think. It may be something his body can't tolerate."

The eunuch's face split in a grin. "Seafood, mistress, I would swear it."

"Great," she moaned, digging through her bag for her inhaler. "Seafood allergies can be fatal."

"Pray that it is not, mistress," Koto said, elbowing the wailing mother aside so Zoe could help the boy with the inhaler. "For his welfare as well as ours,"

It wasn't difficult getting the boy's lips around the inhaler; his mouth was so pursed, it held the tip tightly. She only hoped he could get in a blast of air. Zoe had Koto talk to the boy, letting him translate her instructions as her hands smoothed the tight muscles constricting the child's throat and chest—he seemed more lucid than the bawling women. When Koto nodded, she gave it a try, pumping a squirt of medicated air into the child.

The boy could hardly suck in a breath.

She tried again and again, knowing the amount entering his lungs was so small, repeated tries would be needed before the medicine would take effect. As soon as the boy's throat started to loosen, she sat back on her heels, drenched with sweat, and left Koto in charge.

The big man soothed the boy as gently as could be, taking Zoe's spot, working his massive hands over the cramped muscles of the child's neck until they relaxed. By time the boy breathed regularly, he had fallen asleep. Koto gazed at her, eyes filling with tears, and bowed his head to her.

Once again Zoe heard the startled intake of the women's breath at Koto's gesture. These people have a thing or two to learn about friendship, she thought.

Koto's voice whispered through the air like the wind on dry leaves. "Hakim is a good boy, mistress, and like a son to me. I thank you for his life."

Zoe stood on shaky legs and gave the giant a lopsided smile. "Any time, my friend." She started to walk from the room, but Koto followed close on her heels, stopping her with a firm but tender grip on her arm.

"When the time is right, friend Zoe, I will let you know," he said cryptically. Then he nodded again and strode back into the private quarters to stand guard over the boy.

Zoe wouldn't let herself wonder too much about what he had meant.

14

The Algerians had jeered at Winn on his way to the prison, but that had been a luxury he'd now bear gladly.

He peered through the slit in his cell that served more for air than for the view. The thin slice of fading blue sky and busy harbor mocked the captivity of his men and his mission. He'd come here to clear the way for Decatur, knowing that the Algerine heydey of piracy must come to an end.

With the war against England on its last legs, his mission had been to secure whatever Americans he could with the ransom provided and to note the lay of the land for Decatur's future confrontation with the corsairs. The plan had all been laid out a number of months before, with some time for leeway because of the precarious nature of ships and the seas.

Zoe's descriptions of the communication speakers in her future whetted his appetite. Oh, to see such wonders. Compared to the filth and neglect he had recently experienced, anything outside of Algiers seemed like heaven.

Winn adjusted his pantaloons, hating the rough garments given to him and his men. He looked like a damned native wearing the baggy pants, hooded jacket, and flimsy slippers. But the extra shirt and blouse came in handy during the damp night, when all that lay between him and the dirt floor of the palace dungeons was the threadbare blanket he'd been issued.

He couldn't complain, though—if anything, he was better off than his men, who now resided in the Bilic prison. Most of them had become part of the endless chain gang that clanked through the prison at all hours of the day and night, working to build up the Algerian mole of earth and rocks to extend it beyond the fortified island in the harbor. They would go out to the mountain by dawn to dig and blast, then pull the loaded sleds to the harbor to lay down the rock.

Morning and noon saw them eating hunks of stale bread soaked in vinegar. Dinner consisted of another small loaf of sour black bread each. Already some of the crew had developed sores. He'd even lost one man to a tarantula bite on the cheek.

McCairn had related the story to him on one of his rare visits to the dungeonlike hold. The doctor had some freedom within the palace, having become an important personage after all. He'd told Winn how the unfortunate seaman had survived the horror of the vicious bite, only to be forced to continue working until his head had swollen to nearly twice its size.

Winn cursed the bloody black-hearted dey and his minions, but most of all he cursed himself. Oh, he had followed his orders to perfection all right. And look where that blind loyalty had landed him. As soon as he'd seen that bloody bastard Hammida's face, he should have blasted him and his inferior garish ship to kingdom come.

Hammida had left him alone for the most part, aside from an occasional taunt. For that he was thankful. He needed his strength and mind to release his men. It was a pity he hadn't yet come up with a plan.

While McCairn served to keep him informed, he hadn't seen hide nor hair of Grizzard, that wiley bastard. He wondered what the pirate was up to and when the hell he'd move his arse. Because if he had to live in this hellhole much longer, it wouldn't matter. The place could so easily break the spirit of a man.

Not for the first time, and not for the last, Winn's final thoughts before sleeping turned to Zoe, the *Raven*, and little Adam. He hoped they fared better than he, and he prayed that his rescue by the *Blackbird* would be soon.

Jonathan paced the deck of the *Blackbird*, feeling as one with the ship.

If at times the men looked at him as if he were still "barmy," as they put it, that was fine with him. He'd never had so great an adventure in all his staid English life. Ah, the wind and the sea and the loyalty—if not sidelong looks—of his men. He'd not trade it for anything.

Except, maybe, for Black Jack's treasure.

Above him the sails billowed, sending the ship

scudding along at great speed. He still hadn't gotten the hang of the wheel or come to understand the subtleties of tacking, but he left that in the hands of his more than capable crew. Captain Messier was a self-sufficient sort, and as long as the man paid him respect, Jonathan was content.

He overheard the men talking a time or two, and they'd come to the decision that the blow in the head he'd received from the regent's men had rendered him a virtually different person.

He had his own ideas about what had happened.

His theory had him trading places in time with the infamous Black Jack Alexander. That poor bastard was now somewhere in the future, wrestling with accountants and paying off debts. Jonathan thought he had it cushy in comparison, sailing the seas in the pirate's place.

The only fly remaining in the ointment was his worry over Zoe. Had that been her tumbling beside him through the worm-hole, or was it only wishful thinking on his part? And if she had followed him through, where did she end up? He wished he had the answers but knew he might never learn the truth. God knew it was a precarious life, and the nineteenth century was fraught with dangers of all kinds.

Take, for example, that ship on the horizon. Why, it could be a friend or, just as likely, an enemy. If it was an enemy, they'd have to run like the devil with the wind, since he could now see that several smaller ships followed the large one.

Or, he thought, a slow smile curving his lips, we can always stand and fight.

Given his druthers, he'd choose the latter, since that was what this adventure should be—adventurous. You only went around once, and all that rot. You might as well take a risk now and then.

Jonathan leaned against the rail, staring out at the approaching ships. Hadn't anyone else seen them? He called behind him to Mr. Gartner at the wheel, but the man was busy checking the compass.

"Larmer," Jonathan called out to the beefy fellow who had found him on the strand, "can you make out those ships in the distance?"

"Lor', sir, but if that therapy of Doc McCairn's didn't improve your eyesight. Do you think it might work the same on me?"

"I don't see why not," Jonathan prevaricated, not having an inkling to what the man referred. "Take a look through the glass and tell me if we meet up with friends or foe."

"Aye, sir," Larmer said, raising the spy glass to his eye. "Lor', Cap'n, you be right again. Them is one frigate and three brigs from the Algerine navy."

Jonathan looked at him blankly, and Larmer whispered in his ear. "Corsairs, sir."

"Right," he mumbled. "I'll tell the crew."

"Ya plan to outrun them, sir?" Larmer asked.

"I plan to fight," Jonathan answered, stepping away from the rail and yelling to his men. He began singing in a hearty but off-key voice.

Larmer rolled his eyes to the heavens as Jonathan's rusty notes mentioned honor, battle, and the shores of Tripoli.

"Oh, Lord, Cap'n. I fear ya done it now."

Winn was rudely awakened. The gnarled mug of the vizier wavered before him. It took a few seconds to get his bearing, but then he remembered he was in a hellhole under the palace while his men labored and starved to death nearby. Pulling himself and his thoughts together, he sat up, waiting for the Lilliputian's next command.

"You will come now," was all the man said.

Winn stretched to full height, thinking how easy it would be to snap the rodent's neck. With the guard outside the bars, he wouldn't get far, but the image pleased him. He suspected he was punch happy from lack of food and sleep.

He shuffled out of the prison cell he had called home for the better part of two months and followed the vizier up the narrow stone stairs. One tug and the fellow would fall to his death. Winn refrained.

He couldn't find his way out of his own quarter room, the shape he was in, let alone search the palace for Zoe. He'd have to take things one step at a time, and the farther from the dank recesses of the prison he could go, the closer to his princess he would be.

After trailing his jailor for quite some time, Winn stepped into a great marbled hall that was lined with columns, a guard standing at each one. Sitting upon a carved throne on a dais at the end of the room was none other than Hadji Ali, a fat, pompous, vicious old man and the barbarous dey of Algiers.

Walking slowly in the vizier's wake, Winn saw the gleam of greed in the man's eyes long before they filled with false remorse and humility. The dey nodded to him, and Winn did likewise.

The decadent-looking ruler shifted his heavy body upon his silk-swathed throne and looked him up and down. "That fool Hammida told us that the notorious scourge of the sea, Black Jack Alexander, resided in our prison."

"I am not Black Jack Alexander, Your Eminence." He knew God would forgive him for the bald-faced lie. He believed in a loving God.

The dey nodded.

"We can see you are not, although there is a slight resemblance. Our vizier said the man imprisoned claimed to be one Jonathan Dunham from America, come to offer tribute and ransom. We choose to believe our vizier, especially since we have recently left that scoundrel, Black Jack, on the high seas running from us aboard his ship, *Blackbird*."

Winn hid his startlement and nodded, acknowledging the dey while silently thanking whichever of his men posed for him in his absence. A brilliant idea, if he said so himself.

"It is clear to us that you are not Black Jack. We engaged him in a fierce battle, and from my lookout glass we could see the man who dared to oppose us. Bigger by a head than you, he stood, with shoulders broad as a door. The infidel is easily twice your size, with the most frightening demeanor this side of Mecca."

Winn listened, dumbfounded, wondering who the hell it could be. Considering the dey hadn't caught the *Blackbird*, he figured His Eminence was pouring it on a bit thick. The scoundrel's vizier and court, however, murmured in awe. Winn had the wild desire to confess, so proud was he of his fierce reputation. But logic won out, and he kept his mouth shut as the dey went on.

"Thighs like tree trunks and teeth sharp as pikes, he had. An uncanny, sly devil with the magic eyes of the Jinn. He cast his evil spell upon us, becalming our ships, but soon the ocean boiled beneath us and sea serpents lashed the waves with their tails."

Winn choked on his laughter, trying to keep a straight face. The man was entertaining, he had to give him that, even if he was an inveterate liar.

"But Allah proved beneficent," the dey continued, "showing his kindness to his true followers. In the midst of the battle he sent the infidel sailing away in fright of Mahomet's people."

The room burst out with oohs and ahhs. Damn, but the man knew how to act. The dey focused on Winn, the gaze from his piercing gray eyes burrowing into him.

"We are told that you bring ransom, yet I have seen none of it."

Winn stepped closer and bowed his head. "That is because our sister ship brings it. She was delayed with repairs, but should be here soon."

Actually he *prayed* the *Blackbird* would be there soon. He was also curious as to who had played the infamous Black Jack. He thought it might be his midshipman, Book, a strapping figure of a man.

The dey put on a smarmy smile, treating his potential money giver like a guest. "If you look out from the balcony, you will see the result of Hammida's folly. He is a good high admiral, and for that we will not kill him, but he must be punished nonetheless."

At the dey's command, Winn followed the Lilliputian vizier to where the fresh breeze blew in from the balcony. He stretched his lungs with the welcome air, filled with warmth and sunshine rather than dank and must. Below him along the narrow main street, the people gathered and jeered.

The object of their derision soon appeared.

Reis Hammida, high admiral of the Algerine navy, had been strapped atop a braying jackass, sheep's entrails festooning him like a necklace. The loyal crowd pelted their admiral with stones and excrement while they jeered.

Winn's hearty laugh boomed over the crowd and caught the hapless Hammida's attention. The look he gave the admiral served only to push home a point: You should not play games when you play with the enemy.

That night there was a great celebration honoring the dey's return. Although the old goat hadn't captured a single prize, he had scared off that scourge Black Jack Alexander in a mighty battle, and his subjects rejoiced.

Winn had been given a bath and rich silk raiment. Then he had gone from his now stately quarters to join the dey's festivities.

The women had remained in the harem, preparing for their own celebration. It seemed the dey's son would soon marry the woman who had saved his life. As Winn sat down to the feast, a huge beardless man slipped silently next to him and whispered in precise English:

"Although the dey was assured of the woman's fertility, he would have his boy child remain safe from harm by marrying the American princess in his stead. Unfortunately," the big man said, "there is a dilemma, as she is already married and says she could easily be the poor boy's mother. She cannot contemplate a life with him that only consists of playing go fish."

Winn choked on a piece of sweet bread. It had suddenly turned more dry and sour than that which he had once soaked in vinegar. The giant served him some fruit and placed a bowl of rosewater beside him so that he might bathe his sticky fingertips. Winn went about his business while listening to the man's interesting information.

"This woman saved the boy's life, and has taught him much about medicine and ah-lor-gies. The boy is like my own, and the princess has become my true friend as well. I have sworn myself to her allegiance and have foresworn all others."

Winn nodded, picking up a piece of cheese. "I understand," he murmured, and nodded as if thanking the man for the food.

"There is trouble afoot," the eunuch whispered while he cleared a tray. "A small fire occurred on the *Raven* today. Your men will be aboard for a few days, as they are needed to repair the damaged ship. The boy and I leave with you on the morrow, and the princess will leave with the pirate, Grizzard."

Winn turned upon his fat pillow, body trembling with renewed purpose, meaning to ask about Zoe. But the giant had melted back into the shadows, leaving him only with a heart filled with hope.

Zoe ran into Grizzard in the dark courtyard outside the harem. She could tell it was he by his creative curses.

"And hello to you, Mr. Grizzard," she drawled as if offended, but when the silly man swung her round in the air, her heart nearly burst with happiness.

"Eh, missus, you be a sight for sore eyes, I wager.

That be if I could see ya, what with the moon disappeared from the sky and all. How ya been?" he asked as if they were taking a stroll rather than breaking out of the beautiful palace.

Luckily she had already shooed Raven away and hoped the bird had winged ahead to the ship; otherwise the crow would have awakened the guard upon the reunion with Grizzard.

"Fine, and you?" she asked, wondering where the old salt had gone after that horrendous acting job the last time she'd seen him.

"Been keepin' an eye on that bastard Hammida, fillin' him with nonsense about the cap'n. Could have knocked me over with a feather when that hulkin' giant what's lost his ballocks came prancin' in to let me loose."

Zoe could not imagine Koto prancing, but she blessed Grizzard for going along with the eunuch's ingenious plans. "Koto said you were the one who heard of the plotting Hammida intends." She could barely see Grizzard's nod.

"Know a bit o' the lingo, I do, but didn't let on none. The giant says there be a few men more to get out of the locker what been put up here to tend the dey's monies. Mr. Leetch be one."

"Is that where we're off to?"

"Aye, ta free the jailbirds. Happens to be I have a knack with locks."

"You mean you pick them?" she asked, fascinated by Grizzard's well-rounded prowess as he led her into a dimly lit corridor.

"No, ma'am. Me specialty's pickin' pockets." He held up a ring of keys. "Nobbed the little bugger what carried these before he could squeal by nailing him with a facer. Little turd eater won't see the light till mornin'."

Zoe stifled a laugh and gave Grizzard a fierce hug. "You don't know how much I've missed your cute curses."

"Cute curses, hey, that's a new one. Cute curses," he mumbled to himself, ego puffed up, as he led the way down the long mazelike corridor.

"How can you tell which way to go?" she asked. "Don't you lose your direction?"

"Once 'pon a time I was a rat catcher, get used to the mazes of a house right quick now."

She couldn't imagine calling the monstrous palace a house. Only Grizzard could mangle descriptions in such a way, she thought, halting beside him in front of a locked door. Having found the right key after only two tries, Grizzard pushed open the heavy carved wood. The room stood empty save for the chaplain, who had one foot over the windowsill—the other men were already down on the ground.

"Good evening," Chaplain Amonte said. "Got the message from that big man to get back to the ship. Leetch settled the watch with a whack on the nob, so we thought we'd exit this way. Care to join us?"

"Hell, why not," Grizzard said. "Too many damn havey-cavey turns the other way. Planted a knot on his bean, eh?" he asked the chaplain as they helped Zoe over the sill and down to the ground a dozen feet below.

Grizzard joined Zoe and the chaplain as the others forged their way through the darkness. He nodded his head in approval. "Leetch be a rum cove, I tell ya, though a bit of a turd when it comes to duty."

Zoe clapped a hand over her mouth, trying her

damnedest not to laugh. The chaplain, however, was not as successful.

Zoe pressed against the building, hiding in its inky shadows until the men returned from their scouting. At the crunch of gravel she turned toward the alley, hoping she wouldn't be seen. She tried to drown out the screams and shouting as the crack of rifle fire broke out in the direction of the palace.

The footsteps had grown closer, sounding firm and steady, as if their owners were on a midnight stroll. She was surprised to hear an English accent, and strained to decipher the words of the men as they drew near. A familiar voice grumbled in the night.

"Release me you dammed idiot, or I'll wring your bloody neck."

"Just keep walkin', ya fool, 'cause ye're not goin' back. It's my duty ta see that ye're keepin' that thick head on your shoulders."

"I was never in any danger of losing it."

Oh Lord, she knew those bickering voices. She felt so relieved, she could have wept. She had to stifle her laughter instead, as McCairn's brogue rumbled on.

"Oh, and sure I believe ya." The doctor chuckled. "Fifty guards are not your match. I also believe that I'll invest my life savings in a shipload of haggis, ya daft man."

"Our escape was entirely too easy. What good is it being a pirate, dammit, if I'm not allowed to swash or buckle? They always do that in Zoe's books."

Zoe couldn't hold back any longer. A giggle burst

out and she clapped a hand to her mouth. Winn was upon her in seconds, hauling her out of the shadows.

"I thought the name was Winn Dammit, not Pirate Dammit," she whispered.

Before she could say another word, he latched on to her lips as if to life itself, and gave her a hug that rattled her bones.

"Ah, Princess, I never thought to see you again." He pressed his brow to hers, and she felt her soul reclaim a piece of heaven.

"Winn, I missed you so. Are you all right?" she asked, but McCairn stepped closer, wearing a scowl she could detect even in the moonless night.

"If ya don't mind me dippin' an oar in this conversation, I think it's best we leave."

"McCairn, where's your growl?" Zoe asked. "Don't tell me you're jealous?"

She hugged him soundly until Winn pulled her back.

McCairn found the strength for a mild bark. "Don't be daft, Princess. We best be finding a way to the ship."

"Oh, Koto has that figured out. He'll be here any moment with a tender."

"Koto? You mean that gelded giant?" he rumbled.

"I would prefer you didn't use the word *gelded*," Winn said.

"Well, if she means that eunuch, then she's a noddy to trust him." McCairn's growl had definitely returned.

"She may be a fool with friends like you," a sweet voice whispered from the dock behind them. "But she is not a noddy. I tried to pry a few answers from her about her escape plans, but she's as tight with her tongue as a Scotsman is with his purse strings."

Caty stepped into the dim light of the alley and gave McCairn a meaningful glare. It wasn't her glare, but her looks that did him in. The man stood there as goggle-eyed as a bobble-head doll. Zoe imagined he would have been sizzling if he'd eyed Caty in the hot waters of the *hammam*.

So, doctor, you've met your match, she thought, pleased beyond anything that Caty would be able to pick and choose a man of her own. If McCairn played his cards right, he might just fish up a winner or be caught himself. Zoe chuckled as she watched him—the man was as good as mute.

"What do we do now, Winn?" she asked. "I know Koto has left the rest to you."

"Don't worry, Princess. It's all taken care of. I plan to play the py-rat," he said à la Grizzard. "And since I've been so cruelly denied me swordplay, I think I'll steal meself a ship."

Zoe didn't know if she should laugh or cry at Winn's inevitable humor in the face of such odds. "Now all we need is a little of Koto's hocus-pocus," she said, "and we'll be all set."

"Are you looking for me, mistress?" Koto's dry baritone helped ease Zoe's building tension. "The boat lies this way, with Mr. Grizzard in charge," he said, leading the small group to a tender alongside the dock.

As Winn helped Zoe into the skiff, he ran his hand against the soft silk covering her derriere. The gleam of his wide smile lit the night.

"By the way, nice outfit, Princess."

Zoe gave him a snort and settled into the boat. Then the men put shoulders to oars and sped away in the night like the well-trained seamen they were. Caty admired the doctor's strong arms, Zoe lusted for a glimpse of Winn's thighs, and they all were climbing the ladder to the *Raven* in no time at all.

Leetch was waiting at the rail to greet them, his sandy hair standing out like a halo around his head. The young man's nose had evidently taken a wallop and now had a crooked turn to it.

"Are you alright?" Zoe asked. He nodded.

McCairn tilted the lieutenant's head from one side to the other. "You'll live," he said, "but see me later."

Leetch smiled proudly and nodded again, then he saluted his captain and took the wheel. "Ready on your order, sir."

Just then a burst of gunshot echoed down the alleys to the quay, as a series of small explosions rocked the palace. Grizzard motioned to a huge young man to scuttle the skiff while Koto stepped to Winn's and Zoe's side.

"Best be off," the eunuch said. "I have learned there is an assassination attempt under way. The dey has not long to live. That is why the boy goes with me."

"And Adam?" Zoe asked anxiously.

"Both boys are tucked away in Cookie's cabin, after a bowl of pudding and a warm chocolate drink."

"But the others, Koto?" Zoe asked, worried about the women she'd befriended in the harem.

"Those who wished it have already left the harem. Hakim's mother has returned to her people, and your friends—the three Englishes—have boarded a ship called the *Blackbird* from whence young Book has come." He pointed to the young man helping Grizzard.

"How did the *Blackbird* get in the harbor undetected?" Zoe asked.

"Very clever of them," Winn said. "It seems they sail under Hammida's own crescent. Mr. Book is a wizard with thread and canvas." He smiled a wicked smile. "Since we make way tonight, I sent my captain a message that all's well, and turned them around. We'll meet again at Ravenscourt."

Zoe crinkled her eyebrows, a new worry surfacing. "And the Englishes have sailed with them?"

Koto nodded.

"All three?" she asked.

He nodded again, a slow grin spreading across his dark face.

She turned to Winn. "Did Koto happen to mention their, uh, unusual preferences?" She saw the flash of her husband's devilish smile and shook her head. "Those women will wear out the *Blackbird*'s crew."

Both Winn and the eunuch roared with laughter. Then the captain of the *Raven* ordered anchors cut, and the ship danced merrily into the night.

15

"*And there they be,* all runnin' ding-dong upon the deck, jumpin' overboard like they seen a pack o' ghosts."

"And then what happened, Uncle Grizzard?" Adam asked.

"Uncle Grizzard?" Winn whispered to Zoe as they listened to the old salt tell his tale of adventure. "Would you want your son to call him 'Uncle'?"

"He is not a pedophile, romantically interested in children, if that's what you mean. Just a regular-like py-rat bloke who went sour on women and turned to what comforts he could find at sea, and whatnot," Zoe said, imitating Grizzard's confession to her.

"And whatnot, more than likely," Winn mumbled.

"He told me he was sorry about how we met, that he once loved a lady and she done him wrong."

"Oh, Lord," Winn said. "I'm not sure I can stomach this."

"Told me he sometimes goes for the women but 'likes meself a crummy dame, with lot's o' soft, ripe flesh.'"

Winn rolled his eye, incredulous, but Zoe had more to say. "And he has an interest in meeting up with the three Englishes aboard the *Blackbird*—so he says."

She winked at Winn, whose mouth was agape.

"Are you sure this is Grizzard, and not some Mideastern jinn that has plucked the poor depraved man's soul from his body and now inhabits it?"

"Think about it, Winn," Zoe said, eyeing Grizzard's likewise grizzled body. "Would a genie really want to reside in Grizzard?"

Winn laughed. "It must be Cookie's heavenly food that has me breaking into feverish fits, Princess." He shook his head, amazed at the turn of his thoughts, while Grizzard went on.

"And nary a man jack kicked the bucket. Ya gotta know how to grease a fist or two at times so as not to get a facer from someone else's fist. Just ask poor Leetch." He gave the lieutenant a wink as Adam and Hakim stared in wonder at Leetch's bandaged nose.

"Yup, lads, we was beat all hollow, what with Mr. Leetch's bowsprit all busted to one side. But you know Book, that hulkin' midshipman what seems a bit dense some times?"

The boys nodded eagerly.

"Well, he'd lose his arse if 'twasn't attached, as fat as a hen in the forehead a'times with a habit of shootin' holes in his own ship."

The boys continued their emphatic nodding, much to the nearby midshipman's acute embarrassment. Grizzard remained oblivious. Winn chuckled to himself, glad to be alive, to be back on his ship, but most of all to be with Zoe.

He watched her gazing at the children, looking at Grizzard with more love than the fellow was worth, and realized she held his future in her hands. There were important things to think about, decisions to make. And, by damn, he would make them.

"Book's light heeled," he heard Grizzard say, "for all he is a hulkin' brute."

McCairn took a menacing step toward the captain's table, taking exception to the slur on large men, but Caty grabbed him by the arm and easily held him back. He glared at her until she smiled at him, and then, Winn thought, McCairn blithely wore Sir Reverence on his face.

"And so Book greased the little turd's fist with a false coin, and the bastard let him board without a fight. Then we let Book use his talents to shoot a hole in our skiff. The rest, so's they say, be history. And what do this prove?" he asked the boys like the most principled schoolmarm.

"That it's good to cheat," Adam said.

"Sneaky, sneaky," Hakim crowed in his broken English.

"Right you be, the both of you." Grizzard beamed. "And it shows 'mazingly 'nough that Book has somethin' besides turds in his idea pot after all." Uncle Grizzard tapped the side of his head, and the boys nodded solemnly.

Zoe laughed outright, but Winn cringed, thinking of all the wrong turns opening upon the vistas of the boys.

"I want to propose a toast," McCairn said at the close of Grizzard's story.

"Can we have a drink, also?" Adam asked.

Winn glowered at Grizzard, who hustled the boys along to their bunks while telling them they shouldn't drink "afore ya reach the ripe age of eleven." At Grizzard's words, Zoe practically gagged on her mouthful of rum-laced water. She hadn't felt a moment of seasickness yet and didn't want to press her luck with straight rum.

"To friends," McCairn bellowed, "old and new." His eyes lighted fondly on Caty.

"Prinny will lay an egg if things continue to heat up between those two," Winn whispered in Zoe's ear.

"Lighten up, Winn. They're young, and in love."

"And you can't be old and in love, Princess?" he asked, nuzzling the most sensitive area of her neck.

"I didn't say that."

She looked up at him, love shining from her eyes, and Winn fell head over heels for the same woman for the second time in his life.

"Let them be, it will all work out."

"Will it?" he asked, having serious doubts. "And how would you propose they go about that? Or is a proposal what you're thinking of, my sly princess?"

"Every girl wants a romantic proposal at least once in her life," she whispered in his ear, painting a wet trail down his lobe.

Winn shivered in anticipation, wanting the devil's daughter more than ever. "And how do you think she'll get McCairn to propose?"

Zoe swirled on her seat to face him, mock indignity in her entire countenance. "And what makes you think he'll get her to agree?"

"The man's been an avowed bachelor for thirty

years. I think it more likely it will take her persuading him to get married."

"Well, I have a solution to all that," she said, giving him a sassy wink.

"I don't think I want to hear this one, Zoe."

"Sure you do."

He shook his head, waiting for her next ridiculous idea.

"I told her to seduce him and get pregnant. McCairn's too honorable a man to let her stay single while in a family way, and much too soft-hearted. He's crazy about her anyway, but he's just too stubborn to give in unless pressed to the wall."

Winn winced. "Prinny will cut off another part of my anatomy if he gets wind of this harebrained idea and who concocted it." He couldn't believe the gall of the woman, though knowing McCairn, he knew it might be the only thing that would work.

"And what part of your anatomy will the regent do away with?" she asked sadly.

"With my head!"

"No loss there."

"Zoe. . . ," Winn warned.

"Okay, so maybe I would miss that crummy head o' yourn, if'n the regent lopped it off," she teased. "But there are other parts I vow I'd miss nearly as much."

She sidled up to him, rubbing against him like a she-cat. At the moment several parts of him were most definitely interested in Zoe Dunham.

"Aye, a toast," he said, echoing the doctor's call, hoping to distract Zoe and keep his thoughts from the vicinity of his groin. "To sassy, peppery-mouthed women who make you hot, and happy . . . and to everlastin' love."

"Amen," came Grizzard's rumbly old voice from the doorway. "And to an old man's dream of visitin' with the three English Isles."

Winn, who had turned at Grizzard's entrance, choked on his rum, spluttering it all over his gnarly seaman.

"Ought to learn some manners, boy," Grizzard admonished before heading out the stateroom door.

"Here, here, Winn," McCairn scolded. "Thought I learned ya better when it comes to strong drink."

"He should know," Caty agreed. "The man was weaned on Scotch chocolate."

McCairn threw back his shaggy head and laughed a hearty belly full.

"And what is Scotch chocolate?" Zoe asked.

Caty winked. "Why, don't you know? It's milk and brimstone."

"Mr. Leetch, where is Winn?" Zoe asked the next morning, the thin rays of dawn just lighting the sky. "When I woke up he was gone. I'm worried because he had midwatch. I expected him in our cabin, if not at the wheel."

"I believe he's shooting the cat, ma'am." The young man seemed a bit embarrassed with his answer.

"Shooting the cat? Why? Is it rabid?"

For the first time, Zoe saw a smile creep onto the young man's serious face. He shook his head but took a moment to answer. When he did his voice came out a high, strangled pitch, quite unlike that of the Leetch she was familiar with.

"He's casting up his accounts, ma'am."

"He's doing accounting at this time in the morning? Perhaps the man has taken a fever. This is ridiculous—he needs his rest after being in that horrible prison. Really, this is not the time to take care of business—"

"Aye, it is, ma'am. He's cascading over the railing."

Zoe gasped. "Oh, my. Is that dangerous? I once read where the Vikings used to run a race around the ship—on their oars, mind you. What could he be thinking of? I tell you, men have always been a bit light in the head when it comes to fun and games, and danger."

Leetch started to guffaw, a most unlikely sound coming from such a sober young man. Zoe sauntered to the side of the ship, happy to be out in the fresh air and sunshine and back in her sneakers and jeans. Her Yankees jacket was thrown over her shoulders to ward away the nip in the air.

As she rounded a lifeboat toward the stern, she heard an awful retching sound and hurried to help the poor soul who most likely had overimbibed at the shipwide celeb—

"Winn?" she asked, her thoughts broken by the pitiful sight that loomed before her.

The poor man moaned, his eye blinking and bloodshot. As awful spasms racked his body, she came closer to support his side.

"Shouldn't be here, Princess." He turned away, head hanging miserably over the rail.

"You thick-headed fool," she said, not believing he'd prefer to suffer alone. No man, from her experience, liked to suffer alone. At heart they were overgrown children, no matter their level of sophistication. "What in hell do you think you're doing?"

"It's hell all right, and I'm shooting the cat."

"Oh. I see," she said, finally understanding Leetch's comments. "I take it you are also cascading."

"Right you are, dear."

Zoe pulled out a wrinkled tissue from her pocket and wiped his sweaty brow. She knew exactly how punishing motion sickness could be. "I know you didn't drink that much last night. It's that damn seasickness after being in port again, isn't it?" she demanded.

"No, Princess." He turned his bleary gaze to her and leaned the side of his head against the rail. "It's not that damn-seasickness-after-being-in-port-again. It's that damn-seasickness-every-damn-day."

"Then why didn't you tell me about it? I have extra pills, you know."

"Zoe, it's a long way back to Ravenscourt, and if I am to take you there as I promised, most of the journey is by sea. Can you last that long without your seasickness medicine, or do you have an endless supply? I warn you"—he smiled—"if you answer yes, I'll most definitely think you're a witch."

"If you're this stubborn again, you'll know I'm a bitch. Come here, you numbskull."

She helped hoist him up. The man was as weak as a three-day-old puppy. Leading him past Leetch, who gave a quavering salute—incorrigible boy—she helped Winn down the hatchway and to the comfortable, cushioned chair in his cabin. Then she popped a tiny white pill into his pouting mouth.

"If you haven't noticed yet, you should," she said. "I haven't been seasick since we left the Canaries. Just took a mite getting used to, I guess. I'm like an old salt, now."

"Then what's your theory about me? The longer I sail, the worse it gets."

"Have none."

"None? Why, Zoe, this is a first."

The ship rolled, and she swore she could see his face turn green.

"Serves you right," she muttered, "making fun of me like that. I am not always right."

"Ah-hah! You admit it!"

Zoe scowled. The man had a pompous way about him at times. She didn't like it one bit.

"I didn't say I'm always wrong, either. I most often am right, you know."

"Like you were right about the similarities between me and Jonathan?" he asked, voice growing stronger.

She could tell her pill was taking effect when his mouth started flapping again. She scowled as she answered.

"You both are tall, and have dark hair."

"But what about the eyes, Zoe?" he asked. "You said we both have dark eyes."

"And you do," she said, looking straight into the black center of his eye. She had no idea what he was getting at.

"Well, what about my other eye?"

"What about it?"

"Does it bother you that I wear a patch?"

"Winn, I love you no matter what you wear. Your patch means nothing. I loved you from practically the first moment I focused on your dimpled face."

"I do not have dimples." He pouted like a child.

"You do too. One on either side of your mouth. And you also have a groove that furrows your brow when you're angry . . . like now," she said, smoothing a finger over his brow.

He scowled fiercely. "I am not angry."

"No. I can see that you aren't."

"Well." He leaned his head against the high, padded back of his chair, somewhat mollified. "Would you still love me without my patch?"

Zoe smiled at his worry. Silly man. She loved him to distraction. "I don't know," she teased. "I do find it very attractive. You look like a py-rat, you know."

"Really?" he asked, pulling the word out to a slow, sensual drawl that tingled down the center of her spine and made the hair on her nape stand on end. "Then maybe I shouldn't take the bloody thing off."

"Whatever you want, Winn. It doesn't matter to me."

And it didn't, she realized. Nothing about Winn could put her off. No scar, or white-glazed eye, or empty socket could stop her from loving this man for who he was. If he lost his looks in the next moment, she'd love him as fiercely as she did now, and as she had from almost the moment they'd met.

Although it would be a shameful waste of a pretty face.

"I can handle it, Winn," she said softly, putting all the love she felt into that one look.

"I believe you can, Princess. So I'll tell you it's not as bad as you may think, though a sight like this, I'll warrant, you have never seen. It's part of my character, something that has shaped me since my youth to make me unique."

She waited expectantly as his hand crept under the black velvet patch. And now for a drumroll, she thought as Winn whipped the eye patch off his eye.

Winn blinked once, then twice, unused to the bright light, and turned to Zoe, an expectant smile on his face. "What do you think, Princess?" he asked. But only thin air greeted him.

Zoe had vanished.

Oh, no, he thought. The time tunnel has called her.

Frantic, he pushed himself up from the chair, but when he rushed to the door he tripped over a soft, solid form. Shocked to see Zoe sprawled on the floor, Winn dropped to his knees beside her and shook his head sadly.

Poor mite. She must have expected the worst, when all he had to show her was his other eye. Or maybe it was the eye itself that had caused her to swoon. What had Granny once said? Something about being careful not to scare the bejesus out of those who had never seen a pair of mismatched eyes.

"This isn't like her, McCairn, not one bit. Zoe is healthy as a horse . . . as an ox, even. It's not like her to faint and then take so long coming to."

Winn rubbed his rough hand over his face, worried that Zoe had remained unconscious for an hour before reviving. Hell, even when she had first crashed to the deck, she hadn't been out but for a few minutes. McCairn thought he was an old crone to worry like this, but it wasn't McCairn's wife who had fainted, dammit, and he didn't know about Zoe's precipitous flight through time.

What if this had something to do with her time travel? Perhaps that wormy thing she talked about was coming to suck her in like a silent whirlpool. Perhaps—

"Bring your arse to anchor, man!" McCairn used his normal bellow, shattering Winn's ears in the process. "You'll wear a groove inta the deck."

Winn kept on pacing the length of his stateroom.

"Sit!" McCairn roared.

Winn sat, elbows on knees and head in hands.

McCairn clicked his tongue. "You're up in the boughs over the missus, no use trying to hide it. It's natural for a newlywed couple. But she's awake now, and doin' fine. Imagine, a minor mishap sending you into a hen-hearted tizzy . . . What's wrong with ya, man?"

"She fainted when she saw my eyes didn't match." He knew he sounded like a sad little boy, but he couldn't help it—her faint had unnerved him.

"She was most likely overcome with joy, expectin' an empty socket and then seeing the bluest eye this side of heaven peepin' up at her as if on an angel—"

"A bit long in the tongue, aren't we, McCairn?" Winn drawled.

"Now don't be goin' into a snit. Ain't no use in dwellin' on things. March in there and confront this monstrous mishap between the two of ya."

Winn lifted his head and gave the good doctor a dark look, his scowl deepening when the man shooed him along. He stood and shuffled to the door. With his hand on the knob he paused and looked back at McCairn, seeking fortitude.

"I asks ya, is yours to be a she-house, Captain?"

"And what is that?"

"One in which the wife wears the britches."

Winn smiled crookedly at the doctor. "Zoe already wears britches, and they look right lovely on her, if I do say so myself. I like the way they round over her firm buttocks—"

"Buttocks? Watch what you're calling your wife! Are you daft, man? The woman will take a stick to ya, and you'll be deservin' it with talk like that."

"Buttocks are—" Winn started, but McCairn cut him off with a growl.

"I know what buttocks are. Every schoolboy knows what buttocks are—"

"Where Zoe comes from, it is the word for derriere," Winn explained slowly.

"Then why didn't ya tell me that in the first place? Have ya taken a recent blow to yer head?"

"Only to my heart," Winn said, opening the door. "And the woman who landed the punch is right in there." He grinned as McCairn gave him the thumbsup sign Zoe had taught them.

Winn slipped into the room. He stood there a moment in the shadow of the bookcase, taking in the scene. Zoe was propped up against a pile of pillows like a fairy-tale princess, and that little shaver, Adam, sat by her side. The scene was so domestic, so endearing, that it brought tears to both of Winn's eyes. He opened his mouth to greet them but hesitated when Adam flung himself at Zoe and kissed both her cheeks with loud, smacking kisses.

"I won, Princess, I won," he said proudly, cards scattering in his wake. "Now I am the king of champs at go fish."

"You beat me solidly, Adam. I will have to give you my crown at a special ceremony."

"A ceremony and a crown? Really?"

She nodded solemnly.

"Could we invite Hakim?"

"Certainly. You may invite anyone you want."

Adam looked up at her shyly, then bowed his head once more. He tugged the edge of the blanket with his fingers, and Zoe lifted his chin to face her.

"What is it, Adam?" she asked.

"Can the cap'n come, too?" he whispered.

"Of course he can come. I wouldn't think of leaving him out," she said. "Why shouldn't he be invited?"

"Cap'n's an oak, ma'am, but he's all Friday faced and everything, waiting for you out in the stateroom."

"He's waiting for me?" she asked. "I didn't know. You see, I just awoke before you got here, and wasn't sure what had happened to me."

"You fainted, Cap'n said." The little boy looked at her, face puckered up in worry.

"I know that, Adam, but I don't know why I fainted," she explained. "I thought Dr. McCairn would see how I'm doing and perhaps he can tell me."

"Oh, but the cap'n already told me," he answered in a very serious manner.

"He did, did he?" she asked, tousling the boy's golden curls. "And since when did he get his doctoring degree?"

"He ain't a doctor, Princess. He's a cap'n."

"Oh, sorry. I seem to be a bit confused."

Winn watched, loving her more every second with the way she treated the little boy. He almost said something—almost—but hadn't yet drummed up the nerve.

"That's okay, Princess." Adam patted her hand. "I know you were scared and all. Cap'n says it's because of his eyes."

"His eyes?" she repeated. "What about them?"

"He said his mismatched eyes frightened you, and then you fainted dead away to the floor. You're really not frightened of his lovely eyes, are you, Princess? Cap'n says they make him 'nique, and he's very proud of 'em, ma'am."

The boy started to sniffle, and Zoe hugged him

close, rocking the little mite back and forth. Oh, to be in that spot at the moment, Winn thought. He sighed, a long gusty sound that drew Zoe's attention to the shadowed corner where he stood. She didn't seem to have caught sight of him, so he remained still.

"Adam," Zoe said, "I think your captain is the most wonderful, bravest, boldest, most beautiful man I have ever met. And if he had only one giant eye sitting in the middle of his magnificent forehead, I would still love him with all my soul and all my heart."

"You would?" Adam asked, amazed.

"You would?" Winn echoed, equally amazed.

"Is it your practice to eavesdrop, sir?" Zoe scolded, at the same time beckoning him close with a crook of a finger.

"Only when the things I hear are so flattering."

"Pompous ass—"

"That be pompous arse, missus." Grizzard's gnarly head popped around the door.

"Bloody hell, we're starting a circus. . . ," Winn complained as Grizzard and McCairn sidled into the room.

"Thought you might need fortification," McCairn said, giving Zoe an exaggerated wink.

"What I do need is a little privacy with Winn," she said, narrowing her eyes at the two nosy coots. "You'll be the first to know whether I plant him a facer."

"Go for it, girl," Grizzard cheered her on.

"Whatever happened to loyalty?" Winn grumbled.

Grizzard flashed him a toothy grin. "Why, Cap'n, sir—since the princess came to us, we got smart."

Zoe and McCairn chuckled, but Winn was not amused.

"Adam," Zoe began, trying to direct the boy's attention from the prickly man who owned her heart. The kid needed a responsible role model, she thought, but where could she find one?

"Yes, Princess?" he asked, eager to do her bidding.

"I am as hungry as an ox."

Adam giggled.

"I am, I assure you. Do you think you can grab a few slices of bread, some ham, perhaps a bit of cheese, and make me a humongous sandwich? I am absolutely craving a sandwich this very minute, and I think not even Cookie could make one as good as you and Grizzard. You two have a creative genius about you."

The little boy beamed.

"Aye," Grizzard mumbled, "but not so creative as the tripe that runs so smoothly from your tongue."

Zoe glared at him until he started to move.

"I know when to make m'self scarce," he muttered while pulling Adam's hand. "C'mon, boy, let's make us a sandwich."

"Can we have one, also, Uncle Grizzard?"

"Sure as a turd, boy. Sure as a turd."

"Zoe . . ." Winn looked from Grizzard to her, while painfully biting the tip of his tongue.

"Don't start, Winn. Grizzard has a foul tongue, but a golden heart. Besides, you've interrupted your doctor. McCairn was just bidding us good night."

"No, I wasn't." McCairn placed a hand on the back of a chair as if to sit, but Zoe's surprisingly deep bark had him shuffling his feet nervously.

"Yes, you were," she said, giving him an ominous glare. "You were planning to check my injury in the morning."

"Aye, that I was," he agreed, all grumbly. "I'll be checkin' your abominably thick head in the morning."

"Oh, and doctor?" Zoe called out sweetly before McCairn had shut the door.

"Yes?"

"Make sure you shut the door completely, and—"

"Yes, Yer Highness." McCairn gave her a mocking bow, obviously miffed at being sent away when the going had just got good.

"—kiss Caty good night for me."

He bristled with embarrassment till the color of his face and hair blended. Winn couldn't hold back his laughter and earned himself a scalding look beneath two very red and bushy eyebrows.

The door slammed securely shut.

"Come here," Zoe commanded, every inch the princess of his heart. She patted the bed beside her.

Winn drew closer, hesitating at the last step, the heart Zoe reigned over thudding in his chest. He had been teased about his eyes all his life by everyone from his brutally honest granny on down to the servants' children. Even at school he had been called a queer devil, and his earliest remembrance of a county fair was seeing people make the sign of the cross when he passed by.

"Why didn't you tell me about your eye?" Zoe asked, staring him full in the face. She didn't cringe, or mock, or make him feel uncomfortable. The only thing he saw in her expressive face was love.

"I had an injury—to my left eye, actually. McCairn had heard of a method for strengthening it, as my vision seemed to go double at times. I had been wearing the patch for several months, and out of habit didn't mention it."

"But why would you think I fainted out of fright?" she asked, holding his mismatched gaze with her own.

"All my life, my eyes have caused me heartache. I've been the brunt of humor and speculation since I was a child. I naturally assumed it was too much for you to face."

"Winn, use the brain God gave you. He did give you one, didn't he?" she asked. "You know, as in that old joke—when God gave out brains, Winn thought he said pains, so he told him, 'No thank you. . . .'"

"Never heard of that one. Fairly clever, Princess."

"You haven't?" she asked, clearly intrigued.

"No. Never."

"How about the chicken crossing the road?" An excited gleam lit her emerald eyes.

"Zoe, don't be ridiculous. Why would a chicken cross the road?"

"Why, to get to the other side."

"Oh." Winn chuckled. "A bit on the odd side, no pun intended. But it has its merits."

"I love this. I've never been great at telling jokes," she confessed, "or keeping the punch lines straight, but the old corny ones are right up my alley. Unfortunately, everyone in my time knows them. But," she said with newfound wonder, "that wouldn't be true in your time, would it. All the old jokes would be brand new."

"Princess? . . . Er, Princess," Winn prodded as her thoughts focused on her jokes. He could practically see her brain whirring. "Ahem . . . we were discussing my mismatched eyes."

"Yes, they're quite lovely, Winn," she said in a distracted manner. "I always liked Jonathan's."

"Jonathan's?" he roared. "Jonathan's?!"

"Of course. He evidently inherited your eyes.

Although I'd swear they were the opposite of yours. Now, getting back to the jokes—"

"Zoe!"

"Oh, Winn, I'm only teasing . . . although the mismatched eyes do run in the family. I found them merely endearing in Jonathan, but they are absolutely breathtaking in you, dear."

She pulled him closer, and Winn reluctantly succumbed to her soft embrace. "Not even my eyes are unique," he grumbled.

"Of course they are, you idiot. I've told you before, your one eye was onyx while Jon's was a common sort of brown—"

"Oh," he interrupted, "as Grizzard would say, the color of a—"

"Don't say it," she warned, more than familiar with Grizzard's favorite word.

"—er, mud."

"Very good, dear." She patted his cheek, turning his head to survey his face. "As I was saying, your blue eye is azure with turquoise flecks, while Jonathan's is a washed-out cloudy sky."

"Really?" he asked, somewhat mollified—the woman certainly had a way with words.

"Really," she said.

"Do you love me?" he asked.

"Madly," she answered.

"More than Jonathan?"

"Winn, that is an absolutely ridiculous—"

He clamped a hand over her mouth till she stopped. He wanted her answer, and he wanted it now.

"Yes," she said, shaking her head and sighing with extreme exasperation as he released her.

A slow, satisfied smile spread across his face, and

by damn, he could feel his cheeks dimple. "By the way, Princess. You've seemed uncomfortable lately, as if you had an itch to scratch, but couldn't."

"Winn!" She bashed him with a pillow. "And to think I thought shaving for a bikini was bad."

"Don't worry, I'll help soothe any itches you may have," he whispered, "anywhere they might be." He slid her nightgown off her shoulder and began to nibble up and down her arm.

"Winn," she moaned, enticing him further with that delicious sound. "The sandwiches—"

"Later, Princess. I was asking if you love me, if you will always love me."

He waited for her answer, meeting her gaze, pouring all he felt into his own. Knowing his heart and soul hung in the balance.

Zoe pressed a finger to his lips. "Winn, I love you with my entire being. I will always love you. For all I know I *have* always loved you. Nothing in this world could change that. Nothing."

"Ah, Princess, you are my soul. I was half a man in both body and mind before we met, but you helped me regain my self-worth and confidence. Not through any special methods or madness on your part, only because you are who you are—my sweet, sweet princess, Zoe."

"Winn, let's not get maudlin. This sounds like a grade-D movie."

"That good, eh?" He nuzzled her neck, planting soft kisses on her skin. "By the way, Princess," he murmured against her, "what precisely is a grade-D movie?"

Zoe pulled him close and pressed her lips to his.

"Never mind, Winn Dammit. Just kiss me."

And he did.

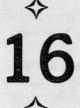

16

"I hate you, Winn. I will hate you forever."

Zoe hung her head over the milk pail they had picked up at the last inn and roundly retched up her meager supper. Winn patted her mouth gently with a hanky, but she pushed his hand away and looked up at him through bleary eyes.

"Why didn't you tell me these roads were so abominable? Why didn't we just sail around the coast?" she asked, but another wave of nausea coursed through her, and she had to rest her head against the cushions.

"These roads are no more abominable than usual. I didn't think about them at all. Furthermore," he scolded her—quite pompously, she thought, "you've been in such a damned hurry to get to Ravenscourt of late that I thought the change of scenery would do you good."

Zoe cast him a malevolent stare, and Winn ran a

finger under his collar as if searching for more air or wishing he was out of the hot seat. She had no sympathy, none at all.

"If I knew you would have such a queasy stomach on the coach, Princess, I would have sailed the damn *Raven* from London right up to Ravenscourt's cove. Had enough of the regent and the corny jokes you taught him," he mumbled. "I was doing it for you, Zoe. You told me you had a terrible urge to return to the tunnel, that you felt as if time squeezed around you."

"Don't remind me," she groaned as another wave rolled through her stomach.

"Besides, you're the one who made me think of the coach, concerned as you were with the possible renewal of my ghastly seasickness." He ran his fingers through his silver-and-midnight hair, and her heart turned over even as she wanted to thump him.

"Why did you have to think?" she asked, not caring if she was being unreasonable. "And why, why, I ask you, didn't you tell me that you're a liar?"

"Liar? Don't you think you're being a bit harsh with me, Princess?"

"Harsh?" she screeched. "I'd like to get my hands around your bloody neck."

"I have nothing to do with your dilemma, sweetheart. If I could, I would have this sickness instead of you."

"If you could have this sickness instead of me, Winn, you'd be the mother of all saints."

"See here now, Princess. You've been around Grizzard too much lately, picking up his nasty language. Get a hold of yourself, and stop all those hatchet-faced looks as well. We'll be out of this coach soon, and you'll be feeling right as rain."

"I'll never be feeling right as rain again. Nothing will ever be right again, you miserable little turd of a man."

"Nonsense, Zoe—"

"Don't you 'nonsense' me, I've been through this before, and it damned near killed me the last time. I'm no spring chicken, Winn—"

"Is this another of your chicken jokes? I told you they were getting stale."

She picked up the milk pail and held it before her. "How would you like to wear this slop on your head? We can play a game of shoot the cat. . . ."

"Now, Zoe, calm down, dear—"

"Don't you tell me to calm down. You're not the one who's pregnant."

"What?" Winn's face paled for a moment, then slowly resumed its windswept color as he relaxed back into the cushions. "Neither are you," he said in a steadier voice. "You only picked up a touch of bad food along the way."

Zoe narrowed her eyes till they were little slits, a habit she'd picked up from Winn. "*All* the food along the way has been bad. That isn't the cause of this malady—you are!"

His jaw hardened. "Zoe, you vowed that no one touched you intimately at the harem. Are you telling me different now?" He grabbed her arm, forcing her to look at him. His anger grew deadly, but she knew it wasn't directed at her. "Because," he said, the edge to his low voice sharp as a knife, "I'll go back and kill the bloody bastard."

"Suicide is a mortal sin."

"I know that."

"Well, you'd have to kill yourself if you were to kill the bloody bastard who knocked me up."

Winn exhaled dramatically. "Zoe, I am sterile. Get that through your beautiful but incredibly stubborn brain."

"I talked to McCairn."

"That's nice."

"I talked to him about your supposed sterility."

"Now, why would you do that?" he asked.

Zoe snorted. Sometimes her husband was a very dense man. "Because, you fool, I suspected I was pregnant before I even left the boat. There was my sudden lack of seasickness and months of missed periods. I may not be a youngster, but I haven't gone through menopause yet," she said, staring him down.

"Lower your voice, the driver will hear you."

"I hope he hears me!" she shouted. "I hope the whole damn world knows that you knocked me up!" Her face was flaming red; she could tell by the heat she felt. She balled her hands into tight fists, ready to take a swing at the man.

Winn looked at her oddly, tilting his head from side to side like a veritable idiot. A tiny frown marred his chiseled features, whole long grooves furrowed his eyebrows. Good. Let him sweat for a change, she thought. After all, she'd done her share of sweating this afternoon and more.

"You're serious about this," he said.

"Damn straight."

"You're sure?"

"Positive."

"Absolutely?"

"Definitely. Hold out your palm for a few more moments, and I'll give you firsthand proof of my morning sickness."

"Oh, my God," Winn said as the reality of the situation struck him. He suddenly grew desperate for air. "Oh, my God!"

He grabbed the bucket from Zoe's hands and joined in her game of shoot the cat. Zoe almost laughed but felt too weak. A pity, since the man deserved it.

"How can this be?" he asked, wiping his mouth with an extra hanky.

"Do I really have to explain it?"

He nodded. She shook her head.

"Winn, you've been jumping my bones practically since the day we met. Don't you think that you can put two and two together?"

"But I'm sterile."

"Evidently not."

He plunked back against the squabs so hard, she could feel it rattle her own teeth.

"Zoe, you sing me small," he murmured.

"In American, Winn."

"You humble me, Princess. You do me proud. I had thought that children were impossible."

"Evidently."

"It seems they're not."

"Quite right." She patted his pale cheek, taking pity on the man. After all, he couldn't help being dense.

"What do we do now?" he asked, a worried frown upon his face.

Zoe grabbed the bucket from his hands. "Pray."

"Winn," Zoe said as she mounted the steps to a slightly newer Ravenscourt.

"Yes, Princess?"

He slid the key into the door, knowing his grandmother would be in Scotland for the season, visiting relatives. Too bad. The old termagant would have met her match in Zoe. He wondered for a moment if the old girl would miss him at all but knew at heart that his disappearance wouldn't affect her any more than his defection to America had.

"I just remembered something—"

"And what's that?" he asked, turning to Zoe.

"I remember something Jonathan once said about you marrying a babe in the woods. Black Jack was supposed to have married an heiress, and they had enough kids to start their own hockey team."

"Hockey team?" he asked, giving her a quizzical look.

"Never mind, it's not important. Let's just say they had a house full of kids. She was much, much younger than him, while I'm three years older than you. Suppose you can't go through the tunnel, Winn? Suppose you change your mind and marry that heiress? Then I'll be alone, unmarried, and pregnant at my age."

"That's ridiculous. I already married you."

"That's right, you did. And you'll stay with me always, like we agreed. Right?" she asked, her panic making her voice quaver.

"My life belongs with you, Princess, in this century or in the next. When I married you I knew full well what it would entail. A mum like you needs her children. That's one of the reasons I love you so." He pulled her to him in a tight embrace, leaving a trail of kisses across her puckered brow.

"You don't have to go with me, Winn."

"I beg to differ, madam. I have no choice but to go

with you, if it's at all possible to do so. You see, I am a man who needs his wife. Besides, Prinny was none too pleased by McCairn and Catherine's wedding. I think it's time I left this century."

"Smart man." Zoe smiled a crooked smile, remembering the temper tantrum Prinny had had when he'd found out about the newlyweds. "Are you scared?" she asked, getting more nervous by the minute.

"Only about you and the babe."

"I love you, you know. No matter what happens. Even if we don't get out of here—"

"No more of this ridiculous worry, Princess. Everything will work out fine. You'll see."

Winn pushed open the massive mahogany front door, and they entered the house together. It was as quiet as when she'd left, the furniture covered in practically the same dustcloths. It gave her the willies to think about what was to come.

"I don't like this, Winn, not one bit."

"Easy, now, Zoe."

"Winn"—Zoe tugged on his arm—"before we go, are you sure McCairn and Caty will be all right?"

Winn drew her close and gave her a hug. "I think so. For all his bark, Prinny doesn't hold a grudge when it comes to those he loves."

"Well, at least he seemed mollified when you gave your shipping business to McCairn."

"Aye." Winn nodded, turning her around to look in her eyes. "The doctor and Grizzard will make a fine partnership—if they don't kill each other first." He loved the sparkle that came to her eyes. "The others will be rich men with all the booty they've earned, and McCairn assured me Black Jack will have his buried treasure one day."

"Did he, now?" she asked. "Then he finally believed our story?"

"Aye. Though he admitted he was most likely daft and sentimental from his recent marriage to Caty." Winn chuckled, thinking about McCairn's initial reaction to the story of Zoe's trip through time. "And with Kato returning with Hakim to his family in Bermuda, everything has turned out so right."

"I just wish I could be as sure about Jonathan," Zoe said.

"Don't worry, Princess," Winn teased, seeking to allay her worries. "If he's related to me, the man can surely take care of himself."

Zoe nodded. "You're right. Jonathan has always managed well on his own. You, however, are a different story. I plan to take excellent and intimate care of you."

"Ah, Princess, we men are all leg shackled now, except for Grizzard and the three Englishes."

Zoe tapped him on the nose while she laughed, spoiling the stern face she attempted. "Watch those lines about being shackled, Flynn."

Winn snorted at the nickname.

"Okay, then," his sweet princess murmured as she stood on tiptoe to rub her soft lips against his, "watch it, Winn Dammit."

Oh, how he loved the minx. He began to return the delicious loveplay, but Zoe suddenly pulled back.

"Wait," she whispered. "I hear something from upstairs."

"It's only your imagin—"

"There," she interrupted. "Hear it?"

"I think so." A dull pounding echoed down the

stairs. "You stay here," he ordered, going to investigate.

"In a rat's ass I will." Zoe headed for the stairs, pretty damn swift on her feet for a pregnant woman who had been through so much.

"Zoe! Bloody hell, Princess, wait for me!" Winn yelled as he charged up the stairs after her.

She'd heard a sound, she knew it, and ignored Winn's warnings as he ran at her heels. "There it is again," she said.

"Zoe. Wait!" Winn called out as she threw open the door.

"Oh, my God . . ."

Zoe could only stare.

In the middle of her bedroom, on her bed, dammit—the same ancestral bed she'd shared with Jon—were two naked people in the last orgasmic throes of passionate lovemaking. She couldn't have gotten out another syllable if her life depended on it.

Even worse, she couldn't move.

Couldn't stop watching, despite her complete embarrassment and Winn's insistent tug on her arm. Her brain and muscles froze solid as she witnessed the scene. It was the familiar sight of the irregular birthmark that pulled her out of somnambulance.

The one upon the left cheek of the man's butt.

Zoe's gaze swept over the woman beneath him. Christ, she was only a girl—couldn't be more than nineteen. But that was full grown in this day and age. The young beauty's eyes remained closed in the last vestiges of passion, oblivious as her lover was to the intrusion.

"Why, Jon," Zoe murmured, breaking through their moans. "I didn't think you had it in you . . . or whomever." She raised an eyebrow as she glanced at the young woman.

The man turned a startled face toward her.

"Zoe. Luv . . ." He groped for words, clearly in a panic. "It isn't what you think."

"Relax, Jon. No harm done," she drawled, and thought it true enough. Her fondness for Jon would always remain, but her body and soul now belonged to the man at her side.

"A friend of yours, dear?" Winn asked. Hot anger laced his voice, giving it a deadly edge.

"Jonathan?" The chit tried to hide under Jon, her big eyes wide with embarrassment. "Who are these people? What are they doing here?"

Jon's own eyes glazed over. "This is my wife, Zoe, and—" He looked at Winn for the first time and was at a loss for words.

"Ex-wife," Zoe addressed the poor girl directly, then stepped aside so Winn was in full view. "And may I present Jonathan Winnthrop Alexander Dunham, ninth earl of Ravenscourt—my husband."

"What?" Jonathan screeched as he wrapped a sheet about him and jumped out of bed.

The poor girl turned completely red, left naked as she was upon the mattress. Zoe tugged a blanket over her and smiled as kindly as she could before turning back to the two men, who circled each other like wild dogs.

"You can't be her husband. I'm her husband!" Jon shouted.

"Ex-husband," Zoe reminded him, stepping between them.

Jonathan turned a painful gaze to her. "But, Zo— we were to remarry when I found the treasure."

The girl took in a sharp breath. "You can't marry her, Jonathan. You're married to me."

Zoe raised a brow.

"It's just temporary, luv," Jon pleaded with Zoe. "I had no idea you were here."

"I'm sorry, old man," Winn broke in. "But there's nothing temporary about our marriage. Zoe belongs to only one man, and that is me, Black Jack Alexander."

Zoe looked at Winn, impressed. With windswept hair, jacket rumpled, stock askew—his earthier aspects sprang to life. A primal maleness, an aura of power, emanated from him to all in the room.

The damn rogue cast the most menacing stares she'd ever seen. It always amazed her when he wore his macho persona—such a difference from the tender soul she'd grown to love. Although, having watched the effect that steely gaze wrought upon people, she had to admit it served a good purpose.

A thin peep came from the forgotten girl. "But Jonathan, I thought *you* were Black Jack."

"Something you'd like to share with me?" Winn asked Jonathan, deceptively soft.

"Wasn't my doing," Jonathan mumbled. "A case of mistaken identity on the part of the *Blackbird*'s crew."

"I see," Winn said as if he didn't. "I take it you were the one who fought the dey?"

Jon nodded, somehow managing to hold Winn's gaze. Perhaps the man was capable of change, Zoe thought.

"I must admit," Winn drawled, "there is a slight resemblance." He drew closer to inspect his rival. "The dey is a formidable foe, and he sang your prowess quite loudly. Perhaps you are a proper descendant, though likely from an obscure family branch—"

"Oh, Lord," Zoe mumbled, ready to strangle him.

"—but how that works in the scheme of ancestry, I wouldn't know. This time-hopping theory gives me a headache each time I think of it." He rubbed the bridge of his nose.

Jonathan's tension dissipated into a hint of a smile. "And this pirating bit"—he looked at Winn with sudden respect—"is a hell of a lot more strenuous than I thought."

Winn stepped back, a smile twitching at the corners of his mouth. "I bloody well agree with you on that," he said, pulling Zoe possessively to his side. "But I think you have your wives mixed up." He glanced meaningfully at the young woman cowering in the bed.

Jonathan turned to her and seemed to come to his senses. About time, Zoe thought. His thick-headedness had always been a major personality flaw.

Jon wiped a tear from the girl's cheek, the expression on his face more tender than Zoe had ever seen. "My wife, Dierdre," he said with a choked voice, as if just realizing the damage his words had wrought. "Countess of Ravenscourt. The former Lady Dierdre—Branbury's daughter."

The girl nodded regally, mollified for the moment.

"Branbury, you say? As in the duke of Branbury?" Winn asked.

Jon nodded.

"Can't see that stickler Robert giving his daughter to a mere earl. A pretty lucrative match on your part, nonetheless." He clapped Jon on the back.

"It was a love match," Jon told him, bristling.

"Good for you." Winn's eyes twinkled as he looked around the room, taking in the obviously new silver chandelier and rich accoutrements. "Doesn't seem to have hurt your pocket any."

Zoe recognized the telltale tic of annoyance on Jon's cheek. When his hands knotted into fists, she ground a warning heel into Winn's toe.

Black Jack indeed, she thought. The man had the devil in him, sure enough.

"Estate never looked better," Winn mumbled, giving her a glare.

Zoe smiled at him sweetly, satisfied that Jon's fists had relaxed. Pigheaded males were a hindrance she'd just as soon avoid. "But we're not here for a visit, are we, Winn?" she prodded.

"Why, no. We're not," he drawled.

Jon shifted to the edge of the bed. "Then why charge in here like this? If you think to take my place, *Grandfather,* think again." His tone filled with angry challenge as he purposely drew his eyes to the silver wings in Winn's hair. "I live here now. And I have the formidable backing of the duke."

"Ah, Jon." Zoe shook her head sadly. What had happened to his lovely promises of a few minutes before? "Money and status always were your top priorities. I pity you, dear." She turned to the girl and envied the youthful energy and determination in her face. "Perhaps you'll have more success with him than I."

The girl looked at her keenly, then smiled in understanding. "Perhaps I will."

Jonathan stood there blankly.

"We are going back," Winn continued, "to Zoe's time. You're welcome to both the title and the estate. Unless you'd like to return with us. . . ."

"Hell no, Grandpa." Jonathan broke out in a silly

grin. "Grown accustomed to the good life." Dierdre whacked the back of his head with a pillow, and Jonathan pulled her to him. "And I couldn't leave my muffin behind."

Zoe stifled a gag as the girl snuggled closer. "Give me a break," she muttered.

"Then it's good-bye"—Winn's eyes narrowed on Jonathan's, his lips curling up with disgust—"*grandson*."

Zoe broke out in fits of laughter. How two men could look so alike, be so alike, and yet be so different—thank God she'd found the right one after all.

"Come, you two. Now that we have things settled, I'd like to be moving on." She walked to the secret panel and popped it open.

"What are you doing?" Jon stood, taking a step toward her.

"Attempting to find that damn tunnel again. It's our only hope to return, and I do so miss the kids."

He had the grace to look sad.

"We'll need to borrow a candle, Jon." She nodded to the silver candlestick beside the bed. "Unless you've devised some sort of generator and wired the passage for light."

Jonathan smiled. "Not yet, luv. Not yet."

Winn took the proffered candle without a word, bristling at their banter. He ducked into the secret passage, looking over his shoulder at Zoe. "I'll lead the way if you can remember the turns, Princess."

She nodded, eager to go yet oddly reluctant to leave. A long chapter of her life was over, and she'd likely never see Jon again. They'd shared so many good times, and those were the ones that now scraped at her heart.

She started for the hidden door, but a tug at her elbow turned her around. Jon stood beside her, a look

of agony mixed with ecstasy shadowing the mismatched eyes that were his family legacy. He caught
her hand.

"Just wanted you to know that I'll always love
you." He squeezed hard, tears filling his eyes.

"Me too," she whispered.

"And the children. Love them for me, Zoe?"

"I will." She nodded, sharpness stabbing at her
throat.

"I belong here now." He smiled sadly. "Never did
fit well in the modern world, did I?"

"No, Jon. You didn't." She wiped a tear from her
cheek. "Just do me a favor and quit the pirating.
Okay? You're not exactly a spring chicken, no matter
how much of a stud you may be." She swept a meaningful glance at the thoroughly confused Dierdre.

Jonathan's smile turned rueful. "You have my
promise, luv. I meant what I said. Swashbuckling's
one damned backbreaking job."

"Tell Winn about that." Zoe laughed softly as she
wrapped her arms around Jon—the husband she
would leave for a final time. An impatient "Harrumph!"
sounded behind her, and she was hauled into the tight
embrace of a very jealous and endearing Winn.

"Our flight leaves *now*, dear." Winn's brows slashed
into a menacing frown.

Zoe smoothed them out with her thumb, pulling
his head down to kiss the tip of his nose. "So it does."

"This is it."

Zoe knocked against the panel on her left. It had
taken longer than she'd thought to find their way to
it. A wrong turn earlier had her confused for a bit, but

once she'd gotten on track only the darkness had slowed her.

"Are you sure?" Winn asked, gripping her tightly by the elbow.

He'd hung on to her through the tunnel as if it meant his life. Zoe knew he was afraid to let her go for fear she would disappear on the spot.

She nodded. "I remember everything about that day." She turned back to him, placing her hands on his chest, heart and soul in her eyes, free for the taking. "It was the day I met you."

Winn dipped his head to hers, capturing her lips, her mouth, her tongue.

Tasting her. Holding her.

Giving himself.

Sharing.

She couldn't get close enough to his warmth. To the essence that was Winn. Life without him wouldn't be worth living . . . except for the children. Zoe pulled back from his embrace, memorizing the features of the man she loved.

"You're sure about this, Winn?"

"Positive."

He kissed her forehead.

"You can still change your—"

"Zoe. Say one more word, and I swear I'll paddle your generous bottom."

Gently he pushed her aside and searched the panel with his tanned, callused fingers—the same clever fingers that worked such wonders upon her body. A dull groan emanated from both the wood and Zoe at precisely the same time.

"'Generous bottom'?" she suddenly asked, Winn's last words finally registering.

She tapped her foot, thoroughly irritated by Winn's ridiculous comment. Hell, she'd never been in such great shape in her life, what with all the acrobatics she'd performed the past few months.

Winn glanced at her as the panel creaked open.

"Lush, Princess." He smoothed his hand slowly, sensuously, against her derriere. Then he trailed his fingers over her rounding stomach. "And ripe."

Zoe dropped her head to his chest. How she loved this man. She'd do it all again, brave hell to be with him. Only one regret burned her soul.

"If only. . . ," she whispered, an ache wrenching her heart. She never thought she could hurt so much.

"What?" Winn asked, holding her gaze as a fat tear coursed down her dusty cheek.

"If only Adam could come with us. I miss the little tyke so."

A soft shuffle echoed behind them, and Winn raised a devilish black brow. "You can come out now," he addressed the darkness.

Silken blond hair shimmered in the candlelight a moment before the little boy in question ran pell-mell from the shadows and propelled himself into Zoe's arms.

"Please don't leave me, Princess," he sobbed. "I want to be your boy."

"Oh, Adam," Zoe whispered through a constricted throat. Tears ran in rivers down the grooves of her nose and dripped, salty, into her mouth. "How did you get here?"

"Stowed away in the carriage boot, ma'am. Couldn't bear to watch you and the c-cap'n go." He looked up at her with tear-rimmed eyes, his plea squeezing her aching heart.

"It's so dangerous, sweetie, and you might get hurt. We explained this to you on the ship." She sought Winn's gaze, torn between duty and desire. His eyes gleamed damply as he turned to the boy.

"Adam," he began. But the boy cut him off.

"You told me a true man accepts defeat gracefully, sir." He released Zoe, swiping at his eyes with the back of a grubby hand and squaring his little shoulders. "If you go without me now, I'll only follow later. I swear it."

Winn looked down at the little boy who stood so staunch in his convictions.

"Well then, sir," Winn addressed him solemnly, "it seems that I must cry defeat." He broke off the boy's victory whoop with a forceful glare. "On one condition."

Adam eyed him warily, then hung his head, too young and unsure to defy his captain further. Zoe waited with suspended breath, her heart hammering in her throat.

"No more of this 'Princess and Captain' nonsense. A proper son addresses his parents as 'Mother and Father,' or 'Mama and Papa.'" Winn winked at Zoe.

"Or 'Mom and Dad,'" Zoe said, scooping the boy into her embrace.

Adam stole a shy glance at them, his face beaming. "I love you, Mom and Papa."

His voice rang sweet and clear in the tunnel as he snuggled closer to Zoe, wrapping his tiny arms around her neck. Then, after a long hug, Winn scooped the boy up, transferring his deceptive weight.

"You're getting a tad too heavy for Mom to carry, my boy. We've discovered why she's getting so fat."

"But she's not fat, sir," Adam protested, casting a critical gaze at Zoe. "Just a bit more round."

Zoe smiled and ruffled his hair. "Bless you, Adam. You're right, I'm not fat"—she glared over the top of his head at Winn—"I'm going to have a baby. That means you will have a big brother and sister, and a little brother or sister, too. Four kids," she muttered to herself. "Who'd ever believe it?"

"Uh, Zoe," Winn said, wearing a wry grin. She knew immediately it boded no good.

"Yes, Winn?"

She didn't like that smug look he wore—the dimpled cheek and devastating smile, the devilish glint to his eyes—not one bit.

"Did I ever mention that multiple births run in my mother's family?"

"Twins?" she choked out from a mouth gone dry as cotton.

He raised a roguish eyebrow, and her stomach plummeted. "Triplets."

Zoe stepped through the portal, mind numb. Winn followed her, wrapping his arms tightly about her and Adam.

"Triplets. . . ," she murmured.

And all fears of her trip through time abated.

Epilogue

Alexander and Alexa looked out the window to the spot on the hill where their parents romped. It was wonderful to see them like this, so different from what life had been like in England.

In all, it had been a wonderful two years—even Alexa had learned how to smile. She was Dad's girl now, happy as could be. For once, Alex thought, they'd become a true family.

He turned his head, shifting his gaze to look up at the portrait above the desk. Time had taken its toll. The painting hung there, rippled, cracked, the glazing dulled; yet nothing could dull the personality of Old Black Jack Alexander, scourge of the seven seas. Black Jack—his namesake and Alexa's. He remembered a time when Dad had idolized his ancestor.

Now it was his father who eclipsed the old man.

Alex looked to the window where Lexa stood

watching their parents. They'd agreed that Mother hadn't changed much in the last few years, except for being happy, that was. But Dad . . . well, he hadn't been the same since he and Mom had returned from their trip with that imp, little Adam, in tow.

He was the latest addition to the family, they'd said, telling him and Lexa that more were on the way. Alex never did get it straight about Adam—where he came from or how they'd found him. They only said that the boy was an orphan and would soon be his brother, which was fine by him.

He always *had* wanted a brother.

He'd never forget that day. How they'd come to school for him and Alexa, pulling them out in the middle of the term, insisting they were needed at home, to the horror of the headmaster. Then whisking them away to the Connecticut hills, so very far from their life in England.

It had taken a while, Alex recalled, before he'd believed it was real. It wasn't until he'd been in public school with a report card of all A's that he realized his father had truly changed. Instead of being pleased by his work, Dad had cringed, appalled at the grades.

"A man must learn how to play," he'd said.

So they'd skipped school the next day and driven to the mall for a day of junk food and laughter and the video arcade. His dad was a whiz at the swashbuckler game and had won a Pirates jacket and given it to him.

"A's," Dad had told him, "we'll reserve for names." And he had—much to Mother's protest. The twins had been named Ariel and Andrew. "After all," Dad had said, "Zither and Zephyr are even stranger than Zoe."

Privately Alex agreed, although he never men-

tioned it to Mom, not wanting to hurt her feelings.
She had enough of a burden, what with caring for two
babies at once. A handful, they were.

But, oh, what fun.

Cute as buttons, and little rascals as well. Already
they were taking apart any gadget they could get
their sticky hands on. Mother said they took after
Dad. But Ariel was the image of Mom, all golden
and smiles, with the widest green eyes you ever saw.

And Andrew, he was the spitting image of Dad. A
big boy already, Alex thought proudly. Most likely
took after his older brother, with the same dark hair
and sturdy build.

At least that's what Mother often said.

But the eyes . . . the eyes were all Dad. One bright
blue and one chocolate brown. Sometimes he felt a
bit jealous that his own were green, until his mom
called attention to the fact that the girls in his class
had a definite habit of staring into his eyes in the
silliest manner.

Well, not so silly, he thought. Mom called it
dreamy. He imagined Andrew would one day get such
dreamy stares.

"Hey, Alex, I've been trying to get your attention!
What are you thinking about?" Alexa asked, coming
over to the desk to join him.

"Just Mom and Dad, and all the changes there have
been." He swept a hand through his hair.

"All good ones, don't you think?" she asked with a
grin.

He loved it when Lexa smiled—she hadn't for so
long. He watched her glance up at the portrait. The
same naughty grin she wore tilted upon Black Jack's
lips.

"You've got a bit of the pirate in you, too, sis," he teased, and watched her blush.

"It's amazing"—she ran a finger over the portrait—"how much he looks like Dad. The right eye blue, the left one brown."

"Funny . . ." Alex stepped beside her, studying the painting. "All those years when Dad was so distant . . ." His voice trailed off.

"What?"

"I got immense satisfaction thinking at least the eyes were wrong—the opposite of Black Jack's."

Lexa turned to him, an odd expression on her face. "You know, I thought that, too." A hush seemed to fall over the room. Even the mild breeze had stopped.

"It *is* the same portrait," he said. "I scratched my initials on it once, before going away to school. Sort of a quiet way to get back at Father," he confessed. Alex lifted the frame from the wall, showing her the mark on the bottom of the canvas.

Lexa nodded, her voice coming out a rough whisper. "I would have sworn Dad's eyes were the opposite, too. And yet, I know the left is brown and the right is blue because they're just like Andrew's, that little pirate and scourge of the house." Her own silver eyes widened.

They turned to the window as one, staring out to where Dad stood with Mom. Alex could hear their laughter on the breeze, a warm sound filled with love.

"He's changed so much," he said.

Lexa nodded. "He always laughs and sings."

"And he even tells us now that he loves us," Alex whispered, his throat tight.

Lexa turned to him and stared. "He's like a different man," she said.

"And his left eye is brown, just like the portrait."

"You don't think . . ." Alexa's whisper faded to silence.

Both their gazes shifted to the wall. Black Jack grinned down at them, a happy soul—but not as happy as their new family.

Alex looked at his sister and shook his head. "Naah. . . ," he murmured.

And knew he really didn't care.

Zoe closed her eyes to the evening sun that angled like patchwork through the leaves.

The breeze swept her face, a soft caress, with each slow pass of the swing. Winn stood behind her, fierce privateer, pushing her back and forth.

After posing the pirate for her wildly successful perfume—Pirate's Passion—he'd since retired his cutlass and patch. Instead he had become a corporate pirate, nicknamed Black Jack Deuce by a loving staff.

He'd pillaged the competition at the first opportunity—stealing the best people from his rivals and reaping the abundant rewards of their expertise; using his skills as an ex-privateer he plundered treasures from the less talented with a ruthlessness he'd never shown upon the seas.

Singlehandedly he'd turned a dozen failing companies into a wildly profitable portfolio. And he had neatly secured the family business from the downward spiral left in Jonathan's wake.

Jon was right, Zoe thought. He never did belong here.

This century was tailored to Winn's natural skills.

In fact, he'd recently turned his formidable talents to the fast-food industry and lent his financial support to a host of budding inventors—junk food being his weakness and gadgets his obsession.

Yes. Winn belonged in the twentieth century. And he belonged here, by her side—as if he had been tailor-made for her.

Zoe leaned back in the swing with complete abandon, trusting Winn to keep her safe. Her hair brushed his chest with each backward swoop, and she breathed in the sharp spice of his scent—the smell of sea, and sun, and Winn.

How the children loved him, she thought. How he filled her heart. Life was sweeter, fuller, than she'd ever thought.

Winn shifted behind her, attuned to her senses, and let out a contented sigh. It was getting late, and she was tired—but oh, so content.

Winn's thoughts echoed Zoe's.

"Ah, Princess. Life is good."

He swept his gaze over his trim lawn and the rolling hills of his beloved Connecticut. In the distance, Long Island Sound sparkled with light. It was nice being near enough to look at, he thought, although his sailing days were long gone.

He missed them sometimes.

But he could definitely live without seasickness.

Speaking of which, Zoe looked pretty green at the moment. He grabbed the ropes of the swing, pulling it to a halt. He hoped they hadn't overdone it.

"Zoe, you don't look too good. Are you all right?"

Winn was greeted by a baleful stare. "If I look as bad as I feel, then I don't know how you could stand to look at me," she groaned.

"Nonsense, Zoe. You're as beautiful as a well-rigged frigate."

"That good, eh?" she mimicked him, a twinkle in her sea green eyes. "Oh, Winn. Must you flatter me so?"

Winn rolled his eyes. "I see you're feeling better now, Princess."

"Much. You're lucky this turned out to be only a virus instead of another baby." She looked up at him with an admonishing gaze. "But now that we're on the subject, I'd feel a lot better if you got yourself fixed. In this day and age we believe in small families."

He felt himself wince. After all, he had promised.

"I confess, I've been a coward. It wasn't long ago I thought myself sterile." He paused, then turned a contrite face to Zoe. "I only have one, Zo. What if the doctor slips?" He hurried on when her eyes narrowed— she'd heard all the protests before. "But I promise you, Princess. The twins are the first and last."

"They had better be the last. Or I'll finish the job Hammida started. As it is, you're lucky they weren't triplets."

Her mouth turned up in a sexy grin as she threatened with her words while stroking his growing parts with her hand. And to think she called *him* a devil.

What a woman, he thought.

What a wife.

More than he'd bargained for and all that he wanted. He hoisted her to her feet and gave her a tight hug before leading her down the path to home.

"By the way, Winn. Speaking of Hammida—" Zoe's voice broke into his thoughts. "I looked up your friend, Stephen Decatur, in Alex's history book. You'll be proud to know the commodore squelched the Barbary pirates in 1815 and, turning the tables on his enemies, demanded tribute from Algiers."

"Ah, Stephen. Always had a taste for irony." Winn smiled, but Zoe's eyes clouded up. "What is it?" he asked.

"Unfortunately, he was killed in a duel, not long after. . . ."

Winn let out a great sigh and shook his head sadly. "Poor Stephen," he murmured, "ever the hothead, dueling for honor." He lost himself in memories for a moment, but she caught his attention with her next words.

"As for Reis Hammida," she said, a rueful twist to her mouth, "that vile man finally paid his dues when he met up with your friend Decatur. A shot from Stephen's second volley cut Hammida right in two. They captured the *Meshouda*, then sailed to their showdown in Algiers."

Winn couldn't help his smile. "Ah, Princess, after all the evil that bastard did, it's gratifying to know there is such a thing as justice." He turned to Zoe, glad of his second chance at life, feeling blessed by all he'd gained. "It's funny . . . seems our minds have been turned in similar directions. Got curious the other day, and happened to look up the history of one Black Jack Alexander."

Zoe stopped short, her natural curiosity getting the better of her when Winn remained silent. "And?" she asked.

"Well . . ." He pulled out the word for suspense, and she thumped him on the chest.

"Spit it out or I'll flog you."

"Zoe," he whispered, pulling her close, pressing his hardening body to hers, "you know how to make a man tremble." He placed a line of kisses along her ear.

"I'm warning you, Winn. My patience is about gone." She tweaked his hair, pulling him down for a quick kiss, then pushed away from his grasp.

"Woman, you are a hard taskmaster. As I was saying"—he caught her hand as they headed up the path—"the rumors about old Black Jack seemed to die down sometime around 1815. The ninth earl of Ravenscourt was totally exonerated by the regent, and with the treaty of Ghent making peace between the United States and England, he found himself with homes on both coasts and became a substantially wealthy man."

Zoe smiled at him. Such a beautiful smile. It did funny things deep in his stomach and tightened his aching groin even further. He hastened his steps toward home, nearly dragging her with him. Hell, he couldn't roll her on the lawn.

Could he?

He looked around, spied Alexander and Alexa watching from the library, and knew Adam and the twins would soon join them after Nanny finished with their baths. No. He couldn't roll her on the lawn—

At least not with the children about.

A mischievous smile lit his face as he thought of what he'd do if they weren't about.

Zoe arched an eyebrow. "What's so amusing?" she asked.

"Thought you might change your mind and want to match Jonathan with children."

She waited expectantly.

"He had thirteen. More than enough for a hockey team," Winn said, and winked. He felt a bit guilty when Zoe blanched, but he couldn't suppress his laughter. She smacked him in the stomach and walked away. He thought her swaying bottom looked exceptionally appealing.

"You promised, Winn, to get yourself fixed. Until you do, we practice safe sex, or no sex."

She looked over her shoulder, eyes heavy, an enticing smile etching her face. Then she licked her lips slowly, enticingly.

"Fortunately, the means to safe sex are within the house. Race you," she said, and lit down the path like a greyhound, laughing all the way.

God, life is sweet, Winn thought once more while he watched her.

By a quirk of fate, they'd met each other.

Through a slip in time, they'd found love.

What more could he ask of life? Look what he'd been given. A loving family. Happiness. A new century to explore. *Fate*—he hoped it had been as kind to Jonathan. Still, he knew he'd received the better end of the bargain.

After all, he had Zoe.

Winn looked around him, breathing deeply, soaking in the earth's warmth as Zoe's laughter echoed down the path. The sky's evening rainbow shifted to twilight, and the first silver starfire touched the heavens.

So beautiful, he thought, the perfect time for sharing.

The perfect setting for making love.

Thoughts shifting to Zoe, he noticed her lead and took off after her, fast on the chase. Never could let such rich plunder pass, he admitted to himself.

The last rays of sunlight gilded the path as Winn closed the gap between him and his wife, her laughter spurring him on. "Ah, Princess," he said as he swept Zoe into his arms. "You do lead me a merry chase. . . ."

Yes. He wanted her always.

Would love her forever.

And as for safe sex—he vowed to practice it every chance he got.

Author's Note

I tried to give you a bawdy, light-hearted story. One that would leave you with a smile on your face and happiness in your heart. This book was my pleasure to write. I hope it was as much fun to read.

Despite my penchant for corny jokes, I strived for historical accuracy. Dozens of books were used for research. Hadji Ali, the dey of Algiers, was described in numerous journals of the time as a less than desirable leader. He was assassinated in 1814. Reis Hammida, the dey's high admiral, was cut in two by a volley of fire ordered by Stephen Decatur.

Decatur, a hero of the Tripolitan War and the War of 1812, made the rank of commodore at a tender age. A true swashbuckler and lady's man, he was killed in a duel not long after he implemented the defeat of the Algerian navy. I think he would have liked Winn and Zoe.

The *Raven* was based on American frigates like the

Constitution. Fast and durable, they harried the English ships of the line, breaking England's long domination at sea. They often held more than 450 men and boys, as well as livestock. The smells must have been horrendous.

The research was exciting, the writing was fun. I've left the high seas for the Oregon trail. And my new hero's a cowboy named West. Enjoy! You can write to me at P.O. Box 3144, Newton, CT 06470–3144. Send an SASE, and I'll be sure to write back.

✧

Glory in the Splendor of Summer with
101 Days of Romance

BUY 3 BOOKS — GET 1 FREE!

Take a book to the beach, relax by the pool, or read in the most quiet and romantic spot in your home. You can live through love all summer long when you redeem this exciting offer from HarperMonogram.

Buy any three HarperMonogram romances in June, July, or August, and get a fourth book sent to you FREE!

Look for details of this exciting promotion in the back of each HarperMonogram published from June through August—and fall in love again and again this summer!

Evensong by Candace Camp

A tale of love and deception in medieval England from the incomparable Candace Camp. When Aline was offered a fortune to impersonate a noble lady, the beautiful dancing girl thought it worth the risk. Then, in the arms of the handsome knight she was to deceive, she realized she chanced not just her life, but her heart.

Once Upon a Pirate by Nancy Block

When Zoe Dunham inadvertently plunged into the past, landing on the deck of a pirate ship, she thought her ex-husband had finally gone insane and kidnapped her under the persona of his infamous pirate ancestor, to whom he bore a strong resemblance. But sexy Black Jack Alexander was all too real, and Zoe would have to come to terms with the heartbreak of her divorce *and* her curious romp through time.

Angel's Aura by Brenda Jernigan

In the sleepy town of Martinsboro, North Carolina, local health club hunk Manly Richards turns up dead, and all fingers point to Angel Larue, the married muscleman's latest love-on-the-side. Of course, housewife and part-time reporter Barbara Upchurch knows her sister is no killer, but she must convince the police of Angel's innocence while the real culprit is out there making sure Barbara's snooping days are numbered!

The Lost Goddess by Patricia Simpson

Cursed by an ancient Egyptian cult, Asheris was doomed to immortal torment until Karissa's fiery desire freed him. Now they must put their love to the ultimate test and challenge dark forces to save the life of their young daughter Julia. A spellbinding novel from "one of the premier writers of supernatural romance." —*Romantic Times*

Fire and Water by Mary Spencer

On the run in the Sierra Nevadas, Mariette Call tried to figure out why her murdered husband's journals were so important to a politician back East. Along the way she and dashing Federal Marshal Matthew Kagan, sent to protect her, managed to elude their pursuers and also discovered a deep passion for each other.

Hearts of the Storm by Pamela Willis

Josie Campbell could put a bullet through a man's hat at a hundred yards with as much skill as she could nurse a fugitive slave baby back to health. She vowed never to belong to any man—until magnetic Clint McCarter rode into town. But the black clouds of the Civil War were gathering, and there was little time for love unless Clint and Josie could find happiness at the heart of the storm.

Say You Love Me by **Patricia Hagan**

Beautiful Iris Sammons always turned heads and was doted upon by her parents, whereas her fraternal twin sister Violet was the quiet one. An attack on their caravan by Comanche separated them irrevocably, but their legacies were forever entwined through their children, and through the love that ultimately bound them.

Promises to Keep by **Liz Osborne**

Cassie McMahon had always dreamed of a reunion with the father she hadn't seen since she was a child. When her hopes were dashed by his distant manner, she found consolation in the arms of a mysterious but seductive stranger. But Alec Stevens was a man with a secret mission. Could he trust his heart to this irresistible woman?

Cooking Up Trouble by **Joanne Pence**

In their third outrageous outing, professional cook Angelina Amalfi and San Francisco police inspector Paavo Smith team up at the soon-to-be-opened Hill Haven Inn. Soon they encounter mischief in the form of murders and strange, ghostly events, convincing Angie that the only recipe in this inn's kitchen is the one for disaster.

Sweet Deceiver by **Angie Ray**

Playing a risky game by spying for English and French intelligence at the same time, Hester Tredwell would do anything to keep her struggling family out of a debtor's prison. Her inventive duplicity was no match, however, for the boldly seductive maneuvers of handsome Nicholas, Marquess of Dartford.

Lucky by **Sharon Sala**

If Lucky Houston knows anything, it's dealing cards. So when she and her two sisters split up, the gambler's youngest daughter heads for Las Vegas. She is determined to make it on her own in that legendary city of tawdry glitter, but then she meets Nick Chenault, a handsome club owner with problems of his own.

Prairie Knight by **Donna Valentino**

A knight in shining armor suddenly appeared on the Kansas prairie in 1859! The last thing practical and hardworking Juliette needed was to fall in love with an armor-clad stranger claiming to be a thirteenth-century mercenary knight. Though his knight's honor and duty demanded that he return to his own era, Juliette and Geoffrey learned that true love transcends the bounds of time.